Mad Dog had never seen a sky so clear, and Angola's bad power grid increased the brightness of the stars.

Jack drove one truck, Mbandi the other, with five mercs piled into one flatbed. Not including their chopper and C–130 pilots, Mad Dog had brought nine men, including himself, to sub-Saharan Africa in search of riches—diamonds—and he hoped to God nine would return. All were foreigners, unfamiliar with the country.

Yet all were hell raisers, trained killers who shot first, shot second, and shot third. There wasn't any time for questions.

He nodded to his men, drawing Doolittle's attention. The translator had a tentative look on his face.

Mad Dog raised his voice above the thrumming engine. "What is it?"

"There is bad energy here."

"You a translator or a psychic?"

Doolittle shrugged. "I see death." Then he smiled and shoved Mad Dog's shoulder. "I see death, and it is you, Sergeant!"

By P. W. Storm

The Mercenaries
BLOOD DIAMONDS

Force 5 Recon
DEPLOYMENT: PHILIPPINES
DEPLOYMENT: NORTH KOREA
DEPLOYMENT: PAKISTAN

THE
MERCENARIES
BLOOD DIAMONDS

P.W. STORM

AVON BOOKS

An Imprint of HarperCollins*Publishers*

This is a work of fiction. Names, characters, places, and incidents are products of the author's imagination or are used fictitiously. Any resemblance to actual events, locales, organizations, or persons, living or dead, is entirely coincidental and beyond the intent of either the author or the publisher.

AVON BOOKS
An Imprint of HarperCollinsPublishers
10 East. 53rd Street
New York, New York 10022–5299

Copyright © 2006 by Peter Telep
ISBN–13: 978-0-06-085739-4
ISBN–10: 0-06-085739-0
www.avonbooks.com

First Avon Books paperback printing: December 2006

Avon Trademark Reg. U.S. Pat. Off. and in Other Countries, Marca Registrada, Hecho en U.S.A. HarperCollins® is a registered trademark of HarperCollins Publishers Inc.

Printed in the U.S.A.

10 9 8 7 6 5 4 3 2 1

For James Ide

Acknowledgments

· ·

Once again it is a great pleasure to have worked with my editor, Michael Shohl, whose encouragement and commitment to my work are truly appreciated.

My agent, John Talbot, has been a continued source of enthusiasm and support, and I look forward to working with him on many more projects.

Vietnam veteran and Chief Warrant Officer James Ide, a fellow Floridian with twenty-one years of active naval service, brought his considerable experience and expertise to this manuscript. Jim assisted me from outline to final draft, carefully reading every page and providing ideas and invaluable commentary. His level of commitment amazed me, and his keen sense of humor kept me grinning through some long writing days. I am blessed to know him.

Major William R. Reeves, U.S. Army, also helped from the beginning stages, contributing to the outline and to the manuscript. He did extensive research on weapons, terrain, communications, and too many other items to list here. Will is one of those selfless individuals who likes to help people, and his willingness to spend so much time assisting me is a testament to himself and to the caliber of officers being produced by the U.S. Army. He's an inspiration, and I'm honored to know him.

Lieutenant Colonel Jack Sherman, AR, USAR, Operations Officer 5th Joint Task Force, read every chapter and gave me character insights and plot details that allowed me to surround my lies with much more of the truth. Like Jim and Will, Jack spent many, many hours assisting me, and thanking him here is the very least I can do.

The listing of these individuals is my humble way to say thank you. None of them were paid. The fact that their names appear here does not constitute an "official" endorsement of this book by them or any branch of the U.S. military.

THE
MERCENARIES
BLOOD DIAMONDS

Prologue

....

Staff Sergeant Michael "Mad Dog" Hertzog bolted across the mountainside and slipped into the cave, keeping tight to the dusty wall as his eyes grew accustomed to the faint light.

Like many of the caves in "the 'Stan," the entrance was L-shaped to prevent bombs and missiles from being sent right down the middle of the opening. He turned a corner and entered a much more narrow tunnel.

There! Five meters ahead ran a bearded man wearing a *pakol* on his head. The *chapan* clinging to this torso and his baggy pants were equally nondescript. He glanced back, spotted Mad Dog, then shouted to his buddies as he slipped into the shadows.

At once the passage grew narrower, the ceiling sweeping down and catching Mad Dog's pack. He hunched over and pushed on, his breath ragged, his pulse drumming in his ears. Tommy's pleading eyes flashed in his mind, and the kid's voice echoed, *"Sergeant, just . . . get 'em."*

Mad Dog shuddered. What was he doing? Throwing away sixteen years in the Marine Corps? Throwing away his reputation as a first-class Force Recon operator, a hard man with a hard job who had never rejected a challenge?

Shit, he was the unconventional warrior perfectly suited to being the eyes and ears of his commander. He was an NCO respected by every officer in his company. They called him Mad Dog because he knew no fear, took every bet, engaged in every dare, pushed the envelope on practical jokes and pushed his men harder than any team leader in the company. He was a thirty-eight-year-old hell-raiser who refused to grow up, reminding his brothers that Peter Pan wears green. The others loved him, respected him, wanted to work with him . . .

But if they only knew how badly he had just fucked up. He had just waltzed his men into an ambush, gotten three of them killed. If he didn't make these Taliban fuckers pay, he wasn't sure he could live with himself. He had never made a mistake like this. Never. He switched out his rifle for a pair of .45-caliber pistols. He was faster and more lethal with them in close quarters.

Another turn, and the tunnel emptied into a wider chasm where the two lanky, gaunt-faced assholes were waiting for him:

One had hunkered down to the right, his AK poised.

The other stood near the wall, his rifle held high.

Neither was aware of the fire burning in his gut, white

hot flames searing away all fear and reason, leaving only the instinct to kill.

He threw himself forward and fired, the sidearms speaking violence in perfect unison. Yes, the scumbags had managed to squeeze their triggers, but not before Mad Dog's rounds had jolted them back, causing their three-round volleys to go wide and ricochet across the cave wall as he slammed across the deck.

Before the dust could settle, he was back on his hands and knees, then clambering to his feet. He had shot and killed both men. That victory registered a mere second, then he charged toward the back of the chasm, where another tunnel waited.

He never reached it. A tingling on the back of his neck told him to hit the deck.

Gunfire ripped through the shadows. Had it come from ahead or behind? Christ, he wasn't sure. Was he shot? He hadn't felt anything. No time to care.

He rolled onto his side, tugged free another grenade, pulled the pin, let it fly, tucked his head into his chest.

The explosion reverberated through the walls and floor like an aftershock, bringing down part of the ceiling. Small pieces of rock continued to fall as Mad Dog finally took a breath and slowly glanced up.

Clear. Okay. Back on his feet. Panting now. Sweat pouring from his brow. No breath. Just gasps. He reached the pile of rubble, picked his way over it, noted how the passage ahead was cast in dim light. An exit was close by.

But then a shadow to his left seized his attention. The grenade blast had left a gaping hole in the wall, revealing a chasm on the other side. Mad Dog fumbled in his pocket, withdrew a small flashlight, shone it into the opening.

About a dozen wooden crates of various sizes, some as small as shoeboxes, others as large as footlockers, lined the wall of the narrow opening. Nearby sat a pair of Nike gym bags bulging at the seams.

Faint voices—the words not English to be sure—brought an abrupt end to his inspection. He rushed forward, deciding another grenade might bring down the entire ceiling and bury him alive. He would shoot or stab the bastards. He just had to find them.

Oh, his ex-wives would be having a field day with this. He took unnecessary risks in the Corps and in life. But weren't the most successful people the ones who took risks? That philosophy hadn't worked in marriage, but he would make it work on the battlefield, even if it killed him.

So he threw himself into the next tunnel, running headlong until he broke into the next chamber and hit the ground. Gunfire sounded from everywhere. He rolled, came up, firing blindly in a circle until his gaze locked on one fighter hunkered down in a corner.

A head shot sent the first asshole slumping as Mad Dog whirled and fired again, his first two rounds missing but a third connecting with the chest of a second fighter who jerked back on rubber legs and crumpled to the dirt floor.

He scrambled to his feet, reached the exit tunnel, dashed toward the light, emerged outside. His shoulder throbbed, then a searing pain cut through. He'd been hit. Fuck it.

The last two fighters were running down the hillside, leaving a dust trail behind them. Range? Fuck, maybe seventy-five meters. He holstered his pistols, slung around his M4 with attached grenade launcher, took aim, and let a grenade fly.

Not a second after the explosion took out one fighter, he brought down the second with a quick triplet of fire.

Then he collapsed onto his ass, exhausted, completely out of breath, every muscle throbbing, the wound knifing hard now. He checked it. Clean entry and exit and not bleeding too badly, just a scratch, really. He'd live. Thank God he had never had kids. Their faces would have kept him back there with Tommy, José, and Dalton, the men he had just lost. They would have called, *"Daddy, don't do it."*

Mad Dog rubbed his eyes, got slowly to his feet, then shifted toward an outcropping for cover. He tugged out his binoculars and surveyed the mountains. Light flashed in the distance, perhaps a quarter kilometer away. More Taliban were moving through a pass. He spent a moment with his portable GPS, estimating their location, then turned back to the tunnel, wincing over his shoulder again.

He reached the section where the grenade had exploded, pushed his way past the opening in the wall and crouched down near one stack of crates. With his KA-BAR he pried open one of the larger boxes, and as the lid fell back, he gasped.

Gold bars. Dozens of them. He frantically opened another crate. Gold coins. One of the gym bags produced cash—American dollars—thousands and thousands of dollars.

He realized only then that his assistant team leader, Sergeant Eddy Yodell, had been calling him over the radio, and he replied: "Alpha Two, this is Alpha One. I'll be there in a minute." Mad Dog quickly replaced the crate lids, zipped up the gym bag.

Back at the boulders where Eddy and Doc were waiting, he dropped to his ass and groaned, "Shit."

"What happened?" Doc asked, noticing the blood on his shoulder and immediately digging into his pack. Frank "Doc" Sanders was a Navy corpsman who had a heart as big as the M–249 automatic weapon he lugged around.

Mad Dog rubbed his eyes and used the quick release to remove his assault vest. Before Doc could begin treating him, he rose and grunted, "Come on."

Ignoring Doc's protests, he led them back into the cave, to the tunnel where he had thrown the grenade. They squeezed into the chasm.

"What do we got here?" asked Eddy. "Little weapons cache or something?"

When Mad Dog opened the crates and unzipped the bags, Doc's jaw dropped, and Eddy thought aloud, "Holy fuck."

Mad Dog's moral compass had never pointed to true north, but he wasn't a street thug or whore, either. No way. "All right, boys. Listen to me. If we turn this over, it'll just get flushed back into the system. Shit, it could even wind up in the hands of the Taliban."

"Well, now we know why they were here," said Eddy. "Probably came to get the stash, only we got to it first."

"Exactly," said Mad Dog. "And the cash came from the CIA, from our local scumbag spook."

"You mean that guy Moody? James Moody?" asked Eddy.

"Don't dignify him with his real name. We call him Jimmy Judas," said Mad Dog. "And that fuck has been using the money to pay off warlords."

"Sergeant, we can't steal it," said Doc.

"The hell we can't," Eddy cried.

Mad Dog eyed the gold and cash. "This is our nest egg, boys. This is the money we need to build our little company after we all get out. And I think it'd be great if some Afghan warlords and the CIA donated to our cause . . ."

After burying the money and gold in the rubble, Mad Dog and his men linked up with the rest of their company, shared the grim news of being ambushed, and returned to Camp Buffalo. Doc wasn't happy, but Mad Dog knew he'd eventually come around.

Then, that night, during the wee hours, with a bogus operations order in hand, they piled into an HMMWV and headed out to recover their stash, with Eddy telling Doc that they would use some of the money to help the widows of the men they had just lost. That made Doc feel a little better, but he was still shitting a brick.

They bounced, skidded, and climbed through some of the roughest goddamned terrain imaginable and wound up having to ditch the truck about fifty meters below the cave entrance. Even with the HMMWV in "Low-Locked full 4WD," it just couldn't handle more than a 60-percent grade.

"Fuck, it's cold," said Doc as he began opening the heavy metal "cruise boxes" they would use to store the cash and gold.

While he and Eddy did that, Mad Dog got the pioneer tools from the HMMWV. The tools included a D-handle shovel, a pick mattock, and an axe. He also hauled their entrenching tools up the mountain and back into the cave. With his flashlight leading the way, Mad Dog and his men returned to the chasm.

As they began carrying out the first crate of gold, a muffled thumping of helicopter gunships sent Mad Dog sprinting for the outside. Four of the godforsaken whirly-birds streaked toward the northeast. Whether they had spotted the HMMWV, whose hot engine would show up in their thermals, Mad Dog didn't know, but it would be wise at this juncture of the operation to get the fuck out, pronto!

The transfer of gold and money into the cruise boxes took another fifteen minutes, with Mad Dog shitting a brick the entire time. He had never been more nervous in his life—and that included the first time he had gotten laid and the first time he'd been shot at. There was so much at stake, a future waiting to happen . . .

Or a career about to end.

Murphy must've had too much to drink and had slept through the night because Mad Dog and his fellow non-commissioned thieves returned to Camp Buffalo without drawing any attention.

They discreetly moved the cruise boxes into the camp's main mess tent. These particular boxes were rectangular, and, when stood on their ends, rose to about table height, which was why many of them had been combined with large cargo lids to make tables so that more marines could be fed at one time.

The Marine Corps and the Navy had a tradition of keeping "special" or difficult-to-acquire spare parts stored in such boxes. These parts were purloined by making a "midnight small-stores run" (outright thievery) or traded for by the age-old tradition of cumshaw. There was a code of honor whereby no one raided another gang's cruise box and the COs never inspected the contents of these boxes during material inspections. Don't ask, don't tell.

The next morning, at 0700, Mad Dog, Eddy, and Doc couldn't resist the temptation of waiting until their "special" table in the mess tent was free. Mad Dog led his men away from the line, and they settled down with their trays.

Doc leaned forward over his breakfast, his eyes wide. "Sergeant, this is crazy."

"Or brilliant. Depends on your point of view."

A long shadow passed over them, and when Mad Dog glanced up, a pit immediately formed in his stomach.

"Well, well, well, if it isn't the Mad Dog himself—and his leg-humping buddies."

Jimmy Judas stood six five but couldn't have weighed more than one-eighty soaking wet. He had the long limbs of an extraterrestrial, and though he was bald, he had grown a ponytail wired with gray to compensate—which it didn't, of course. When he flashed that yellowing, chipped-tooth grin framed by his scraggly beard, Mad Dog wanted to stand up and kick him in the balls. But Moody had no balls. He was all mouth, a pilot fish dressed in local garb who wanted to play with the big boys, but he was just another company scavenger, playing both sides against the middle, fucking everyone over and cashing in at the end.

"Hey, Judas?" Eddy called. "Eat me."

"Gentlemen, I thought we agreed. No hard feelings."

"We spend two weeks reconning that village based on your intel," said Mad Dog. "And what do you come up with? Jack shit. Wild fucking goose chase. You wasted the tax payers' resources. So . . . I thought we agreed that you are an incompetent asshole."

"My intel was good. Your timing wasn't. Now let me ask you something. That wouldn't have been you guys burning the midnight oil in a hummer last night . . ."

Mad Dog's lips came together, and he looked to see if Doc or Eddy wore guilty expressions; they didn't. "Wasn't us," Mad Dog answered.

"Yeah, because I'm privy to a lot of information, stuff from chopper pilots, copies of fake OPORDs with the names of marines who don't exist on them, you name it. And I was up real early this morning. Real early. I had a very interesting conversation with one of our allies, a warlord named Hamid Hekmatyar."

"We know who he is," said Mad Dog.

"Well he's blown a nut. Someone stole his money. He told me he stashed it in a cave not too far from where you guys were ambushed yesterday."

"I *wish* we had your buddy's money," Mad Dog said with a laugh. "I'd spend it all on hookers and booze, and when the money ran out, I'd charge the rest to the company account, just like you do."

"Hekmatyar is a crucial ally. If he finds out his money was stolen by Americans, he'll cut us off and get back in bed with the Taliban."

Mad Dog sipped his coffee. "That fuckin' rag head is a drug pusher. And so are you. So get the fuck out of here."

Judas smirked. "I'll be watching you, *Sergeant*. I'll be watching all of you."

"Whoa," Eddy said with an exaggerated shiver.

All three soldiers burst out laughing as Judas left.

Mad Dog waited until the agent was out of earshot, then he sighed deeply. "Fuck . . . This is not good."

* * *

Later on that day, Mad Dog stood outside his tent, peering through his binoculars at Judas, who was seated behind the wheel of an HMMWV and taking a long pull on a bottle of Coke. The agent was about to leave the camp, probably heading off for a meeting with that opium pusher he financed.

"He's drinking it now," Mad Dog told Eddy.

"Asshole."

"He'll be shitting for a week," said Doc. "That oughta take his mind off us."

"I wish I had something better, something a little more mature."

"Hey, even if this doesn't work, it's funny," said Eddy. "He's already as skinny as a green bean, so he might as well be the right color."

Mad Dog lowered his binoculars and faced them. "Just two more days, boys. If we can lay low for two more days, we'll be in good shape."

"Laying low is no problem, but that fuckin' patrol tomorrow is," said Doc.

"Yeah, I know," moaned Mad Dog. "I'll see if I can get us out of it."

Eddy snorted in disbelief. "How?"

"First play the sympathy card. If that doesn't work, I got some dirt on him."

Mad Dog volunteered himself, Eddy, and Doc for all the shit jobs around the camp, so long as the CO wouldn't send them out in the field. After all, they were scheduled for R&R in just two days. Getting killed before they had a chance to ship their loot out of the 'Stan was unacceptable, even if that meant swallowing their pride and being accused of having lost their edge by their fellow marines.

The CO finally agreed, sans any threats—which was too bad, because Mad Dog was hoping to see the look on the man's face when he told him that he knew about the affair. To his credit, Mad Dog had employed an expensive, high-tech thermal video camera normally used for special recon missions or for blackmailing one's CO because you never knew when you'd need a favor. The footage had been converted into an mpg file easily emailed to one's spouse.

Not going there was for the best, though. Too personal. Too dark and dirty.

So for the next few days Mad Dog, Eddy, and Doc played professional maids for the rest of the company, cleaning weapons, filling sandbags, and helping the new replacements become quickly acclimated to life in the 'Stan.

They had neither seen nor heard from their favorite CIA agent, and that was good. Mad Dog thought of asking a few of the doctors if Judas had come in complaining of a stomach virus or other gastrointestinal aliments, but he figured he'd leave well enough alone. Judas was off somewhere, squatting and groaning, and he didn't need someone asking after him.

The enormous C–5 Galaxy arrived on the tarmac, on schedule. The plane was rotating broken and worn-out APCs, bulldozers, and other heavy equipment to Germany for recycling and was cause for the men to delay their R&R. Still, Mad Dog, Eddy, and Doc couldn't just stroll onto the plane. Everything that left the country was checked by the military police. They used dogs to sniff out explosives or drugs being shipped back to the states or other destinations. They also made sure no arms or ammunition was heading out. You didn't want that shit hitting the streets of Miami or Detroit or D.C.; they already had their share of illegal ordnance.

The customs MPs were pricks of the first order, and, other than caskets, checked it all. Mad Dog had considered shipping the loot with some poor bastard's remains, but that meant the stash would wind up at Dover Air Force Base in Delaware and still be under military guard 24/7.

Thus, the day before, Mad Dog had made it a point to bribe one of the MPs. It was cheaper, faster, and easier. Well, not quite as cheap. The prick was also a negotiator of the first order and upped his price twice. Mad Dog gave in. Ten thousand fucking bucks to the wind. But it worked.

Mad Dog, Eddy, Doc, and their four cruise boxes hitched a ride, and, amazingly, left Afghanistan without being caught. They were so giddy that even the C–5's crew inquired about their grins. "Just glad for some time off," Mad Dog told them.

The C–5's final stop was in Friedrichshafen on the northern edge of Lake Constance, where the three box-toting musketeers got off, carrying a set of "official orders" and military ID cards. A ferry ride across Lake Constance put them in the land of Swiss chocolate and Rolex watches.

The Gnomes of Zurich converted the gold to U.S. dollars for a fee, but in the end the trio netted $25.34 million. Numbered accounts were non-interest-bearing: the price paid for anonymity, which, of course, translated into more money for the gnome. Everyone won.

With a few urgent phone calls back to the States, Mad Dog had set up a dummy corporation with the help of an old high school buddy turned Harvard grad lawyer, Bryan Johnson, aka "Catfish." Mad Dog, Eddy, and Doc now had the seed money to buy controlling interest in the fledgling International Philippine Group Bank (IPG). Mad Dog's goal was to have IPG expand its interests into military and security operations. Under his guidance and influence, the business would thrive.

They left Zurich and stayed in Baden-Baden, where they spent another two days at one of the spas, bathing in natural spring water and being pampered by some really husky, really ugly women. But those broads had great hands, and every muscle in Mad Dog's body felt loose by the time they left.

What he had forgotten, though, was that they had given Jimmy Judas the shits, and with all that shit around, some of it was bound to hit the fan.

During the next two months, several warlords filed charges of brutality and excessive force against Mad Dog, Eddy, and Doc. Two weeks after they had returned from their R&R, the shit had indeed hit the fan and become an international shitfest that Mad Dog just knew was instigated by Judas.

A three-month-long investigation had begun, during which time Mad Dog and his team had been making routine patrols through the villages within a two kilometer radius of the camp because that had become the quiet zone, with no fighters spotted for weeks. The brass didn't want them getting too close to the Taliban for fear of another incident. Mad Dog's talents were being wasted, and he had voiced those concerns to the CO, whose deaf ears had remained deaf.

Mad Dog's attorney had told him that the Corps wouldn't have enough evidence to warrant a court-martial or even a Letter of Reprimand. Mad Dog, Eddy, and Doc would confess to being a little too exuberant and a little too efficient.

However, the commandant of the Marine Corps and even the secretary of defense were involved, and they knew that appeasing the Afghan locals was necessary since the relationship between the U.S. and Afghanistan was already strained because of little problems like killing people with food drops.

Consequently, there was a good chance that Mad Dog, Eddy, and Doc would be cashiered out with an administrative discharge (for the good of the service) under honorable conditions, in lieu of a court-martial. The Corp's decision was supposed to come in any day now.

What no one could predict, however, was that the Taliban would return to the quiet zone around Camp Buffalo, to the most innocent of villages, where, only minutes before, they had shot a farmer. Mad Dog reported the attack, said that his team had already taken out two fighters. They were hunting down more. He cringed as he waited for a reply.

"Alpha One, you break off that attack!" barked the CO. "I say again, you break off that attack, over!"

Suddenly, gunfire splintered pieces off of the cart behind which he'd sought cover.

Cursing under his breath, Mad Dog keyed the mike. "I say again, we are taking fire, over!"

"Break off the attack!"

"Sergeant, he's telling us not to fight?" asked Watkins.

"You heard him. If Bravo was out here, he wouldn't be saying that. But it's us. The politically incorrect team. And now we're fucked."

"What're you going to do?"

Mad Dog's face flushed, and suddenly he damned radio protocol to hell, damned it all to hell, figured this would be his last act as a United States marine. "Herschel, I got three kids in a hut right here, we're pinned down, taking fire. I ain't breaking off the fucking attack!" He slammed down the microphone.

"Holy shit, Sergeant," said Watkins. "You're the coolest fuckin' dude I know. And sorry for cursing, Sergeant."

"Just shut up. Go to the hut, let me know how the interpreter's doing with that farmer. I have to get Doc back here."

"On my way, Sergeant!" Watkins darted off, drawing another spate of gunfire.

Mad Dog himself raced toward the hills, a round striking two rocks less than a meter to his left. He lowered himself to one knee, took aim at the shooter who peered out from behind a boulder, fired.

Down went the asshole. Oh, he'd had no idea how extensively marines trained on the range, no idea that every marine is a rifleman, no idea that Mad Dog was standing on the shoulders of every United States marine who had thrown himself into the fight and had given his life for his country.

And, of course, the asshole would never know.

Carbines resounded somewhere above him. Mad Dog turned and charged after the racket, picking his way past a steep slope to where a little cut formed a path.

He slowed, sidestepped his way up the hill, using the cut as a source of cover. He arrived on yet another ridge where in the distance Eddy and Doc lay on their bellies, trading fire with a shooter poised between two rocks, one slightly overhanging the other.

His breath nearly gone, Mad Dog reached a ditch, dropped onto his gut, called into his mike: "Doc, I need you back at the hut. Farmer's been hit. I'm right behind you, coming up. Eddy, give him cover."

They didn't answer. Just acted. Eddy opened up. Doc hauled ass, dashing by Mad Dog, who at that second sprinted up to join Eddy. He slammed down at his assistant's side. "You're taking way too long to kill this fuck."

"I know."

"Cover me."

"Roger that."

He took off like he was wearing cleats and about to round the bases.

Eddy's gunfire sliced past Mad Dog's legs.

The Taliban dickhead wasn't returning fire, too scared to peek out from behind his rock with all those rounds ricocheting and sparking around his head.

Mad Dog veered to the right, dove for home plate, hit the ground in a pile of dust at the base of the rock. He crawled forward, each movement silent and carefully measured as the bad guy chanced a few shots at Eddy.

"Eddy, keep firing until I say," Mad Dog whispered into his mike. Then he dragged himself on his elbows a little farther, came completely around the rock, and spotted the ragged-looking fighter. "Okay, Eddy, stop!"

In one fluid motion, Mad Dog sprang to his feet, glided up behind the shooter. Shifting his hands to the barrel of his carbine, Mad Dog flipped the rifle around and raised it high over his shoulder.

Thud! The rifle's collapsible stock connected with the scumbag's skull, his head swinging sideways at an improbable angle.

As Mr. Taliban shrank to his gut, Mad Dog seized the guy's weapon, yanked it away, then dropped both rifles and grabbed the asshole by the neck.

Setting his teeth, Mad Dog began choking the shooter, grimacing over the man's stench as blood oozed from a deep gash on his head. Then he hauled the dazed man to his feet, grabbed a pair of plastic zipper cuffs from his assault pouch, and bound the fighter's hands behind his back. With one hand wrapped firmly around the back of his prisoner's neck, Mad Dog led him toward Eddy.

"Son of a bitch, you actually caught one," said Eddy, who rose slowly to his feet, his gaze darting from hill to hill.

Doc came humping up the ridge, his face long. "Farmer died. Shit . . ."

"Sergeant, if you'd like, Doc and I'll escort the prisoner down the hill and hold him," said Eddy. "Herschel's probably been screaming for a SITREP."

Mad Dog snorted. "Damn, this ain't the way to fight wars."

"And you got a better way? How? As mercenaries?" asked Doc. "You're dreaming."

"I didn't say that."

"Good, because this shit ain't going away. Maybe you'll get the job done better because you won't have to fuck with laws, but this kind of shit? Damn, the world is cruel and unfair."

"Well, Jesus Christ, Doc, that makes me want to put on a happy face," said Eddy. "And by the way, asshole, you ain't cashing out your share. You're in the business, whether you like it or not."

"We'll see."

"And we might be in business sooner than later," said Mad Dog. "Especially after this. Come on."

A small crowd was gathering in the village below, ten or fifteen people, the women already wailing, the men shouting in anger, an icy wind whipping over the whole scene.

"Sergeant?" Watkins called.

"Yeah, I know, the CO's been howling."

"He's on his way out here."

Mad Dog was about to react—

When a horrific explosion lifted from the road at the base of the hills, stealing everyone's attention.

It was a bomb, possibly a land mine. Afghanistan was littered with them, antitank, antipersonnel, you name it.

Or it could've been an IED remote detonated by more Taliban assholes hiding in the hills.

The distance between Mad Dog and the expanding cloud of black smoke seemed like nothing as he ran with all his might. Watkins was screaming about more mines, but all Mad Dog could think of was getting to his boys, his business partners, his friends and brothers.

He was crying by the time he reached them, because in his heart of hearts he knew what had happened.

Doc was already dead. Shattered. Almost unrecognizable. Eddy was still alive but bleeding profusely from his severed legs and shredded left arm. Part of his face was gone. He had but seconds to live.

Mad Dog could barely look upon his friend. He took

Eddy's remaining hand in his own, coughing at the horrible smell and smoke burning his eyes.

"Two more widows," said Eddy. "You'll take care of them, won't you, Sergeant?"

Mad Dog was too choked up to answer.

He didn't remember being carried down from the hills, barely remembered the conversation with Jimmy Judas, who had come to gloat and tell him that he was being discharged.

Mad Dog would always love the Corps, but it was time to go home and start anew, guided by the memory of brothers in arms.

Chapter 1

....

"The Dog Pound"
Talisay City
Cebu, the Philippines
Present Day
1750 Hours Local Time

"Hey, Dan? You know who called me this morning?" Mad Dog asked as he ambled into the guesthouse and crossed to the living room.

Gunnery Sergeant Daniel M. Forrest III, USMC, retired, leaned back in his recliner. "Hold on a minute. I'm in the middle of something."

Old "Diaper Dan" was checking his blood sugar, squinting at the device's little readout until he remembered to put on his bifocals. While he could no longer control his bowels and was dying slowly from complications related to diabetes (he'd already lost a few toes), he was as lucid as ever. He had spent seventy-five glorious years trouncing around the planet, having fought in Cambodia, 'Nam, Bosnia, and even the first Gulf War, serving as an advisor. He was a hard man who would go out with a tremendous fight.

When Mad Dog was thirteen, his father had passed away from cancer, and Dan, a next-door neighbor who was in the Marines, had taken Mad Dog under his wing, inspired him, served as a father and role model.

What was more, Dan was the marine who had taught Mad Dog everything he knew, a tactical genius who, unfortunately, had been left all alone in the world. His wife had already passed on, they'd had no kids, and he had a sister who had died six years prior in a car accident.

And so, as Dan had begun the final chapter of his life, Mad Dog had taken in the old solider, promised him that he would live on the estate (aka the Dog Pound) until God called him home. Two pretty nurses, brown-skinned locals who rotated throughout the week, cared for him. Each morning when one came, he showed her his bottle of Viagra and was willing to show her more. Though wizened, he still had a thick shock of white hair and an amazing gleam in his blue eyes.

The old coot had actually sweet-talked one nurse into bed by promising her a rich woman's life, and Mad Dog had walked in on them bumping uglies. He had been forced to fire the girl—and she was a girl, just twenty—and warn Dan against taking any more pills and taking advantage of the help.

Dan had been furious, said he was leaving, but had changed his mind an hour later.

The truth was, Mad Dog didn't keep Dan around because he felt bad for the guy (although that was true) or because he felt responsible for the man (that was also true). Dan was one sharp motherfucker. Whenever a job was on the table, Mad Dog always took it to Dan. More often than not Dan would come up with tactical solutions to really complex logistical problems. The old guy knew his shit. Period.

So as he waited, Mad Dog took a moment to reflect. His dream to have the International Philippine Group Bank's interests expand into military and security operations had come to pass. He had taken on several side operations, serving as a military trainer in South America and the Philippines in order to sustain IPG's cash flow during the early years after 9/11.

IPG's success facilitated the founding of the Olongapo Procurement Center. OPC served (on a commission basis) as a Philippine Army Contractor (PAC), an advisor, and a procurer of military armaments for the Philippine Army via the international marketplace.

Tagalog Aviation was founded and became a wholly owned subsidiary of IPG. TA had a fleet of five planes providing charter and freight services. TA charter offered vacation packages with four-star accommodations at IPG-owned hotels in a dozen key cities throughout the world.

Mad Dog tacked on freight costs in addition to commissions for services rendered to the Philippine Army. IPG allowed Mad Dog to electronically transfer large sums of money anywhere in the world. OPC provided him with the necessary arms licenses and contacts to procure state-of-the-art hardware. TA gave him the mobility he needed to show up at anyone's doorstep, locked and loaded.

Old Dan finished checking his blood sugar. "Now what were you saying?"

"Jack Palansky. You remember him?"

"Palansky. Oh, I remember that asshole. Big Polack.

Kinda dumb looking face. Little pudgy. Stupid laugh he had. Good rifleman, though, I remember."

"Yeah, well he's working for an Australian company called Morstarr. They're mining diamonds in Angola. He was hired by the CEO, a guy named Kidman, and went there to train their security force. Typical merc job, but then they asked him to stay on as head. Gave him a really fat bonus." Mad Dog crossed over to the sofa, plopped down, and scratched his head. He had maintained his high-and-tight crew cut, though it was mostly gray now. The gold skull earring betrayed his departure from the service. "So, anyway, Jack's got a problem there. Someone stole about three to four ounces of diamonds. Stuff's worth approximately twenty-five million, that is, after expenses to cut and polish."

"And Palansky's in charge of security there? Shit, he's a Polack, all right."

Mad Dog sighed in frustration. "Listen, Morstarr needs us because the thieves are well armed and the terrain is dangerous. Jack doesn't trust all of his people, and he trusts the local police and military even less."

"How much?"

"They'll pay an even two mil to recover—plus Jack says he'll pick up our travel expenses and bribes, but that's it. Bottom line: no diamonds, no money."

"Fuck that. You want the usual five hundred Gs just to go there and take a look around—because those rocks are long gone."

Mad Dog shook his head. "Jack thinks they're still in Angola. For some reason, the thieves are laying low."

"Angola . . . now there's a fun place. Decades of civil war, thugs running wild, fighting over diamonds. Poverty, disease, shit. You want to go there on a goose chase?"

"I gave Mr. Bibby a call, and he tapped his contacts at the diamond cartel in London. No one's been approached yet about the buy of a lifetime. He also checked with some people in Antwerp and in Jerusalem to see if the cutters and polishers have been given any heads-up for an influx of new work."

Over the years, Mad Dog had used his contacts within the military community to carefully recruit a team of first-class operators from all branches of the service. While he preferred Americans, he recognized the need for international operators, leading him to hire Mr. Alastair Bibby, formerly of MI6, the British secret intelligence service. Bibby was a character, all right, an intelligence specialist who abhorred most of the other team members, deeming them heathens and barbarians, though he seemed to tolerate Mad Dog well enough. However, even Mad Dog wasn't allowed to call him Alastair. It was Mr. Bibby, thank you.

"You want to take this on, it's up to you," said Dan. "But I don't like it."

"Maybe you're right. Could be a waste of time—or it could earn us two million big ones."

Dan thought a moment. "Did Palansky say anything else about the thieves?"

"He thinks they're the same band who tried hitting them a few times in the past."

"Locals? I doubt it."

"Well, here's the thing. They couldn't pull it off until now, so Jack thinks they got help from the inside."

"Well, I don't buy that some local yahoos got lucky and stole twenty-five million in rocks."

"Like Jack said, they got help."

"So he's giving you gas money and greasing palms up

front. No diamonds, and you lose big time. The boys will still need to be paid, and that's big-time overhead."

Mad Dog thought of the pictures hanging in his living room, focused on one in particular, a shot of himself, Eddy, and Doc eating breakfast at the "special table" before they'd flown off to Germany. They might not be his partners in the flesh, but he continued to seek their guidance. He heard them bickering over the job. Eddy was ready to go full throttle. Doc, like old Diaper Dan, had his reservations.

"Sometimes you just go with your gut and take the leap. It's a good payout."

"And you know what? Even if it winds up costing us, so long as no one gets hurt, it'll still be worth it."

"How you figure?"

"Come on, Michael. Running around in the jungle and hunting other guys? Playing with big bombs and big guns? That shit is fucking fun! I wish I could go with you!"

Mad Dog grinned and felt the rush—just a hint—but the rush nonetheless.

Dan nodded. "All right, so you're going, leaving me here all alone in paradise with two young broads."

Mad Dog widened his eyes and waved his index finger. "Hey, I find out you went online and bought more Viagra—"

"Yeah, yeah."

Mad Dog rose. "So how is your blood sugar?"

Dan made a face.

"You've been sneaking ice cream again. I told you!"

"Get out of here. Go run around Angola and bring back some money so you can support the old burden."

Mad Dog went over to Dan, put a hand on his shoulder. "You're an old fuck. But you're not a burden."

* * *

Mr. Alastair Bibby was already in the Philippines when Mad Dog had called him regarding the diamond theft in Angola, thus he was the first to arrive at the Spanish-in-fluenced colonial-style home with guest house.

Bibby wanted to buy a house on Cebu himself, and he had been shopping around the island for the preceding few days. He would never stay with Mad Dog when he was in town, despite the six bedrooms, all with ample guest accommodations. He wanted to avoid the others as much as possible.

Deep down, Bibby was ashamed of what he had become, and he recognized quite clearly that he was living in denial. He thought he could make the situation better by placing himself above these callous killers, when he, in fact, was as cold and capable of murder as they were.

He had a history to prove it. After resigning from MI6 because of "personality differences" between himself and his superiors, he had gone to work for one of England's most notorious mercenaries, Colin Ricer, a man who had nearly caused two international incidents, one in Papua New Guinea, the other in Sierra Leone. After leaving Ricer's group, he had learned about Mad Dog from a mutual acquaintance, Mr. Waffa Zarour, a Palestinian man who had been educated in Saudi Arabia and who had opened up an Internet café in Ram Allah, ten miles north of Jerusalem.

Zarour, nicknamed "the Waffle Man" by Mad Dog, was one of the team's best informants in the Middle East and belonged to a private network of spies who sold information to everyone, including the Israeli army, and, unfortunately, terrorist groups. While at MI6, Bibby had done quite a lot of "business" with Zarour, and when he had left Ricer's group, Zarour put him in touch with Mad Dog.

And so for the preceding two years, Bibby had been collecting a paycheck from IPG and had participated in four major jobs. Sure, he had been tempted to join a much larger Private Military Company (PMC), but many of those lumbered along on bureaucratic treads, just like MI6. If Bibby was going to dedicate his time and efforts toward something, he wanted to be sure that the outcomes would be real and significant. That was the idealist in him. At thirty-nine, he was getting too old to just take the money and run. What he left behind was equally important.

At least that much he shared with Mad Dog and the others. They could affect change. They had, and they would again.

With all that in mind, he spoke briefly with Mad Dog, helped the man contact the rest of the team, then returned to his hotel. In the morning, the team would assemble for the obligatory briefing, then they would chopper up to Manila.

Bibby spent the rest of the evening coordinating their trip to Angola. You couldn't kite around the world without proper cover, and he would make sure that all those ducks were in a row before they departed.

Several calls and chat sessions via his satellite-linked computer put the wheels in motion.

The next morning, as was his wont, Mad Dog had the caterers prepare a massive gourmet breakfast, and as the men slowly arrived, one by one, they immediately tore into fresh fruit, eggs, croissants, and crisp bacon. Heavenly scents wafted through the house, and it was all Bibby could do to hold back from gorging himself. He rarely ate breakfast. Only tea, thank you. He sat in a corner, watching his socially inept colleagues chew with their mouths open and swear, like, well, mercenaries.

To his left were Wolfgang and Sapper. Bibby wasn't thrilled with those Neanderthals being on the team. He had repeatedly shared his concerns with Mad Dog, arguing that both men needed to take their positions more seriously.

The bearded and long-haired Tommy Wolfgang was a former master gunner in the U.S. Army, and while he had considerable experience with vehicles and weapons systems, his claims of being a "real demon" with the deadly arts had thus far gone unproven. He was an impressive shooter, though, carrying both the RT–20 Antimateriel Sniper Rifle from Croatia (a 20mm rifle that he used to destroy big targets like APCs or anything else from a distance) and the H&K G36C, his primary weapon, a 5.56mm Commando carbine with a dual sight system and more. Both guns were as big and loud as their operator.

Sapper, whose real name was Daniel Culpepper, was a former army combat engineer, the team's demo guy, and resembled a black prizefighter with diamonds in his ears and a tattoo of black flames rising up his neck. He carried a Barrett M468 6.8mm SPC carbine with an integral M203 grenade launcher to lob explosives farther than he could throw them. He also packed lots of 40mm buckshot rounds in addition to the HE grenade rounds, and he was probably the most heavily armed man on the team. Sure, he could blow up and kill with the best of them, but his bloated ego often clouded his vision.

Wolfgang and Sapper were Bibby's biggest annoyances. The other six were all assholes, but they were serious about what they did and had true talent. Moreover, not all of them were recruited for every job. Wolfgang and Sapper were always around and simply too full of themselves. Even more disturbing was the fact that Wolfgang constantly vied to become assistant team leader, voicing his desire after every major operation.

Interestingly enough, Mad Dog had decided early on that leadership roles and increased bonuses would go to people on the basis of their ability, rather than on past service rank or seniority. True pirates of the Caribbean functioned that way. Mad Dog remained a strong leader and clung tightfistedly to the business-side of operations. That was understandable. Still, based on his own experience, willingness to listen, and willingness to let others demonstrate their prowess, he always received unanimous approval. His men didn't just follow him because he had the money; they followed him because his skills in business and in war had earned their respect.

Bibby's past successes, coupled with his intellect, had in the past year garnered him the title of assistant team leader. Fire Team leaders were also selected by Mad Dog. It was important for the team to function as a cohesive unit, despite personal differences. Mad Dog was all about unit integrity, which he firmly believed separated the combatants from the corpses.

"Why, hello there, old chap," called Wolfgang, who wore a good portion of his croissant on his beard. "Having a spot of tea, are we?"

Like some Americans, Wolfgang enjoyed speaking with a British accent and didn't realize how foolish he sounded.

And Bibby always threw it back in his face. "Nah, motherfucker," he said like an Italian American New

Yawka. "I'm drinkin' my fuckin' tea while you scumbags eat like a buncha gavones."

"Come on, Ally, you know you love us," said Sapper. "We're just doing our thing. Someone has to provide the entertainment around here, and it might as well be you."

Bibby lowered his voice and spoke normally. "Well, if that's the case, then let me entertain you with a warning: I'll expect nothing but the best out there, especially from you, Wolfgang. Your inability to grow up has worn thin my patience. There's a lot of money at stake, not to mention our lives. Now, if you'll excuse me." He headed across the room, to where old man Dan had staked out a position near the coffee pot.

Mad Dog finally arrived and gave everyone the requisite briefing, with Bibby stepping in to provide what intelligence he had already gathered. Wolfgang and Sapper folded their arms over their chests and looked unimpressed.

After the meeting they took careful inventory of their gear, packed it into a trio of Land Rovers, and headed off for the chopper, piloted by their rotary wing expert, Dick Gallway, aka "Night Stalker," a former captain with the Army's 160th Special Operations Aviation Regiment who had flown in Somalia and had some interesting tales regarding the whole "Black Hawk Down" affair.

Once in Manila, they boarded a C–130 that Mad Dog had purchased eighteen months prior. With Bibby's assistance and contacts, he'd had it surreptitiously upgraded to the J series along with a customized avionics package that would make the USAF drool if they knew it existed. The plane was painted with a big TA (Tagalog Aviation) on each side of the stabilizer and was referred to by Mad Dog and the other gorillas as "Tits & Ass"

Airlines and flown by a retired Air Force pilot named Gerald Styles, who also flew vacation charters for Mad Dog but who refused any job dangerous enough to interfere with his golf game. Mad Dog respected that. The guy was sixty-one. So Mad Dog routinely lied about the dangers involved. That got Styles in the cockpit every time.

They took off at midnight for the four hour, 1,287-nautical-mile leg to Kuala Lumpur, Malaysia. An hour layover there was necessary to repaint the T's to emerald green and the A's to powder blue on the stabilizers to signify "Thailand Army" military colors while the ever-conservative Styles topped off fuel tanks.

Why were these changes to the aircraft necessary? Because Bibby had made a deal with his MI6 contacts on Diego Garcia to make a refueling stop at the joint U.S.-UK air and naval refueling and support station. Thailand was conducting joint covert counterterrorism ops with the UK, and they would exploit these exercises by appearing as just another Thailand military aircraft.

They got out of Kuala Lumpur under the cover of darkness with no witnesses to their custom paint job.

The Diego Garcia leg was 7.5 hours, 1,862 nautical miles, at below best altitude to evade nosy radars. Styles told Mad Dog he'd have to keep it under 260 knots because of turbulence at low altitude.

"Even then it'll be one hell of a bumpy ride, fighting head winds all the way," warned the old pilot.

From Diego Garcia, they made the five-hour, 1,609-nautical-mile jump to Antananarivo, Madagascar. After refueling, repainting the TAs once more, and securing the latest intel, the smoothest leg of their trip began. It was a 6.5-hour, 2,081-nautical-mile run at best speed, over the mountains to Luanda, Angola.

During the last hour of their flight, Mad Dog leaned over and asked Bibby, "Jack's got us covered on the ground? No questions? No interference?"

"He promised."

"Great."

Bibby hesitated. "Can we really trust him?"

Mad Dog smiled broadly. "Oh, I think we can. He was a marine."

Bibby nodded slowly, but a question that had been burning inside since he had first learned about the job finally reached his lips. "Mr. Hertzog, what if your friend Jack stole the diamonds?"

"That would be interesting, wouldn't it?"

"He told his boss about IPG and the services we provide so he could exploit your trust in him. He sends us chasing false leads, while he gets away."

"If he took the diamonds, he would've boogied in a second. He's a hit-and-run kind of guy. Forget it. We can trust him. Period."

Bibby leaned back, removed his small glasses, then rubbed aching eyes.

By the end of the hour, everyone was sitting upright, eyes wide, as rubber struck tarmac, the plane slowed, then taxied toward the gate at Luanda 4 de Fevereiro (LAD).

"Hey, Michael, we got a welcome wagon outside," said Styles from the cockpit. "This is weird. Everything was cool with the boys in the tower."

"Yeah, look at that," said Wolfgang. "All the pretty lights—just for us."

Bibby stood and went to one of the windows. A horde

of local police cars was rolling up to the plane. "Well, he's moved the goal posts on us, hasn't he?"

Mad Dog frowned. "What the fuck?"

"You said we could trust him. Period," said Bibby. "Bloody hell!"

"Doolittle?" Mad Dog called.

"Yes, Sergeant. Coming, Sergeant."

The translator had never stopped calling Mad Dog by his rank, and the man had never corrected him. He must have liked the reminder. "Let's see what's going on."

"This I don't like," said the translator. "Being detained is not good. Not here."

"It's just a mix-up. We don't even know if we're being held yet. Maybe Jack arranged this. It's an escort."

"A police escort for a planeload of mercenaries?" asked Bibby. "I find that hard to believe, even more so because Jack never mentioned this."

Mad Dog winced. "Mr. Bibby, come along, please. Everyone else, sit tight. Keep your weapons holstered. We'll be right back."

The conversation with the airport security chief was, well, it wasn't a conversation at all. He decided to arrest everyone, even after Bibby insisted that Morstarr had made "arrangements" for their arrival.

Mad Dog ordered the men to surrender, drawing groans from everyone except Bibby, whose face was locked in a smug expression.

Their weapons, cell and satellite phones, jewelry, and other personal items were confiscated, then they were escorted from the plane and, one by one, ushered into a small room, where each was subjected to the humiliation of a strip search.

Bibby ground his teeth as he removed his shirt and

trousers, dropped his boxers, and glowered as the guards made a perfunctory inspection of his person. Even they seemed uncomfortable with the process.

He was allowed to re-dress, was cuffed, then transferred to a holding facility—a narrow, windowless, roach-infested room with no chairs—until the authorities could decide what to do with them. Guards were placed around the plane.

Wolfgang was thrown into the room, a pink lump forming on his forehead.

"What happened?" Mad Dog asked.

"When I bent over so they could check my crack, I farted in their faces."

A few of the other guys laughed. Mr. Bibby did not.

The job had come to a complete standstill because Mad Dog had placed too much faith in one man. Never before had he made such an error. Bibby was seconds from meltdown.

"I bet this is all your fault, Bibby," said Wolfgang, shambling over, his head turning even more red. "Old Jack there probably couldn't understand your accent."

Bibby pushed off the wall, brought himself to full height, and walked over to the man, wrists straining against his cuffs.

Wolfgang grinned and said, "What're you gonna do, bite me?"

Before the man could finish, he was on the deck, having been head-butted so hard that for a second, his eyes rolled back in his head. Bibby had targeted Wolfgang's lump, of course.

He hunkered down, his own forehead smarting. "Please, Wolfgang. It's *Mr.* Bibby. I insist."

To hell with unit integrity. At least for the moment.

Chapter 2

Luanda 4 de Fevereiro (LAD)
Luanda, Angola
Present Day
0630 Hours Local Time

Rookie, who had been sitting on the floor next to Mad Dog for the past two hours, leaned over and said, "You told me, and I quote, 'Don't worry about going to jail. We don't break the law so much as navigate around it.'"

"I said that?"

"Yeah, you did."

Takahiro Masaki, a former member of the army's famed Delta Force, had been recruited only a month earlier after one of Mad Dog's other guys, Bobby Foyte, an army Ranger who'd developed a bum knee, decided to make playing the market his full-time career.

Masaki was thirty, had strong Japanese features, a spiked haircut that added an inch to his five-foot-eight frame, and had left the army for something different:

better pay. Getting busted had never been on his To Do list; it wasn't on Mad Dog's either. What the hell had happened to Jack?

"You told me I'd be like Bruce Lee with a Beretta."

"I never said that."

"You told me there'd be big commissions on top of my base pay. *Big* commissions, you said."

"I might've said that."

"You told me I could do this for a couple of years and be set for life, just like Foyte."

Mad Dog raised his brows. "Bobby knew how to invest his money. He's helping me, too, keeping some of it in the family. But as Scarface once said, you gotta make da money first."

"Well, what the fuck, Dog? This kind of shit is totally unprofessional. I thought I signed on with first-class operators! How do we make the money in here?"

Mad Dog stiffened. "Just chill out, Rook. For some reason, Jack didn't get to these guys. I don't know why. Be patient. He'll be here."

"Why, because he's a marine and won't let you down? Fuck man, we're all mercs now. He fucked us over."

"No," Mad Dog said emphatically. "He did not. If we recover the diamonds, he gets a bonus for recommending us. So he's got no reason to fuck us over."

Unless Bibby was right and Jack had a master plan that involved using Mad Dog and his team as a diversion. Shit. You never knew.

"Hey, Bossman, you want me to educate him?" asked Pope as he crouched down before them, sweat beading off his enormous shaven head.

Rookie laughed. "Yo, dude, you know the story of David and Goliath?"

"I know I can squeeze you like a packet of soy sauce. I'll squeeze and squeeze till you pop!"

Billy Pope had been a lieutenant commander in the Navy who had served on both SEAL and SDV teams. He had been trained extensively in submarine insertion and extraction, was an expert rifleman, and liked to show off his Ninjutsu and Israeli Krav Maga skills whenever he had the chance. However, Mad Dog had never seen him squeeze another man like a packet of soy sauce. That was a new one on him. At six six, two hundred and seventy pounds, Pope was the biggest, most evil-minded motherfucker on the team. Sure, he looked like a big ape with no neck, but he was smart, too, an information specialist who could crack into computer systems as effortlessly as Bibby.

"Hey, Dog, you want some dirt on our famous fire team leader?" asked Rookie. "You know what he's got in his ruck? A fuckin' Barbie doll. I swear to God. He's got a doll in there! He plays with dolls! Not blow-up ones. Little ones! Weirdest fetish I've ever heard of!"

Pope thrust himself forward, into Rookie's lap. "You went through my ruck?"

"You went through mine!"

"To make sure you weren't packin' too heavy!"

"I wasn't fuckin' born yesterday! And I would've left your stuff alone if you hadn't made a career out of picking on me. I'm the new guy. So fucking what? I'm Delta Force, cockbreath. You will respect that. You can call me rookie all you want, but my real name's Godzilla, understood?"

"Your breath smells like Godzilla's," Pope said, grinning at Mad Dog. "But you got some balls—small ones, but you got 'em. You might die second instead of first, as I predicted. But you will die if you go through my shit again."

"Lay off him," Mad Dog told Pope. "He's got the record just like you. He'll prove himself."

Rookie shook his head in disgust. "I hope you guys can prove something to me, because so far, this is bullshit."

"I wouldn't worry about that, little man," growled Pope. "Not at all."

"Oh, I'm worrying. So far we got bad contacts, we're in jail, and I'm working with a guy who carries around a Barbie doll."

Mad Dog knew about the doll and he, too, had asked Pope why he carried it; he'd been fed the same line of shit, but you knew there was a whole story behind it, one better left alone until the man was ready to share.

"Enough with the doll," snapped Pope. "It's a good luck charm. That's all."

Rookie snickered. "Fag."

Pope's eyes bugged out. "Fuck you. Back in World War II, my great-grandfather was shootin' you people out of trees."

"Hey, enough with that shit!" cried Mad Dog.

It was amazing how one snafu could set tempers ablaze. Problems usually didn't occur so early in a job; that was part of it, yes, along with the uncertainties, but his guys usually weren't so tense.

Without warning, the door swung open, and in walked Jack Palansky. The marine-turned-security-guy appeared just as Dan had described him: "Big Polack. Kinda dumb-looking face. Little pudgy." And he issued that stupid laugh, which was too high-pitched for a man his size. Still, Jack was a green marine to the core.

Mad Dog wormed his way to his feet. "Hey, Jack. I'd shake your hand, *but I'm fucking handcuffed*!"

Jack raised his palms. "Roger that. Sorry about all

this. We had a little communication breakdown between the security chief and his brother-in-law. Their bad. Not mine. I got it all straightened out."

Mr. Bibby stepped between Mad Dog and Jack. "Hello, Mr. Palansky. I'm Alastair Bibby. *Mr. Bibby.* And I must say we have a low tolerance for inefficiency, because as you know, it gets blokes like you and me killed."

"Nice to finally meet you, too," Jack said with a smirk. "We'll be on our way now." He turned to the others. "Welcome to Angola, boys . . ."

"Yeah, I hate it already," said Pope.

A couple of aging, Russian-made, eight-wheeled BTR–60s, armored personnel carriers that were beat up to shit but still ran, waited for them on the tarmac. They inventoried and offloaded their gear into the vehicles, then set out for a full day's drive west to Saurimo in the province of Lunda Sul, which lay in the northeast region of the country. There, about thirty-five kilometers from Saurimo, Morstarr had set up its mining operation in one of the world's largest, most productive diamond mines.

While that area was diamond-rich, its inhabitants were still dirt-poor. Because the province was so remote, everything had to be flown or trucked in, though the roads were little more than broken tar and dust. Water and fuel were incredibly expensive. An ongoing operation to rid the roads of landmines was still in effect, though Jack assured everyone that his drivers knew the safe routes and that once they were in Lunda Sul, they would be safe. Neither the government nor any of the rebel groups, past or present, had bothered to plant mines that far out.

With time to kill during the road-trip phase, Mad Dog ordered his men to apply their war paint, which in this case was a specially formulated sunless tanning solution that would darken their skin to a medium black. From a distance, they would pass for locals, but up close they would need to say they were mestico (a mixed European and native African) which made up about 2 percent of the population. Still, a few people like Mr. Bibby just couldn't pull off the black thing, war paint or no, so they'd keep him in balaclava to hide his face whenever they could.

On the other hand, Sapper, who was, of course, black, would fit in (though the tattoo on his neck might need some explaining). He made a point of ribbing the other guys about how much better they looked as black men.

When Mad Dog was finished smearing on his own war paint with Jack's help, he grabbed a bottle of water and said, "So, Jacky boy, bring me up to speed."

"I've had my guys go to some of the rural villages between the mines and the Congo border."

"And?"

"Well, that's a big area, tough, about a hundred klicks out to the Congo."

"You do any more air recon since we talked?"

"We've done some, but the transport pilots we've been using are glorified cab drivers. Don't know how good their eyes are. Don't know if we can really trust them, either. And their flight paths are always the same, so the bandits know how and when to lay low. Yesterday we paid one guy to do a few passes along the border, but he didn't see jack."

"This is getting better all the time."

"I'm worried that if we do any more air recon, we might put them on the run."

"Maybe. So tell me about these villages."

"First thing you notice is all the women. A lot of the men were killed off during the civil wars. It's pretty sad.

There's no sanitation, and it's amazing the people actually survive. But they don't, not really. Most die before they hit forty."

Mad Dog nodded impatiently. Had Jack taken conversation lessons from old Diaper Dan? Was he doing a humanitarian-aid commercial? "You telling me you don't have a single lead?"

"Not a one."

"Jesus Christ, Jack."

Mad Dog's friend smiled knowingly. "Relax. We've bought some eyes in those villages now."

"That's it?"

"No, that's not it. I do have a place for you to start, little town about three hours out I call Jumoke's Place. My men gathered some intel on one of the bandits who was seen there the day before the robbery. The old lady, Jumoke, is real nosy, and she likes gifts. We tried, but we couldn't get much out of her. She knows more than she's saying—at least my guys think so. She needs a bribe. And she's the one who thinks they haven't left. She seems real certain about that—which makes me believe she's in bed with them, until someone else pays her more."

"All right, I'll cough up some of your boss's money. We'll see her first. Do a little recon before we come a knockin'. Soon as we get to camp."

"It'll be dark by then. A lot of 'em go to bed at sundown. Maybe you should, too. You jet lagging?"

"Yeah, but we'll catch a few Zs right now. We didn't come here to sleep."

"God equals Gold, Oil, and Diamonds. Seems old Mad Dog's got dollar signs in his eyes."

"Used to be American flags—for both of us."

"Times change."

"Times do. But not us. Couple jarheads."

Jack grinned wearily. "Ooh-rah."

Morstarr Base Camp
Near Saurimo, Angola
1530 Hours Local Time

Angola's northeast region was mainly a plateau, with altitudes about a kilometer south of Saurimo. A series of major, north-flowing rivers traversed the countryside and created valleys generally 150 meters deep into the plateau. They were heading to the southern edge of the rain forest belt, and vegetation varied between relativity thick forest cover to thin woods covering grasslands to wide open stretches that unrolled in lazy bumps toward the horizon.

The rainy season ran between October and April, and a brief shower had just ended as they neared Morstarr's base camp nearly nine hours after they had left the airport. Mad Dog would have much rather flown, and there was a Boeing 727 cargo plane that made the run, but Jack had argued against it for security reasons. Too many curious eyes, too many people to bribe, and too much commotion at the airstrip.

Besides the trio of Quonset huts that the company's management team used as field offices, a small cluster of about a dozen clay huts with thatched roofs stood near a dense tree line, already falling into a steamy darkness. Those huts housed the mine's security team of fifteen men, local recruits who loitered outside the huts, half-dressed, smoking, and drinking sodas, their brows full of sweat.

Jack said two of the huts had been emptied out and that Mad Dog and his crew could have them. Inside they would find Morstarr security uniforms ordered to size.

Once they unloaded, the team would begin fieldstripping, cleaning, lubing, and performing functions checks on all weapons as soon as they got them unpacked to ensure they worked and hadn't been tampered with by those bozos back at the airport.

While the team got busy on that, Mad Dog went off with Jack toward a hundred-foot-deep pit that spread out from the camp like an impact crater. Three feet of rainwater had collected in several of the corners, the mud assuming a dozen shades of red as the sun continued to set. Four giant backhoes, along with at least as many six-wheeled dump trucks, bulldozers, loaders, tractor trailers, and other heavy machinery and conveyor belts stood inert like gray-and-yellow monoliths. The crews had retired for the evening.

Mad Dog was impressed with what he saw and even more impressed with the Cuban cigar that Jack shoved into his hand. "They got a big operation here, eh?"

"This is one of three sites," Jack said, lighting up his stogie. He handed the Zippo to Mad Dog. "You know anything about diamonds?"

"Yeah, I learned a little when I was buying all those wedding rings." Mad Dog took a puff, sighed in ecstasy.

Jack laughed. "At least you gave it a try. But, hey, you see down there, we got these pipe-shaped igneous rock formations? They're called kimberlite. That's where the diamonds take shape."

"What are you, a scientist now?"

"This is fascinating shit, man. Listen. Did you know that 70 percent of stones they haul out of here are considered gem quality? Diamond for diamond, that makes this place—"

"A gold mine?"

"I was going to say an incredibly profitable mine, one of the most profitable in the world before Mr. Fucking Wiseass interrupted me. That's a good cigar, isn't it?"

"The best."

Jack lowered his voice. "Hey, I was thinking about something. You came a long way out here, and like I said, I think those diamonds are still floating around. But if they aren't, there might be a way to get some . . . payment . . . anyway."

"Oh, yeah?"

"I put this security team together. I know their strengths and their weaknesses. So does the company's CO and his team. Like I said, I think one of those suits is in bed with the bandits. They knew just when to hit us and how."

"Or that could just be a coincidence. Or . . . and I'm just thinking out loud here . . . maybe the chief of mine security is in bed with the bandits."

Jack chuckled. "You know, right now, I wish I were. Because that's what I'm getting at. There's no reason for you—for us—to walk out of here empty-handed. I mean, Michael, every day I've been here the thought has crossed my mind."

"So you're saying that if me and my guys can't find the diamonds, we can steal some with your help?"

Jack pulled the cigar from his mouth, stared at the glowing tip. "Morstarr's a huge company. Those suits are fucking each other over. One of 'em set up this whole thing. What say you and me fuck the fuckers?"

"I didn't come here to steal, Jack. I came here to recover and collect the reward."

"But you're a merc now."

"Which means I got no code, right? Bullshit. I'm not like those other assholes. That's why I attract first-class operators. I'm not afraid to break the law, but if I can get results without going criminal, that's what I do. There's too much marine in me. So if I walk out of here with nothing, then that's that."

"You fuckin' amaze me."

"The amazing part comes when me and my boys come back here with the stash in hand and the two mil transferred to our account."

"Hey, Zog?"

Mad Dog turned to face Boo Boo, who was trudging up the hill, wearing the same khaki shirt, trousers, baseball cap, and green jacket as the Morstarr security team.

Vincent Orrello was the oldest guy on the team, at forty-eight. He'd been an army medic in the first Gulf War, then he'd spent another ten years as a firefighter/paramedic assigned to some of L.A.'s toughest hoods. That he had no special-forces training was not a handicap, according to Mad Dog. Orrello practiced street medicine, the kind of down-and-dirty tactical stuff mercs needed if anyone got hurt. Sure, Ranger medics and other SpecOp medics knew their shit, but Orrello had also seen his share of trauma and had developed enough personal tricks to write his own protocol manual. Better still, he'd dealt with all kinds of people under stress and was a smooth negotiator when dealing with the "mentally impaired." His monotone voice, unflinching eyes, and keen intellect soothed savage beasts, be they mercenary, military, or civilian.

The medic must have already inventoried his Special Operations Forces Medical Equipment Set (MES). That done, he had no doubt tested their micro Reverse Osmosis Water Purification Unit (ROWPU) in case they had to purify their own drinking water (you *did not* want to drink the tap water in a place like Angola). Custom made and about the size of a suitcase, the unit could produce enough potable water to refill the Camelbaks, canteens, and water cans for the entire team in less than twenty minutes from literally any water source. The last thing they needed was to get sick, forcing Boo Boo to play nursemaid to a bunch of queasy killers.

Though he saved lives, Boo Boo wasn't afraid to take them. He carried an H&K MP–5K-PDW "Personal Defense Weapon," a compact submachine gun that could be folded and neatly slung over his shoulder or back, or fired with one hand when carrying someone in a fireman's carry. When it came time to rock 'n' roll he would unfold the shoulder stock for accuracy and in a pinch add a silencer onto the muzzle. Presently, the weapon dangled from his shoulder.

"What's up, Boo Boo?"

The hairy Italian's expression was steel. "The DVD player in our hut is broken. No porno for us."

Jack frowned. "DVD player? There's no—"

Mad Dog held up his hand, exceedingly familiar with the medic's dry sense of humor. "What?"

"One of Jack's guys has a bad laceration on his leg. Tripped over some equipment or something. I think he was drunk. He's been hiding it. But it looks pretty bad. One of the other guys wants me to treat it. Figured I'd ask first. We ain't UNICEF. What say you?"

"Go ahead. Fix 'em up." Mad Dog regarded Jack. "If it's okay?"

Jack nodded. "Thanks, Boo Boo."

The medic glowered at Jack, then hustled off.

"He hates people," Mad Dog explained.

"What a fuckin' bunch. But that's what makes you so good, huh? Everyone's nuts."

"Cranky, too."

They left the pit and returned to the huts, where Jack introduced Mad Dog to a slender, six-foot-tall black man with a goatee, Jack's right hand.

In broken English, Mr. Ari Mbandi explained that he had been a sergeant in the army before retiring to work for Morstarr. He said with no real remorse that his ex-wife, who now lived in Luanda, had stolen all of his money and that he was working as much overtime as possible to help his sister pay for an expensive transplant operation for one of her daughters. Jack said that Mbandi was, without question, the hardest-working, most keen-eyed guard they had, and it was he who nearly foiled the robbery. Nearly.

"I am happy to catch these thieves," he said.

Mad Dog nodded, then gathered his people in one of the huts, his gaze falling upon each of them, ticking off names in a mental roll call and imagining their thoughts:

Mr. Bibby sat on a folding chair, trying to lose himself in his satellite-linked laptop because the others smelled so bad.

Wolfgang was stroking his chin, pissed that he'd had to trim his beard and that they hadn't seen any pussy thus far.

Sapper still wore his shit-eating grin because, in his words, he was now the "best-lookin' nigger" of the bunch.

Pope clutched his 9mm HK MP5N submachine gun with integral flashlight like he had already taken it to dinner and the movies and was getting blue balls because they had yet to get it on.

Rookie looked equally impatient as he shouldered his Remington 870 shotgun, a Marine magnum version painted a splotchy camo to resemble an old throwaway.

Doolittle sat cross-legged, engrossed in a local newspaper, a MAR 5.56mm or "Micro-Galil" which could pass for an AK–47 strapped to his back, yet the rifle still fired the 5.56mm rounds that many of the team members used.

Boo Boo was pulling off a pair of latex gloves but figuring it wouldn't be long till his hands got bloody again.

And last but not least, Cap'n Drac, aka Larry Bowler, was thinking, *It's come to this shit?* as he thrust out his lips in a vain attempt to look "more black."

Drac had been a captain in the Air Force and member of a Combat Controller Team that had been attached to one of Pope's SEAL teams. The two men went way back, and it was Pope who had actually recruited him. Drac was the team's link with the air, though for this job, he'd basically serve as an infantryman with a keen interest in how the bad guys intended to smuggle out the diamonds (he argued for air, of course). He was a twitchy, beady-eyed bird who talked in clipped sentences, cutting himself off, his mouth never catching up with his head.

Back when Drac was preparing for duty with one of Pope's SEAL teams, he'd done a little reading on SEALs in Vietnam and learned about their choice of the 5.56mm Stoner M63 weapon system. Another old but good system, he had to look long and hard to find one, but he had, and Mad Dog had satisfied his appetite.

Currently he carried his Stoner in the M63A short-barreled configuration with a 150-round drum attached. Shipping cases held the other accessories to convert it into a carbine, rifle, or light machine gun, depending on the mission. If it was good enough for SEALs in Vietnam, it was good enough for him.

Mad Dog's mercenaries were locked and loaded. "You want the good news or the bad?" he began. "Strike that.

First the good news. You all look fuckin' beautiful. I want to spank all of your asses and put you to bed."

That drew a few hoots and guffaws, especially from Sapper.

"The bad news is we got about two and a half more hours by car till we reach our first objective, probably an hour on foot to close in for surveillance."

Long faces, loud moans.

Mad Dog continued: "We'll do our radio check once we ditch the vehicles. Jack and his assistant Ari Mbandi are coming with us on this first leg. They'll stick with my fire team."

Mad Dog had organized the group into three fire teams, each with three men. While the traditional military fire teams included four to five operators, Mad Dog had found that smaller, more dispersed groups worked better for conducting the kinds of surveillance and raids mercenary work required. Still, his teams were not much different than what he'd been taught.

The Marine Corps organized its fire teams using the mnemonic ready-team-fire-assist, which described a column as

1. a rifleman out front to serve as scout,
2. the team leader, who was also the grenadier,
3. the automatic rifleman, and
4. the assistant automatic rifleman, who carried additional ammo.

Mad Dog had simply eliminated the assistant because, like Force Recon teams, he didn't want his men engaging in prolonged firefights. Their radio call sign was "Blackhound," and the table of organization was simple:

Fire Team #1		Fire Team #2		Fire Team #3	
Mad Dog	BH1	Pope	BH4	Wolfgang	BH7
Bibby	BH2	Sapper	BH5	Drac	BH8
Doolittle	BH3	Rookie	BH6	Boo Boo	BH9

Mad Dog let Jack take over to describe the village and the old lady Jumoke, then they hustled out of the hut.

About friggin' time. Mad Dog felt so wired, so electric, that he could've powered a small city. They piled into a couple of sputtering Toyota pickup trucks (the APCs ran much too loudly and burned way too much fuel), and headed off down a dirt road as the sky washed from purple into something deeper but not quite black. Mad Dog had never seen a sky so clear, and Angola's bad power grid increased the brightness of the stars.

Jack drove one truck, Mbandi the other, with five mercs piled into one flatbed, four in the other. Not including their chopper and C–130 pilots, Mad Dog had brought nine men, including himself, to sub-Saharan Africa in search of riches—diamonds—and he hoped to God nine would return. All except Sapper were *chindeles*, white men, but all were foreigners, unfamiliar with the land and its people.

Yet all were hell-raisers, trained killers who shot first, shot second, and shot third. There wasn't any fuckin' time for questions.

Maybe just one: where the fuck are the diamonds, asshole? Tell me now, or you're dead . . .

He nodded to his men, drawing Doolittle's attention. The translator had a tentative look on his face.

Mad Dog raised his voice above the thrumming engine. "What is it?"

"There is bad energy here."

"You a translator or a psychic?"

Doolittle shrugged. "I see death." Then he smiled and shoved Mad Dog's shoulder. "I see death, and it is you, Sergeant! You are one ugly motherfucker!"

The little man burst out laughing as Mad Dog hoisted his middle finger and cracked a deep smile.

Mr. Bibby sat sullenly, finding no amusement in Doolittle's teasing, his submachine gun propped upright and balanced between his legs. Being a tasteful Brit, he carried a Sterling L34A1 9mm with silencer. An oldie, but a goodie, the Sterling was a classic, rugged, highly reliable British weapon that added an air of sophistication to any firefight. To finish out his kit, he carried a Browning Hi-Power 9mm pistol and a Sykes-Fairbairn British commando dagger, both highly civilized weapons that he deftly wielded. Mad Dog just wished the guy wasn't wound so tightly. Maybe one day he'd let down his guard and admit he was just as much a buccaneer as they were.

"Hey, Mr. Bibby, you all right?"

"Just thinking, Mr. Hertzog. That's all."

" 'Bout what?"

He wriggled his brows. "Shiny little rocks."

"Jumoke's Place"
Approx. 55 Kilometers West
Saurimo, Angola
2325 Hours Local Time

Just about the time Mad Dog's ass was really going numb, the tiny speaker in his ear crackled to life:

"Blackhound One, this is Morstarr One, over?"

Mad Dog had given Jack and Mbandi intrasquad radios, high-tech, lightweight, wireless earpieces with small boom mikes that crept halfway down their cheeks. They could be set as voice-activated or keyed by a little remote clipped to their belts.

"Go ahead, Morstarr," Mad Dog answered.

"We'll be pulling off the road, right over that next hill coming up. Boys, you'd best be ready, asses and elbows."

"You heard the man," Mad Dog boomed, playing up the cliché. "Fire Team Two's got the left flank, Three's got the right. One holds back. Hasty one-eighties when you get in position. Are we Lima Charlie, over?"

They sounded off one by one, all radios checking out perfectly.

The trucks came up and over the hill hard, spun to a screeching halt, and Mad Dog levered himself out of the flatbed, hitting the ground, and dropping ankle deep into a puddle. Shit.

His pulse was bounding, his senses fine-tuned, reaching out, the contrast set real high, trees and more puddles coming at him in sharp relief as he jogged into the forest, Doolittle on one side, Bibby on the other, their rucks thumping in muted taps, their breaths heavy.

He took in a long breath through his nose, smelled the rain, the mud.

Old Dan had been right. This was fun. Life was beautiful.

ChapteR 3
·······························

ad Dog could barely look upon his friend. He took Eddy's remaining hand in his own, coughing at the horrible smell and smoke burning his eyes.

"Two more widows," said Eddy. "You'll take care of them, won't you, Sergeant?"

Mad Dog shuddered and thought, *Not now!*

The flashbacks struck at the worst times, and anything at all could trigger them. Simple things.

Even just running.

And suddenly he was back in Afghanistan, oblivious to his current surroundings, every sense locked in the memory's grip as his gut twisted and his friend begged with dying eyes for him to do the right thing.

Not now!

He raced up to the stand of trees overlooking the small

village, crouched down, then shuddered again as he reached into his ruck and tugged out his Fraser-Volpe binoculars.

You're good, he told himself. *You're okay. Focus.*

The binoculars were gyro stabilized to eliminate motion blurring, had an attached eyepiece turning them into night-vision goggles, and had a camera attachment so that any member of the team could shoot digital images and/or real-time video of unknown individuals and transmit them via radio back to Mr. Bibby for data-base comparisons and to update their intel files.

However, the phosphorescent images currently piped in through the binoculars weren't worth transmitting and said one thing: shit hole. Mad Dog didn't need a reminder that people still lived like this, even in the twenty-first century. He'd visited holes around the globe; they were always sad, never new. The dozen or so clay huts were in ill repair, a few walls crumbling, some roofs beginning to fall off. Garbage was piled into a big hole behind the place. Laundry lines spanned the gaps between huts, hanging above woven baskets and chipped clay pots. They had no power, no plumbing, nada.

Mad Dog continued his scan, panning to the center hut, where two lanky men sat in old rocking chairs, each with AK–47s lying across their laps. Both looked fast asleep and cast in a flickering glow by a small lantern at their feet.

Mad Dog lowered his binoculars and grinned at Jack. "I see their security detail is in place."

Jack returned the smile. "These little villages don't usually post guards outside, which says they've had some visitors and might be expecting us."

"Yeah, but I doubt the beer's cold."

"Blackhound One, this is Blackhound Four," came Pope's voice over the radio. "We're in position. Got two guys with rifles by the middle hut. I'm betting you can see 'em. We observe no movement out back yet, over."

"Roger that. I got 'em, too. Just sit tight."

"One, this is Seven," called Wolfgang. "Ditto over here. Two sleeping beauties, otherwise this place is dead."

"I hear you, Seven. Standby." Mad Dog glanced back at Bibby and frowned. "You picked a funny time to check your email."

The Brit was sitting on his haunches, his compact laptop with ten-inch screen balanced on his hip and dimly lit so as not to betray their location. He tugged down his balaclava, pursed his lips, then issued a long sigh before speaking. "Mr. Hertzog, I've enlisted a few of our friends in Manila to tap into Morstarr's landline and wireless communications, and I've just received an email of their records for the past forty-eight hours."

Jack's partner, Ari Mbandi, suddenly crouched down beside them. "Excuse me. Trouble. Listen . . ." His big eyes lifted to the tree limbs, then he pointed emphatically ahead.

A faint clicking noise came from somewhere behind the huts, and to the uninitiated, it sounded like a nocturnal creature, perhaps an owl or rodent.

Jack grabbed Mbandi's wrist. "You told me the bandits had clickers."

"Yes! They use them to communicate with each other."

Another clicking answered the first and originated east of the village.

"Yes, it is them! The bandits!" cried Mbandi. "Mr. Palansky, come!"

Before Mad Dog could stop him, the black man sprang from the trees, heading straight for the long shadows and deeper pockets of gloom behind the huts.

"Jesus Christ, Jack!" Mad Dog stage whispered. "Is he sure?"

Jack shook his hands in frustration. "It could be them. But why the fuck would they come back here?"

"Who knows? But your boy will blow our cover if we don't rope him."

"Aw, shit." Jack lifted his own rifle and nodded. "Guy wants to be a hero. I'll get him."

"You stay right fuckin' here."

"My guy. My problem. Tell your apes to hold back till I confirm."

"Doolittle? Go with him."

The translator rose. "Yes, Sergeant."

Jack shook his head. "I don't take help. You know that."

With a wink and a sigh, the former marine was gone.

"Sergeant?" Doolittle called, ready to give chase.

"Let him go. He knows what he's doing. And we can use his guy to walk point for us. That idiot dies, and at least we know the bandits are here."

"But are they the right bandits, the ones with the diamonds?" asked Doolittle.

"Yeah, I hear you. Doesn't make any sense, unless they needed to come back here for something . . . what?"

Mad Dog quickly updated Pope and Wolfgang, whose tone matched his own: pissed off and impatient. Would their first contact with the locals immediately devolve into a world-class cluster fuck? Stranger things had happened.

Wolfgang said he spotted Mbandi racing toward a hut

closest to the tree line, where two dogs began barking and tugging at their leashes. "You want us to move in, over?"

"Negative. Hold position. Standby."

"Roger that."

"Shit. We should've come here alone," Mad Dog said under his breath.

"Maybe the bandits hid the diamonds near here and are protecting them," said Doolittle.

"Why? Why not keep them on the move, get them out of the country?"

"I don't know."

"Uh, excuse me, Mr. Hertzog," called Bibby. "I was going to say that there are at least a dozen calls from Morstarr's office in Luanda to several numbers in the Congo." He rapped a knuckle on his laptop's screen. "That's very unusual, and it's worth checking out. Perhaps the diamonds are headed there, and there's someone from Morstarr who's helping the smugglers, someone who made those calls."

Mad Dog rolled his eyes. "Yeah, good, but can you wait till after we kill the bad guys?"

"It's all about timing, Mr. Hertzog. We could wait now and pay later."

"Fine. Do it. Just hurry it up."

Bibby's fingers worked rapidly on the keyboard. "It's the only thing that looks suspect so far. I'll have our friends do the legwork. No harm in checking it out."

"Unless you get shot while typing."

Bibby cocked a brow. "I trust you'll cover me."

Rookie was carrying a mix load of #4 buckshot, OOO buckshot, and sabot slugs for point and long-range targets, and he was itching to get into a fight no matter what kind of ammo he used. They hadn't come all this way and brought all of these guns for nothing.

But there he was, gripping binoculars instead of his rifle, a spectator biting his tongue, wishing Mad Dog would give the word and let him breathe fire.

He listened as Pope and Wolfgang kept feeding reports back to their fearless leader. They'd lost sight of Mbandi, weren't sure if he'd gone into the forest or had ducked into one of the huts.

The two guys in the chairs, however, were on their feet with rifles at the ready.

Nearby, an old woman, possibly the Jumoke that Dog's friend had mentioned, hobbled out from one of the huts, carrying a kerosene lantern in one hand, a walking stick in the other. She squinted into the darkness.

Rookie was about to report her appearance, but his instincts took over. Pope was seeing the same thing, and it was better Rookie ditched the NVGs for his rifle now.

Mad Dog tried for a third time to reach Mbandi over the radio, then Jack.

Unable to contain himself anymore, Rookie left the tree where he had paused, dodged left, then sprinted over to Pope, who was still lying on his gut and peering intently through his own binoculars. "Hey, man . . ."

Pope scowled at him. "What the fuck?"

"This is bullshit. We have to move in. Something's wrong."

"Get back in position!"

"I'm telling you, this is going south!"

"And I'm telling you—"

Pope's sarcastic expression vanished as gunfire woke in the jungle ahead.

"See?" cried Rookie.

The disembodied voices of nearly every guy on the team broke over the radio: "What the fuck? Who's firing? Is that you, Seven? Six, are you firing? Hold your goddamned fire!"

And then an absolutely beautiful order punctuated a few seconds of silence: Mad Dog wanted Pope and Rookie to disarm the two guys out front. "Don't shoot 'em," he insisted.

Finally, it was game on. 'Bout fuckin' time. Rookie shouldered his rifle. He doubted either of the Angolans would pose a major problem. This would be routine but fun nonetheless.

"Hey, little shitbird," rasped Pope. "You take 'em both down. I'll watch."

"You serious?"

Pope's lips cracked in a sinister grin. "Test number one. Let's move!"

Two more triplets of automatic weapons fire boomed through the valley, trailed by the muffled cries of several babies and children from inside the huts.

"Who the fuck's still shooting?" Boo Boo asked.

"Fuck if I know," answered Wolfgang. "Maybe our bandits are right there in the woods. What do you think, Doc?"

"I think you're right. There is definitely someone in the woods who is firing a weapon."

"You dumbass."

"You mean *wiseass*. And it ain't the bandits. No way. It's just some fuckin' clown who probably thinks *we're* the bandits. Just like the good old days back in the hood."

"Fire Team Three, this is Blackhound One. Move in and clear those huts on the west. Get everybody out and into the clearing on the right. Go now!" ordered Mad Dog.

"Well at least we're off our asses," said Wolfgang, wanting oh so badly to take out those gunmen with his big, fat, RT–20 splatter-your-brains sniper rifle. He would sign his autograph in a special ink called blood.

But no such luck. Pope and Rookie would handle the Angolan gunmen . . . graciously . . . of course.

"Hey, man, I'm like, I'm ready, let's do this," said Drac, tripping over his words as usual, but never his feet. He glided out of there, his Stoner leading him like a compass needle, the cardinal points all labeled "D" for death. Man, if he didn't look plucked from a Vietnam war movie and dropped into Angola. All he needed was some Doors or Stones tune serving as the soundtrack to his advance: *I can't get no, na na na . . .*

Wolfgang gave a little howl, his trademark war cry, as they rushed down toward the huts. He swung his ball cap on sideways, gangbanger style, then hocked a big loogie and leapt over a ditch.

Like three men guided by a single intelligence, they fanned out, reached the first hut with its rickety wooden door, and huddled against one wall.

Wolfgang's fist shot into the air: wait!

A baby screamed from inside, the cry as quickly strangled.

Another round of gunfire woke thunder in the woods.

Wolfgang glanced over his shoulder. Pope and Rookie were stealing toward the villagers with the AKs.

After another long breath, Wolfgang nodded to Drac, while he and Boo Boo took either side of the entrance.

Drac booted in the door, splinters flying as Wolfgang

and the medic whirled and charged inside, hollering, "Hands up!" as the women and children shrieked.

It was all fucking chaos.

And that was fine by Wolfgang. He couldn't be happier.

Sapper understood why Mad Dog had given Pope and Rookie the honor of disarming the two gunmen. Rookie needed to prove himself, and Pope needed to be there for insurance.

Yes, Sapper understood, but he wasn't happy about it, either. He covered both men with his carbine, imagining that at any second he'd be ordered to put the attached grenade launcher to work. There was no greater pleasure in the world than lobbing grenades with an M203. What about sex? Believe it or not, that'd be number two on his list. He was a pyro, a demo guy, an engineer through and through. The black flames on his neck communicated that to everyone.

In fact, he wanted so badly to launch a grenade that he literally heard the order come in and fired at the tree line. Boom! White flash! Fucking hooah!

And damned unprofessional, shit!

"Hold that goddamned grenade fire," screamed Mad Dog over the radio.

"Oops," Sapper muttered, then took off running down a narrow path that cut through the trees and led down toward the huts, where Pope and Rookie were a half-second away from contact.

A bark sounded nearby, then suddenly a big, black dog was on him, trailing a snapped rope—

And Sapper found himself flat on his ass.

*   *   *

It was the grenade's explosion that gave Rookie the advantage. Both Angolans craned their heads for a look.

He came up behind the first, well versed in the techniques of disarming men, techniques taught to him by experts from around the globe. Some of them he practiced in his sleep, visualizing himself snatching weapon after weapon and smirking at his stunned opponents.

In truth, though, it was all instinct. He no longer had to think about where that muzzle was pointed; he knew just how to snatch the gun while simultaneously delivering a stunning kick to the man's groin.

Which he did. Expertly. Even as the guy doubled over and groaned, Rookie used the weapon as a hammer on the back of the guy's neck, carefully applying enough pressure so he wouldn't kill him. Down number one.

And that took the better part of two seconds. He cockily tossed the rifle to Pope, who nearly dropped it, then rushed up to the next guy. One, two, three. Weapon removed. Man down. No time for him to take a breath. No time for his prey to react in defense.

Rookie gasped and faced Pope. "Fuckin' A plus-plus on that exam. Fuckin' gold star."

"Sloppy. B plus, asshole. Let's clear these huts!"

Rookie frowned and whirled toward the first door. "Shit, Pope, you must be blind."

Sapper would have killed the dog if it hadn't started licking his face. He almost laughed aloud, then bolted up, and finally reached the rest of his fire team, just as they were entering a hut.

"Were you covering us or jerking off?" asked Pope.

Wearing a crooked grin, Sapper answered, "I don't know the difference."

Then he smashed in the door and came face to face with a woman wearing a tattered, sun-bleached dress and pointing an AK–47 directly at his head.

Her hands trembled. Not good.

He glanced at her, then down to her swollen belly, two little boys clinging to one of her legs. She hollered something in Portuguese.

"Don't shoot!" he cried, removing one hand from his weapon and lifting his palm.

Before he could fully lift that hand, Rookie had slipped in behind him and was wrenching away the woman's rifle, which went off, sending rounds punching through the roof.

The woman yelled again, took a swing at Sapper, who grabbed her wrist as Rookie retreated behind them like a Ninja thief, AK in hand.

At least six more women came up behind the first, all wearing the same scowl.

Sapper released the first woman, who reached down and picked up one of her kids.

Meanwhile, another villager, the oldest and heaviest woman of the group, shouldered past the others and came up to Sapper, wearing an improbable piece of headgear: a N.Y. Yankees ball cap. She just leered at all of them, then shook her head.

"Outside. *Now!*" cried Pope.

"They don't speak English, you knucklehead," said Rookie.

Sapper did remember one word from the language book he had spent about five minutes studying: "*Desculpa.*"

I'm sorry.

The woman looked daggers at him, and then, in heavily accented English, said, "Fuck you."

"Outside!" yelled Pope, gesturing with his rifle.

"Hey, Mama, I just work here." Sapper tilted his head toward the door, then ushered out the old Yankee fan.

"Yo, Sap, you got a new friend, eh?" asked Pope. "But I don't think she's your type."

Sapper just grunted and swatted at the mosquitoes buzzing around his nose.

Mad Dog sent Doolittle and Bibby toward the center of the village, where the rest of his guys were corralling the men, women, and children they'd forced from the huts. There weren't many, maybe twenty in all, and Jack had been right. Mad Dog only counted four adult males in the entire group, two down for the count, thanks to Rookie. Jack and Mbandi were still nowhere to be found.

So Mad Dog ordered Pope to break off from the others. The former SEAL would accompany Mad Dog into the forest, where the gunfire had finally ceased.

"How far out you want to go?" asked Pope as they ran.

"Not too far. Stay close."

They rounded a stand of trees, then Mad Dog tried once more to contact Jack. The son of a bitch wasn't answering. He ordered Rookie to take over for him.

"Roger that," the guy answered, unenthused but cooperating. "Morstarr One, this is Blackhound Six, request SITREP, over."

"Hey, wait, I got someone!" yelled Pope.

Mad Dog paused, turned right, falling in behind Pope, who had veered off to the left, past a row of shrubs, the forest much thicker now, with fronds, tall grasses, and thickets weaving through the trees.

A salvo of gunfire shattered the quiet, the shooter's muzzle flash giving up his location: about fifty yards out.

"There!" cried Mad Dog.

As one round struck a tree trunk to his left, he flinched and ducked behind the next one.

Pope finally got his chance to get it on with his date. He triggered his HK MP5N submachine gun, laying down a vicious stream of fire that spread toward the horizon. Smoke rose from the weapon and brass clanged as he fired once more.

That second volley away, he came up beside Mad Dog and fired again, just as Mad Dog cut loose a grenade from the launcher attached to his own carbine. A chest-pounding thunderclap echoed the rattling.

"He's a dead fuck now," grunted Pope.

Mad Dog stole a look with his binoculars.

"You gotta be kidding me . . ."

Not a goddamned thing. No body parts dangling from tree limbs. No dead shooter, damn it.

Pope snorted. "We missed?"

"I think so."

Mad Dog gave the hand signal, and they advanced. Cautiously.

"No way we missed," said Pope. "No way."

Mr. Bibby had Drac, Boo Boo, Rookie, Sapper, and Wolfgang set up a perimeter, while he and Doolittle tried to calm down the villagers. Doolittle spoke rapidly with the old woman wearing the Yankees cap, who identified herself as Jumoke.

"Careful what you say," Bibby warned the man. "We all work for the company and are trying to recover the diamonds. That's all you say. Tell her we're sorry for waking them up."

Doolittle complied. The woman made a face, not buying that for a second. She raised her voice, unleashed a rapid-fire retort, then removed her cap, whacked Bibby on the head.

"She wants to know why we're all wearing face paint," said Doolittle.

"Oh, she said more than that, I'm sure. Tell her we are a very special security team of men from all over the world. Then ask her what she knows about the bandits."

"I already did," said Doolittle. "She says we've beaten her men, and she will not talk. She says the other man, the American, was already here and that we should know better than to come again."

"Tell her that it's in the best interests of her entire village if she talks. Tell her we can help them buy many supplies and help get the children vaccinated. Is she not aware of the measles epidemic here?"

Doolittle translated. The woman folded her arms over her chest, took a step toward Bibby, bit her chapped lip, thought a moment, then said, "No."

Pope caught a glimpse of something shiny in the dirt, leaned down and picked up a shell casing. He swung around, saw droplets of something in the moonlight, flicked on the flashlight attached to his submachine gun. Blood.

Mad Dog arrived out of breath. "What do we got?"

"Got some casings. And we did hit him. Blood trail leads off this way." Pope started away. Their wounded prey was close. He could almost smell him, knew the danger would increase tenfold now. As always, he thought of his guardian angel:

Here we go, sis.

When Pope was a kid, his family spent a lot of time at Daytona Beach. One weekend, when he was twelve and his sister, Cheryl, was eight, they had gone swimming, and Cheryl had been carried to Heaven by the rip currents.

Yes, the water had taken her life, but not before she had given him the doll.

He would never tell these assholes about her, never soil her image by mentioning her in the same breath as them, never tell them that his parents had put him in charge of watching her, that she had died because he had been too busy trying to body surf.

That he had become a U.S. Navy SEAL was a great irony, because he had spent most of his youth hating the water, absolutely hating it.

He still remembered leaning over Cheryl on that beach, staring into her blank eyes, her face cold and blue, her body perfectly still as the ocean rushed up behind her head. People were screaming. A lifeguard shoved him out of the way. Pope's mother grabbed him by the shoulders. "I told you to watch her!"

I'll become a SEAL. I'll be closer to her, be able to tell her how sorry I am.

And so he had. And so he did.

It's okay. You'll be safe, his sister whispered as he paused once more to study the blood trail, saw how it jogged off to his left, up and over a dark mound of earth about three meters high. He waved over Mad Dog, and together they ascended, came down—

And found their shooter lying face down in the dirt, a blood stain on his back, his legs bleeding.

"Oh, fuck," gasped Mad Dog. "It's Mbandi."

Pope rushed to the guy, rolled him over. Mbandi was still breathing. "Dude, what the fuck? You were shooting at us! Jesus . . ."

"I'm . . ." He couldn't finish.

"Mbandi, did you see them? Were the bandits here like you said?"

The Angolan grimaced, all teeth, the agony overcoming him.

"Mbandi!"

"Still got a pulse," said Pope, his fingers pressed firmly to Mbandi's neck. "He's lost a lot of blood. Better get Boo Boo up here."

While Mad Dog hollered for the medic, Pope reached into his ruck and pulled out one of two big trauma bandages from his own first aid kit. He used his big SOG SEAL knife to cut off Mbandi's shirt, then placed the bandage on the shrapnel wound caused by Mad Dog's grenade. It was nasty, like pressing a wad of paper towels into a plate of spaghetti.

"You fuckin' dumb yokel," Pope whispered. "Why didn't you answer us?"

Pope tilted Mbandi's head, removed the ball cap, noted that the man was not wearing the intrasquad radio mike and receiver they had given him. Maybe it had fallen off while he was running? Who knew? It'd be a goddamned shame if they had killed him. Classic fuckup. But he'd been firing at them. If he was as good as Jack said, then he should have been smarter.

Mbandi jerked violently, gasped, then settled back down.

"Just hang in there, bro. Help's on the way."

Boo Boo hated using the GPS, but it was either that or wander around an Angolan forest, at night, with shooters still lurking around.

So he dug out the little piece of shit, fired it up, and followed the coordinates that Mad Dog had given him. He moved hard and fast, mindful of his step but figuring that if anyone was trying to get a bead on him, he'd literally give them a run for the money.

Weaving a serpentine path, he realized he had strayed too far east, turned, rounded a tree, and spotted an odd silhouette in the distance, off to his left.

The closer he came, the more he realized that he wasn't seeing part of a fallen tree but a figure on the ground. He switched on his flashlight, came upon the man, who was lying prone, his back a bloody mess.

The guy wore a painfully familiar uniform, and Boo Boo didn't need to roll him over.

Emotions were something the medic kept in tight check, his face almost always stoic, a wax mask. But inside, his gut was twisting, and he felt really bad, not for himself, but for old Mad Dog, who'd be hit hard. Boo Boo cleared his throat, then keyed the mike.

Mad Dog's heart dropped as Boo Boo's voice came over the radio. "Roger that. I'll be right there."

He sprinted away from Pope and Mbandi, coming up

over the next rise and spotting the dim light, where Boo Boo was signaling.

When he reached the medic and glanced down, his knees weakened, and time stopped.

"I'm sorry. Real sorry."

Mad Dog leaned down and pushed away the ball cap shading Jack's face. The man had been shot three times in the back, goddamn it.

"Looks like close range," said Boo Boo.

"He wouldn't be this stupid," Mad Dog said. "Not Jack. No way. No fuckin' way."

It took another moment for him to compose himself. He rubbed his sore eyes, then told Boo Boo to go after Mbandi, that he'd carry Jack to the village. The medic nodded solemnly and left.

Mad Dog hoisted his friend across his shoulders, then shifted unsteadily back up the mound.

It was happening all over again: friends were dying before his eyes, and just as before he felt completely helpless.

But that feeling wouldn't control him, not if he had anything to say about it. The fucks that had killed Jack would pay. If Doc could keep Mbandi alive, he might have some answers.

Mad Dog had to keep it together. For the sake of his men. Good leaders did not break down in the face of adversity. They did not let themselves become overwhelmed by emotions.

They forged on, no matter how hard, no matter what.

He would.

Chapter 4

....

"Jumoke's Place"
Approx. 55 Kilometers West
Saurimo, Angola
0110 Hours Local Time

Mad Dog sat on a creaking wooden chair inside Jumoke's hut. The woman had removed her Yankees cap, had set it down on the table between them, and folded her arms over her sizable chest. She was no happy camper.

Doolittle stood behind Mad Dog, translating, while Mr. Bibby sat in another chair, gaze glued to his computer screen. All of their faces were glossed with sweat and gleaming in the lantern light, while moths circled overhead.

"Why isn't she answering," Mad Dog asked Doolittle.

"I don't know."

Mad Dog held up his bloodstained palms. "You tell her the blood of my men is on her hands, too!"

Doolittle did.

Jumoke grabbed one of the Camelbaks off the table and took a long pull on uncontaminated water. She finished, sighed, and spoke very slowly, her voice almost a whisper.

"She says it's not her fault that our friends died. She says none of her men would have shot them. She says she wants us to leave. She can't help."

"Bullshit." Mad Dog rose from his chair, leaned over, and got directly in the woman's face. "You *will* help us. How much?"

Doolittle translated the words in the same tone, growing as heated as Mad Dog.

Jumoke shook her head, rubbed her big eyes, then threw up her hands. The words came so quickly that it seemed even Doolittle had difficulty keeping up.

Wolfgang and the rest of the guys had thoroughly searched the huts for any other weapons, had found and confiscated a few more pistols and rifles, then had ordered the villagers back inside, while they returned to their positions along the perimeter.

He and Drac, however, had taken up posts outside Jumoke's hut, scanning intently and bullshitting with the rest of the team over the radio:

"That's a . . . that's a goddamned shame about Jack," said Drac. "He and Mad Dog knew each other for a long time."

"Yeah, now what?" said Rookie. "If Dog can't get that old bitch to talk, we're fucked. And what if she doesn't know anything?"

"Then maybe Bibby can run what we got, see what's up," said Sapper, hunkered down across the clearing. "This shit didn't go down for nothing."

"No kidding, assholes," said Pope. "Jack was murdered. That's fuckin' clear. He was getting too close, and they wanted him dead. Clear as day to me."

"Who did it?" asked Boo Boo.

"You want my theory?" Pope began, not giving anyone time to protest. "I think fuckin' Mbandi did it. Somebody got to him. He led Jack into the woods and whacked him. This way they could blame it on the bandits. They all use the same weapons, same ammo, and Mbandi's clip was empty when we found him. They knew Jack was getting close, and they got him wet, mafia style."

"Yeah, too bad we can't ask him," said Wolfgang. "But dead men tell no tales."

"Hey, I tried," snapped Boo Boo. "He was a real bleeder."

"But the clicking. We all heard it," said Wolfgang. "Somebody was out there, signaling."

"Mbandi either paid someone here to wait for us and make the noise, or maybe a few of the bandits were here to help him out," said Pope. "They're all poor. And they're easily bought."

"You think Zog'll walk away from this?" asked Boo Boo.

Wolfgang gave a loud snort. "He's on a rampage now. First he just wanted money. Now he wants revenge. You know what that equals? One fuckin' mad dog!"

"What about the company? Kidman could pull us off," said Sapper. "Their head security guy gets whacked, and his second is accidentally killed."

"Yeah, maybe, uh, they'll want to cut, you know, their losses," said Drac.

"We'll find out soon enough. But I don't think that'll happen," said Wolfgang. "If Kidman was aggressive enough to hire us in the first place, he'll want us to stay on the job. We got more to lose than he does."

"Shit, that's right," said Rookie. "All we're going to collect here is a standard paycheck. No big commissions. Nothing . . ."

"Shut up, whiner," said Pope. "You ain't played with us long enough. We're just getting started."

Mad Dog's fingers dug into his palms, and he shifted on the seat, ready to rise once more. "You tell her again that we're not leaving till she talks."

Doolittle nodded, challenged the woman once more, then glanced at Mad Dog.

Jumoke slowly closed her eyes, took in a long, deep breath, then muttered something.

"She wants enough food, water, and kerosene for the entire year. And she wants a truck."

"Tell her we'll get it all to her—if she tells us something we can use."

After listening to that, Jumoke spoke once more, and Doolittle's brows shot up. "There are five bandits that she knows of. All are Angolans and she thinks at least one or two used to work for Morstarr."

Jumoke's voice grew more intense, as did Doolittle's. "She says they paid her so they could stay for two days and keep out of sight. They didn't know these men had stolen diamonds until after they had left and the American man showed up and told her."

"Did she know where they were going?"

Following a moment's translation, Doolittle nodded. "She overheard them talking. They were supposed to meet friends at a small airstrip by the Congo border. But their friends were late, so they decided to stay here."

Mad Dog turned to Bibby. "Pull up satellite images of this entire area. Find that airstrip."

"I've already downloaded those images," said Bibby. "And I have that airstrip," he said, tapping an index finger on his touchpad. "About seventy-five kilometers southeast of here. Just big enough for a small plane."

Jumoke interrupted with a flurry of words.

"What?" asked Mad Dog.

"She doesn't think they went there," said Doolittle.

"Why?"

"Because three of them came back just a few hours after the American left."

"They forget something?"

"No, they were looking for their other two friends. She says they were crazy, screaming at each other, waving rifles and scaring the children. She and the others hadn't seen the other two, but they accused her of hiding them for a bribe."

Mad Dog thought a moment. "Wait. A double cross? Could be. Two of 'em got greedy and took off with the stash. Not hard to believe."

Doolittle translated. Jumoke nodded.

"Now it's coming together. Five guys rip off the diamonds, head toward an airstrip, then find out their ride off will be late. So they wait here. Then they go off, and two guys vanish with the stash. The others come back looking."

"Correct," said Bibby. "That explains why they didn't leave the country. They were trying to find their former friends. But it doesn't answer the most important question: where are the diamonds?"

"Fuck. Back to square one."

A glimmer came into Bibby's eye. "Not exactly."

Delta Force Team
Congo Border
Fifty Kilometers South
Lucapa, Angola
0115 Hours Local Time

Captain Danny "Bender" Benson and his three Delta Force troops were heading south along the Kasai River, which separated Angola from the Democratic Republic of the Congo. They had procured an old pickup truck in the town of Lucapa and were braving a rainstorm while en route to a small village called Tongaso, directly east of Saurimo.

Bender and the rest of his men were black and two, Thorn and Dzoba, spoke fluent Portuguese. They were armed to the teeth, dressed like locals, and were ready to get some. And get some more. Delta Force didn't come to the jungle to fuck around, no sir.

Indeed Bender's wrecking crew had been in Angola for about a week now, crossing the border into the Congo and questioning locals in the small villages along the river.

Fact: The country was currently being run by a military regime with a terrible human rights record, and there was serious unrest in the villages—the numerous villages of the have-nots.

Fact: A young, ambitious guerilla, Mboma Kisantu, along with his small but loyal group of followers, was already engaged in skirmishes along the huge DROC-Angolan boarder. Kisantu used Angola as a refuge each time the DROC military came after him, and he was raising a few eyebrows back in the States.

Fact: the INTEL geniuses at JSOC and the Defense

Intelligence Agency feared that Kisantu might have ties
to al Qaeda, whose leaders might help him fund a coup.
Afterward, they would place Kisantu in the DROC as a
puppet president sympathetic to them.

A recent theft of diamonds from an Australian mining
company had thrown up the warning flags. Those rocks
could be used to help fund the coup. Moreover, if the
DROC were in the hands of al Qaeda, they would tap the
country's resources to fund their activities.

Consequently, Bender and his men should learn what
they could, take out Kisantu, and stop the smuggling operation at all costs. Beers and whores to follow . . .

The truth was, Bender was more interested in hunting
down Kisantu than chasing smugglers. Terminating that
guy would be a nice feather in his cap. Still, if they could
locate either Kisantu or the diamonds, one might lead to
the other. And if they brought down a coup attempt and
thwarted a smuggling operation, hell, it didn't get any
better than that.

Bender was a senior captain, rapidly approaching the
rank of major. He had been a Special Forces A-team
commander and then had tried out for Delta. He, like
many superior SF guys, had had to try out several times
before passing the Delta selection—it was that damned
hard. On top of that, most of Delta was made up of
NCOs, and he'd had to earn their respect. However, his
background in SF, plus some prior experiences leading
an A-team into Afghanistan weeks after 9/11 had made
the transition far less bumpy. Thorn, Dzoba, and Greene
were seasoned troops who seemed to like him and
wanted to notch their belts as badly as he did.

Thus far, though, they had been doing little more than
playing TV detectives, going from clue to clue and meet-

ing a handful of colorful characters. Since the CIA and other national intelligence agencies still hadn't learned to share information efficiently, the team resorted to the usual: going out and finding "actionable intelligence" on their own.

The best lead they had came back in Lucapa, where they had learned that two men had stopped for water while on their way to Tongaso. The locals had never seen them before, but one old man firmly believed they were members of the rebel group. Why? Because he had confronted them and had asked. They had grown very defensive, suspiciously so.

Consequently, Bender and his boys were taking a little road trip. Couldn't hurt.

He leaned back in the truck's passenger seat, stuffed a wad of chew into his mouth, then widened his eyes as the dim headlights picked out the road ahead, mud puddles swelling in the heavy rain.

"Jumoke's Place"
Approx. 55 Kilometers West
Saurimo, Angola
0118 Hours Local Time

They were still in the hut, talking with the old woman, and Bibby was emphatic: "It's no coincidence that Morstarr has been calling the Congo. Someone at the company is in bed with our thieves."

"You're assuming our bandits have ties to the Congo?" asked Mad Dog. "Spell 'em out for me."

"Whomever has been making the calls from Morstarr has been using their general line, so as not to point suspicion his or her way. And while the names attached to those numbers in the Congo belong to yet another mining company, which seems perfectly natural, I've emailed our mutual friend Big Booty at JSOC for their INTEL."

Mad Dog grinned inwardly. Big Booty could best be described as Oprah before the diet and feisty as hell. Mad Dog was embarrassed to admit that he had actually slept with her, but after a nice dinner with mutual friends and four beers, her bed was the next logical place.

And sometimes big girls were more appreciative. She certainly had been.

At the time he had known that she worked for JSOC, but he hadn't realized she was privy to so much valuable information. That was a most happy coincidence. They'd had no hard feelings in the morning; in fact, for the past couple of years Mad Dog had provided her with "holiday money" and a little phone sex now and again so long as she leaked information his way.

Bibby went on: "She's provided us with an interesting set of events that occurred prior to the diamond theft."

The Brit described the political situation in the Congo, as interpreted by the INTEL folks at JSOC. He described a guerilla named Kisantu, detailed his actions and the possibility of a coup being funded by the stolen diamonds.

"So the two guys who ripped off the others are loyal to Kisantu," Mad Dog concluded.

"That's the theory."

Mad Dog rose from the table and turned to Doolittle. "Ask her if one of the men is willing to drive back to Morstarr's camp. We can't leave Jack and Mbandi here."

While Doolittle did that, Mad Dog told Mr. Bibby to contact the mining managers using Jack's satellite phone directory. Bibby would notify them of the deaths and request that Kidman himself come out to the site. Someone at Morstarr had a lot to gain from the coup, and Mad Dog hoped to God it wasn't the CEO himself.

Doolittle cleared his throat. "Uh, Sergeant, she says she will get one of the men to drive back—if they can keep the truck."

"Tell her it's not ours to give away, but she'll be getting a brand-new one, along with everything else she wants. You tell her I'm a man of my word."

"I will."

Before the translator began, Mad Dog proffered his hand to Jumoke. Tentatively, she accepted.

Tongaso, Angola
Near Congo Border
0140 Hours Local Time

Jaga and Savimbi were young men in their twenties who were full of fire, idealists who were desperate to save their country—and they had found a way to help.

They had found Mboma Kisantu.

The Congo would change forever under their great leader's guidance. They respected him more than any man on Earth and had vowed to help him achieve his goal.

Thus, they were on a great mission, the most important mission of their lives:

They had teamed up with the local bandits as Kisantu had asked; they had stolen the diamonds by relying upon the transfer schedule that Kisantu had given them; and they had, in turn, made their break and stolen the diamonds once more from the rest of the group, those naïve fools who thought they would be escaping by air.

As instructed, the two men had hidden themselves in the jungle for one day, then they had fled to Tongaso, where they were to await transportation arranged by Kisantu.

Unfortunately, the rains had driven them closer to the village, forcing them to seek shelter in a hut on the edge of town. The women inside had glared at them, and the men were full of questions. Jaga concocted a story about how they had been searching for a lost child, and that they would resume their search in the morning. They just needed shelter for a few hours until the storm passed.

He leaned against the hut's half-open door, smoking a cigarette, while Savimbi slept on a small mat behind him. The other two families were sleeping on the far side, though one older woman sat up, her legs pulled into her chest, her eyes narrowing with suspicion.

Jaga offered her an uneasy grin, then glanced at his friend. He knew that Savimbi had stored the diamonds in a small leather pouch that he kept in his hip pocket.

After a last drag, he flicked his cigarette away, then leaned down and reached toward Savimbi—

A hand shot out and seized his wrist.

"What are you doing, Jaga?" Savimbi's eyes seemed to glow in the darkness.

"Nothing," Jaga said, wrenching free his wrist.

Savimbi studied him a moment more, then said, "Call them. See if they'll answer this time. Find out where they are . . ."

"Jumoke's Place"
Approx. 55 Kilometers West
Saurimo, Angola
0150 Hours Local Time

Pope flicked a glance skyward and muttered a curse at the black clouds that had smothered the stars. Being tired was one thing. Being wet and tired was, well, two things—two things that really pissed him off. He helped Wolfgang load the bodies onto the flatbed, then covered them with a few old blankets. Jumoke's man would take them back to camp in the morning.

"I feel like we should say something," said Wolfgang as he slammed closed the tailgate, rain dripping from his nose.

"Rest in peace," Pope grunted.

"Well, that's fuckin' brilliant."

"Hey, fuck you."

Wolfgang flashed a twisted grin. "Well, someone's a cranky motherfucker."

"I just hate this rain."

"I love it. It'll finally cool off this goddamned sauna. I just wish . . . I don't know . . . Jack buying it . . . damn, that's such a waste."

"Those fuckers set him up. No doubt."

Rookie jogged over, backhanding water from his eyes. "Hey, Mad Dog wants us in the hut." His tone grew sarcastic. "Apparently, we're moving out."

"And I was just getting to like this place," said Wolfgang.

They trudged back to the hut, ducked inside, and listened as Mad Dog spoke tersely. "There's a village called Tongaso, couple hours east of here. The name came up in the phone transcripts between Morstarr and the Congo. That town could be a rendezvous point. We might be too late, but, hell, it's worth a shot. Jam into the one pickup, and I hope you're not afraid to get wet."

"So we're still on a wild-goose chase?" asked Rookie.

"No, Mr. Masaki, we are not," snapped Mr. Bibby. "Nor have we been. Our INTEL is good. Our timing may be good, as well, so long as we don't waste any more of it."

Pope placed a hand on the back of Rookie's neck, squeezed, and whispered, "What Prince Charles is trying to say is shut the fuck up and get in the truck."

Kisantu Transport Truck
En Route to Tongaso, Angola
0152 Hours Local Time

Roufai's job was to pick up two men in Tongaso and take them back to Kisantu. That's all he knew. And that's all he wanted to know.

The truck had hit a rut in the road, one so deep that it had broken the old cattle truck's axle. He had been under the vehicle for the better part of the day, had finally given up, and had called Kisantu to say they would need to send another truck to pick up the two men in Tongaso. Kisantu, of course, had been furious, but what else could he do but send another truck?

In the meantime, Roufai and his partner, Kwezi, had decided to wait for that second truck. They were taking turns sleeping in the cab. At least they had shelter from the rain, though the air had grown thick, even with the windows cracked open.

The heavy rain pounding on the windshield had torn

Roufai from a most pleasant dream involving a young woman he had met a few years ago. With a groan, he realized he was in the truck, sleeping beside his smelly, unshaven accomplice.

For a moment, he thought he heard an engine, and then headlights suddenly appeared in his rearview mirror. The replacement truck had already arrived!

"What do we got here?" Bender asked as they came up behind the truck, whose driver's-side rear wheel was lost in the muck, the vehicle listing badly to that side.

"Could be our boys," said Thorn, who was at the wheel.

"Looks like the truck they told us about." Bender checked his GPS. They were about three hours away from Tongaso.

"Hey, look!"

"What the fuck?" gasped Bender as a guy leapt out of the cab and began waving his hands.

"Oh, this should be good," said Thorn.

"You ain't kidding."

Thorn brought the truck to a squeaky halt, then reached for his Mark 23 pistol.

"Don't draw," said Bender. "We're friends. Remember?"

The trooper sighed, nodded. Bender's own P220, a .45-caliber pistol that he kept concealed under his shirt, rubbed his side and begged to be fired.

But not yet. He held his breath and hopped out, while behind him, Greene and Dzoba hopped down and hustled off to establish a perimeter. Rain or no, anyone could take a pot shot at them, if only to kill them for their valuable weapons.

Thorn, who spoke Portuguese, opened his mouth.

But the driver rushed forward, his voice rising and falling like an opera singer's. He gestured to the truck, to the sky, to the truck once more.

Finally, Thorn turned to Bender, wearing an odd expression. "He's says he's surprised that we brought such a small truck and that we brought two other men. He says that Kisantu must be getting paranoid and cheap."

The driver spoke again, tilting his head toward the cab. Thorn followed him back there, where the driver shook the shoulder of another man sleeping in the passenger's seat.

Meanwhile, Bender came up behind Thorn and lowered his voice. "He thinks we came to pick him up. Let's confirm where he was headed without tipping him off. Can you play that?"

"I can play that." The trooper went to work.

The driver's partner, a hairy little guy with a pistol strapped to his waist came out and waved at Bender, who slapped the guy on the shoulder, as though they were old friends. *Hello, you little motherfucker.*

The guy was talking fast, even as Thorn was speaking to the driver. Bender smiled and nodded. *Give me a reason to shoot you.*

Thorn broke off from the driver and returned to Bender. "You know, we've been trying way too hard to gather INTEL. We should've waited for it to come to us. I mean, you are *not* going to believe this." The man chuckled through his words.

Bender tensed. "Thorn, what the fuck?"

"Dude, uh, sir, we hit the jackpot. These guys *were* on their way to Tongaso, but they obviously got stuck. They think we're the replacement truck."

The tension eased in Bender's shoulders, and he slowly smiled as Thorn continued:

"We're supposed to go there and pick up two men. Now if you think about it, if someone stole the diamonds and needed to get back to the Congo, this would be a pretty clear rendezvous point. Also, picking up those guys must be pretty important to send a second truck. I'm betting those two guys are carrying the diamonds."

Bender sighed. "Be nice, huh?"

"No shit."

"Well, fuck, this is outstanding. We go there, pick up the guys with the diamonds, then we let them lead us back to Kisantu. Doesn't get any easier than that."

"I know. But I already get a sense that our buddy, the driver, doesn't quite trust us. They expected a bigger truck and two guys. That's what they were told. I told them we were just sent here. We didn't know about that."

"Yeah, well, we can't kill 'em yet. We don't know if those guys in Tongaso know where Kisantu is, but it's safe to assume that these guys do."

"That's right."

Bender thought a moment. He didn't like playing a game with armed men. He always liked being in control of the situation. Perhaps, it was time to drop the smiles and raise the weapons.

"All right, Thorn. Here it is: We disarm 'em, collect their phones and whatever else, tie 'em, and take 'em along as a human GPS, know what I'm saying?"

"Yeah, good. And Dzoba will get 'em to tell us where Kisantu is. He's an evil fuck."

"That he is."

"I'll take Shorty. You take your buddy."

They faced the two men and grinned. Thorn uttered a few words in a jovial tone, then stole a glance at Bender, who nodded.

"Oh, amigo, me gonna fuck you up," Bender said, then tripped the guy, disarming him before he hit the ground.

A shot rang out, and Bender whirled to his right, saw Thorn struggling to bring down the other guy, who still had a pistol locked in his grip.

"God damn it, Thorn," Bender cried.

But in the next second Thorn had taken the weapon and driven the man to the ground. "Sorry, Bender. He's a slippery fucker."

"I don't care. Secure him, and let's move! Dzoba? Greene? Back to the truck!"

The driver began screaming, and Bender recognized a few words: "Who are you?"

"I'm the guy who's taking you for a ride," Bender muttered.

Chapter 5

....

En Route to Tongaso
Near Congo Border
0340 Hours Local Time

Mr. Bibby sat in the truck's passenger seat while Pope guided them over a mud-laden road that cut through the grassy hills. Rain bands swept through, and the water rose nearly a foot in some low spots.

Twice Pope had veered onto the embankment to avoid the massive puddles, nearly throwing the others out of the flatbed.

In the mean time, Bibby had lost the satellite link for a few minutes and was trying furiously to reestablish a connection. Blasted computers were a blessing and a curse. He was ready to crush the thing with his bare hands.

A sudden turn to the right threw him against the door. "Mr. Pope, would you please?"

"Hey, I'm doing the best I can!"

"Do better."

Pope grunted, then gestured with his head toward the laptop. "So, what do you like better, Mr. Bibby—banging heads or banging keys?"

"I've never thought about it. Does it really matter? You think I'm better suited behind a keyboard? Should we go to the range and prove you wrong?"

"I'm not trying to bust your balls. I appreciate what you do, you know that."

"I don't need compliments. I need a connection."

"You know what bothers me about you?"

"Should I care?"

"There it is—your attitude. You're a merc, just like us. Matter of fact, you've gone farther over the edge with Ricer and his boys—fucking big-time criminal activity— which makes me think, why the hell does this guy need to be so proper? And don't tell me it's a British thing."

"Actually, it's a Bibby thing—because it's easy to lose yourself here. And you're right. I was there once, seen and done things I just . . ." He closed his eyes for a moment.

"You got nothing to worry about. We're all upstanding citizens."

"One look at you, and I worry. I really do."

"Oh, give me a break. If we were dumbass scumbags we wouldn't be making this kind of change."

"Mr. Pope, when I was eighteen, I had dreams of serving my country, becoming a great hero for England. I was going to be the next James Bond."

Pope chuckled. "So what happened, Mr. Bond?"

Bibby clenched his teeth. "You bring people together, and they create these enormous mechanisms in the name of efficiency. And soon the mechanisms control everything."

Pope grinned knowingly. "The one I come from is called the military industrial complex. They tell you to do things, but they don't give you the right tools because the tools are too expensive. I can't tell you how many times I've heard that."

"You dream about something for most of your childhood, and then you learn that there is no Santa Claus, that doing the right thing is impossible without doing the wrong thing. As you might say, that fucking sucks."

"That's exactly how I'd put it."

They were silent for a few moments, the truck rattling as they took on more ruts and pot holes, while Bibby steadied the computer on his lap.

"Can I ask you something?" Pope began. "You're not gay, are you?"

Bibby's gaze never left his computer screen. "Feeling lonely, Mr. Pope?"

"Seriously."

"Would it bother you if I were?"

"I'm not homophobic, I mean not in a violent way."

"In what way, then?"

"Tell me you're not gay. Come on, please."

"What makes you think I am?"

"There's been talk. I mean, I've never heard you mention a wife or girlfriend."

"Well, if you think about that further, you've never heard me talk about my personal life, at least not until now. I'm a private man. Most people can appreciate that."

"Yeah, I do. And, uh, hey, I didn't mean to pry."

"Yes, you did."

Pope looked guilty. "You just wonder, you know?"

"Well, Mr. Pope, if while showering you drop your Barbie doll, you can retrieve it with confidence around me."

Pope recoiled, looked embarrassed. "Touché. And thanks." He leaned forward and flicked a glance at his GPS. "We should be getting close now."

"And we have a link," Bibby said.

"I'll call the Bossman. Blackhound One, this is Blackhound Four, over."

Mad Dog had been sitting between Wolfgang and Sapper, his head hanging low as he drifted in and out of sleep. He felt so exhausted that he thought of telling Pope to get off at the next exit so they could find a nice hotel rated Excellent by the AAA. Pope needed to make sure the place had a Continental breakfast and a fitness center. And oh, yeah, a nice pool, too.

Just then the former SEAL's voice crackled in Mad Dog's ear. They were nearing Tongaso. "All right. Lights off. Slow down. When we get within a couple hundred meters of the first hut, we pull off the road and go. Recon first, fire teams two and three on the flanks—and hopefully no one goes running off this time. Everyone get ready."

His voice had been a little too bitter, but his men probably expected that.

After checking his weapon, Boo Boo, who sat opposite Mad Dog, leaned forward and said, "There's a lady named payback, and she's a real fucking bitch, right, Zog?"

Mad Dog nodded halfheartedly. Nothing would bring back his lost friends. Killing those responsible made you feel good for a few hours, but then it was over, all you had were your memories.

However, you could harness the anger and frustration, use them to your advantage, so long as you didn't flip out and do something stupid.

He gave his carbine another once over, then rolled out the kinks in his shoulders as the truck slowly veered off the road, heading toward a large stand of trees. "All right, gentlemen. Here we go!"

Bender, Thorn, Greene, and Dzoba, along with their two new "friends," were still heading toward Tongaso. Thorn was back at the wheel, while Bender repeatedly checked his widescreen PDA. The unit displayed a full color moving map and imbedded GPS that was also night-vision capable for those operations. The map helped him identify potential ambush sites, choke points, detours, and escape routes. Their present location was symbolized in the center of the display, and the grid coordinates and waypoint information were displayed at the top and bottom. They could download new map data by tactical satellite (TACSAT) whenever they needed it.

Thus far Dzoba hadn't pried any significant information out of their buddies, only that Kisantu had established a small camp in the jungle somewhere west of Kamina. From there he had been launching his raids up and down the border, sometimes fleeing into Angola to somewhere south of Tongaso.

Kisantu's two men knew exactly where he was, of course, but they weren't saying just yet. Dzoba had told them that if they didn't talk, they would not like the consequences . . . and for now, he'd left it like that. The trip back from Tongaso would prove interesting, if not bloody.

"How close are we now?" Thorn asked.

Bender checked the GPS. "I figure about fifteen, twenty minutes."

"You want to ride in like nobody's business?"

"We'll drop off Dzoba and the cargo outside of town,

establish a rally point. We three ride in, and I'm betting those two guys will come running out to meet us."

After a second's thought, Thorn grinned.

"We pick 'em up, take them back to the rally point, relieve them of the diamonds—if they got 'em—then take along one guy, probably your buddy the driver, to lead us back to Kisantu."

Thorn wriggled his brows. "I . . . like it! Props to the boss for a good plan."

"Yeah, it sounds good in theory. If it plays out like that, I'll be amazed. Something will go wrong. But for now, we pretend we're tactical geniuses."

"Hey, we don't have to pretend."

"Okay, Thorn. If you say so. Just expect a few fuck-ups, and we'll all be okay."

Tongaso was a lot larger than Jumoke's Place, with twice as many huts and even a few chicken coops and large vegetable gardens. Rookie darted behind the coops and crouched down beside a rickety wooden fence that stood near a string of huts. He attached the night-vision lens to his binoculars and began scanning each hut, probing the doorways, the openings, the shadows.

He was breathing hard, the adrenaline coursing so hotly through his veins that he shuddered. "Blackhound Four, this is Blackhound Six. Got four huts on my side. All quiet over here, over."

"Roger that," said Pope. "Hold tight."

Rookie zoomed in on a shadow near one door, zoomed some more, and bingo, he had a target. "Blackhound Four, I got a guy in the second hut, my side. He's standing there, smoking. Can't get a shot of his face from my angle, over."

"What's he doing up so late?" asked Sapper.

"Blackhound Six?" called Pope. "Remain in position. Just keep your eyes on him, that's it. Don't fucking move. Don't fucking breathe. Got it?"

Rookie snorted. "But if I close in, maybe I can steal a pic for Blackhound Two, over."

"Negative. Stay put."

"Roger that." Rookie moved in a few meters anyway, but he still couldn't get a clean shot of the guy's face.

Mad Dog and Doolittle slipped behind the hut and peered in the open window.

Three women and a half-dozen children slept soundly on small wooden racks. A boy about twelve or thirteen, all long limbs and neck, rolled over as a sudden gust of wind rattled the thatched roof, carrying with it rain from the overhanging trees.

The boy opened his eyes, looked at Mad Dog, who put a finger to his lips. He reached into his breast pocket and produced a ten dollar bill.

The kid's eyes grew wider.

Mad Dog waved him outside, where Doolittle was waiting to whisper in the kid's ear.

"Are we good?" Mad Dog asked the interpreter.

"I think so."

"That was fast."

"He's seen men with guns before. He's only surprised. Not scared."

With a slight grimace, Mad Dog slowly removed his hand, half-expecting the kid to scream.

But he didn't. He spoke slowly, though Mad Dog kept his hand close to the boy's mouth.

Doolittle's tone grew excited. "He says two strangers did come earlier. They were looking for a lost boy."

Mad Dog's pulse bounded. "Ask him where they are now."

Doolittle translated, and the kid answered quickly.

"What?" Mad Dog demanded.

"He says they're still here, and if we want, he'll take us to them."

"Beautiful. Tell him to hang on." Mad Dog reached around and keyed his mike. "This is Blackhound One. Everybody hold position. Three and I are moving in on two targets, could be our guys."

Doolittle whispered something to the boy, who nodded.

"What did you say?" asked Mad Dog.

"I told him if he does what we ask, we'll give him some money to help his family. I'll take it out of my cut."

"This place is getting to you, too, huh?"

"Yes, it is." Doolittle gestured to the boy, and Mad Dog released him.

"Tell him not to run off," warned Mad Dog.

"He won't. He doesn't like these strangers."

The boy turned back and muttered something.

Doolittle frowned. "He says they're not nice like we are, or the other man whose been here for a few days now."

"The other man?"

With a wave, the boy urged them around the hut, uttering a few words in reply to Doolittle's questioning.

"He'll take us to him, too."

After learning some most unsettling news, Bibby stowed his laptop in his ruck and covered Mad Dog, Doolittle, and the boy from his position near the tree line opposite the village. "Blackhound One, this is Blackhound Two, over."

"Little busy right now, Two," answered Mad Dog.

"Latest INTEL from Big Booty. There's at least one team of Delta Force troopers operating in this region. They're targeting Kisantu and the smugglers, over."

"Well that news could've come earlier," answered Mad Dog. "Can't worry about 'em now. Stand by, out."

Bibby shook his head in disgust. There were too many players on the field now: mercs, locals, Kisantu's rebels, bandits who'd been ripped off themselves, and now Delta Force troops. Toss in the local police and the DROC military forces, and they'd be set for a real game, scorecards most definitely required.

Better still—no one would know who was who. Kill everyone, figure out who they were in the morning—just like the "good old" days.

Mad Dog, Doolittle, and the boy turned a corner, out of sight. Bibby slowed his breathing and just waited.

Jaga had finished his entire pack of cigarettes and was about to turn from the doorway when he saw something glimmer near the fence. He frowned, squinted through the rain, and then, as though he were watching it all unfold on a movie screen, he saw a dark-skinned man gripping a rifle rise slightly and ease forward. He recognized that ball cap.

Should he rush into the hut and warn Savimbi? Or should he just remain there so he wouldn't alert the rifleman?

He debated that point for about three seconds before turning and dashing inside. He booted a snoring Savimbi in the ribs and whispered, "Trouble! We have to go!"

As Savimbi sat up, he reached for his pocket, felt the diamonds, then grabbed his rifle as Jaga seized his own. They fled around the back of the hut, stomping through the mud as Jaga led them toward the river.

"Who was it?" cried Savimbi.

"Security from Morstarr, I think."

"How did they find us?"

"I don't know. Just run!"

The second he saw the two men flee the hut, Rookie began screaming his head off on the radio as he hauled ass and spotted the guys in the distance.

He had loaded sabot slugs into his Remington for just such an occasion. Leaping up and over a small rise, he came down, paused, took aim—

Fired!

Had he struck his mark? Shit, too dark.

A volley of incoming fire sent him diving to his gut.

No, he'd missed.

He ticked off three seconds, and fuck it, bolted up and returned to his sprint.

Those assholes wouldn't have run if they didn't have something to hide. And they most definitely had guns. He had guns. They didn't feel like talking. Neither did he.

But damn it, they descended into a little ravine and vanished. Rookie came up and over another mound of clay.

Both boots gave out. He dropped onto his butt, skidded down the mound, and reflexively tucked his rifle into his chest as he began rolling through the mud.

"Hey, Rook?" called Sapper from somewhere behind him.

He finally came to a halt, but he couldn't see through

all the mud in his face. "Two guys running," hollered Rookie. "They were heading toward the river. Go!"

He struggled to his feet, wiping the muck from his eyes. He blinked, looked up into the falling rain, then his vision cleared. Sapper had just run past him, and he fell in behind the man, charging toward the next hill. He thought he heard the river somewhere beyond.

AK fire popped near his feet. He veered left, answered with two rounds of his own.

Then Sapper wailed a curse and opened up.

They both did, muzzles flashing and smoking.

The AK fire died off.

"They're on the run again!" hollered Rookie.

Mad Dog had ordered Doolittle to stay with the boy and question the people inside the hut where the strangers had just been. Then he called for Bibby to join him in pursuit, while Wolfgang, Drac, and Boo Boo of Fire Team Three remained in position, out of sight to continue reconning the village in case some unexpected bullshit went down.

Those shots had no doubt awoken the entire place, and you never knew who else had guns and who felt like squeezing off a few rounds.

He swore as he ran around the huts, seeing two silhouettes in the distance: Sapper and Rookie. They had been so fucking close, and now . . . shit, they were losing them.

Still some unknowns. A pair had fled, but were they the right pair? Probably. Did they have the diamonds? Mad Dog couldn't be sure. Perhaps they were decoys.

No, it couldn't be that complicated. They were waiting to get picked up, and they had waited a little too long.

Mad Dog hoped one of his own guys hadn't been sloppy enough to tip them off—but that seemed the case. Fucking Rookie.

While sidestepping along the next rise, he ordered himself not to slip like an old fart. He slowed, measured his steps a bit more, his boots sinking up to his ankles in mud, his nose filled with that damp, earthy smell.

Damn, his muscles didn't like that shit. The wind tugged hard at his shoulders, the rain blinding him for a few seconds. Nature was really pissing him off.

More gunfire. And a grenade from Sapper's weapon.

Whoosh! A bright flash outlined the treetops, followed by a crack of thunder, almost on cue.

"Anyone still got eyes on them?" Mad Dog called.

"I do!" yelled Sapper. "They're running toward the riverbank."

"Don't lose them!"

"I'm trying! I'm trying!"

It was all for Wolfgang's entertainment pleasure: the women with their colorful headgear running around with lanterns, the children with wide eyes huddling in doorways, the dogs barking, and the men screaming as a few came outside with pathetic-looking clubs they had carved themselves. The Flintstones were angry, all right.

"Now that's a fucking wake-up call," he muttered into the radio. "Look at 'em . . ."

"What the fuck," cried Boo Boo, and for him to get excited, something was most definitely wrong. "A pair of headlights coming down from the north."

"Yeah, I see 'em, too," said Drac.

"Coming right down the road," added Boo Boo.

Wolfgang lowered his Commando carbine, lifted his binoculars, squinted as his eyes slowly adjusted.

Damn, just a blur. He removed the night-vision lens; it was no good now because of all the fog and rain, and while he could switch to the ATN 250 thermal eye camera, which could see through the soup, he didn't need it. The regular lens showed him enough. "Three guys in a pickup truck. Could be the rebels. Probably come to get 'em." He heaved a sigh, swearing through it a few times. "We got here just in time. I think. You hearing this, Blackhound One, over?"

Mad Dog was indeed. But he was all about pursuing the other guys, along with Sapper and Rookie, his legs working like well-oiled pistons, his gaze riveted to the rolling course ahead. "Roger that, Seven. Maintain position. Just watch 'em. Don't engage. Don't blow cover. Flies on the wall. You fuckin' hear me, over?"

"Roger. Fuckin' hear you, out."

Don't engage? Wolfgang thought. *They so much as wave a weapon in my direction, and I'll cut those assholes into digestible chunks and lie about it later.*

Okay, time to break out the big girl. He swapped his carbine for the RT–20 sniper rifle, then came farther around the tree, polishing the trunk with one shoulder. He'd blow up the whole fuckin' truck and those scumbags with it. He and his big girl, his lady of love.

"Okay," said Boo Boo. "Here they come."

With his submachine gun clenched in his grip, Mr. Bibby wove a much wider path north in pursuit of the two men. They might attempt either a river crossing or a double back into the jungle.

If they tried the latter, his course should intersect theirs.

If they tried to hide along the riverbank, Mad Dog and the others should find them. The operative word, of course, was "should."

Running in the rain and mud, at night, in a foreign country was nothing new or particularly distressing to Bibby. Ironically, he felt invigorated, set free from his technological leash to roam and shoot freely.

That, too, was a Bibby thing.

Just before Mad Dog had called, he had torn off the hot and restricting balaclava and replaced his glasses before joining the party. He could finally breathe.

And that was all he heard at that point: his pulse and labored breath. The boots coming down into the mud. The rattle of his pack as the rain stung his cheeks.

He came into a gully at the base of a rocky slope. Clusters of trees with huge, sagging limbs ringed the slope's crest. He would head there to gain an excellent view of the riverbank. With a concerted effort to control his breathing, he increased his pace, traversed the gully, then broke into a hard sprint. Bloody hell, the slope was steeper than he'd thought.

Once at the top, he paused, fished out the thermal camera, and began a slow pan. "All right, you bastards," he whispered. "Where are you?"

When Pope was finished with Rookie, there'd be nothing left but sushi. The noob had pushed his luck and moved in, alerting their bad guys.

The facts were clear:

The men had fled from that side of the town, and the guy Rookie had observed was probably standing watch while his buddy caught some sleep. There was no rocket science involved, no deep fucking thoughts to figure out what had happened.

Mr. Bad Ass Delta Force trooper had blown his first mission as a merc. He'd let his ego get in the way.

Pope shouldn't be mad. He'd seen it coming. Maybe he was mad because he'd been powerless to stop it. He couldn't be a fucking babysitter. You had to place trust. You couldn't operate without it. He had to trust Mad Dog for picking Rookie, and he had to trust the guy to operate like a professional.

Well, fuck, that hadn't worked!

Now he was left bringing up the rear, trying to ensure that the runners didn't turn tail and suddenly head south. He kept a steady pace, turning down toward the river-bank, following the trees, and frightening sleeping par-rots as he hustled by.

He was aching to fire his submachine gun and even thought of Rookie standing before him, making up lame excuses a half-second before a volley erupted across his chest, shaking him as though he were being electro-cuted.

But then again, who was Pope to judge? He'd made mistakes himself. Terrible ones.

Bender hopped out of the pickup, one-handing his sub-machine gun as he shut the door. Thorn came up behind him, his shorter gun in hand as a half-dozen villagers, including two men wielding clubs, started toward them.

They'd heard the shots in the distance on their way to the village, and Bender had dropped off Greene to see what the hell was going on while they continued. Dzoba and their two buddies were back at the rally point, waiting.

Those shots couldn't have been good, and Bender hated mysteries. He could understand if they'd been fired upon, but seemingly random shots meant they were walking into a hot zone. Perhaps a very hot zone.

"All right, here we go," muttered Thorn.

"I love my job," sang Bender.

Thorn spoke to the first man, a bare-chested, broad-nosed guy with a gold hoop in one ear. Funny how jewelry, like drugs and American pop music, found its way even to the most remote regions of Angola. The guy's face creased more deeply, either in confusion or frustration, Bender wasn't sure.

Thorn nodded, turned back to Bender, and they stepped away from the crowd. "I asked him about two strangers. He says they were here. Now he thinks they've run away. They heard shots and came out."

Bender swore through his teeth. "Which way they headed?"

"Follow the shots, I guess."

"All right, tell these people we're, uh, sorry about the inconvenience. They can write a letter to their local government official or whatever."

Thorn made a face. "You really want me to tell them that?

Bender puffed air and threw up his hands. "Just . . . just hurry up!"

Wolfgang noted the expensive, sexy weapons carried by both men standing near the truck.

Conclusion: These rebels either had some pretty fat bank accounts or they weren't the rebels at all but Bibby's Delta Force operators.

Sure, they dressed like everyone else, drove a piece of

shit, and were even black, but that hardly meant they'd come from the Congo instead of Fort Bragg. They had probably assumed they could pack some slick firepower around locals who didn't know an AK from an HK.

But Wolfgang could recite the specs on both guns the way old ladies recite the Holy Rosary.

"Blackhound One, this is Blackhound Seven, over."

"Go ahead," came Mad Dog's breathless reply.

"I don't think the guys in town are rebels, man. They could be Delta, over."

"Are you sure?"

"No, I'm not sure. But one guy's got a full-size HK416 with Trijicon Advanced Digital Optic Gunsight, cyber-optic triangulation unit, and 40mm grenade launcher. The other guy's got the Kurz version—and you know what those weapons are saying to me? Delta, man. Delta."

"Dude, you're a fuckin' gun geek. But you'd best be real careful out there. Just keep watching, Blackhound One, out."

"Hey, Seven," Drac called. "Looks like they're leaving."

"See that."

"You want to follow, circle around, keep them in sight? I mean, I do, come on, over?"

"Roger that, Eight. You and me, go. Nine you hold back here."

"What? No fun for me?"

"You might need to come up if someone gets scratched, over."

"Yeah, yeah," moaned Boo Boo.

Wolfgang started along the tree line, reaching Drac's position in less than a minute. He still had the truck in sight as it rumbled back up the dirt road, pushing north through the darkness, the headlights easily discernable.

Be nice if they could grab their own truck and follow, but . . . fuck it. That's what they'd need to do, in case these guys really hauled butt. Wolfgang and Drac could keep a safe distance, run dark. He fought for breath as he slapped a palm on Drac's shoulder. "Let's go back for our ride."

"You forget something?"

"No, asshole. We'll follow in the truck."

"How?"

Wolfgang thought his fellow fire team member had suddenly gone retarded. "What?"

"Fuckin' Pope's got the keys."

"Aw, shit. All right. Let's go."

They ran hard, with Drac really putting on the pressure. Wolfgang needed to lay off the carbs for a while.

The road snaked off, winding westward for a hundred meters before turning back north. If he and Drac cut through the forest, they might reach the truck just as it came around the bend. After that, who knew what?

Then again, Wolfgang had a few ideas of how to slow them down, if not engage them.

Too bad Sapper wasn't with them. The engineer would get a real rush when Wolfgang's plan exploded into action.

Hell, if they couldn't play with boobs, bombs were the next best thing.

Chapter 6

· ·

Tongaso, Angola
Near Congo Border
0440 Hours Local Time

Mad Dog came charging up to Rookie and Sapper, who were squatting out of breath near the riverbank, binoculars pressed tightly to their eyes.

"Don't tell me what you're going to tell me," Mad Dog began.

He turned as Pope came thundering down toward them, baring his teeth. Pope saw what had happened and had one word for it: "Bullshit!"

"They must be in the water," said Sapper. "No fuckin' way we could've lost them."

"Well, we did, asshole," spat Rookie.

Pope stomped up to Rookie and wrenched away his binoculars, tossed them on the dirt. "You moved in when I told you not to."

"Fuck you, Pope." Rookie seized Pope's collar.

Pope's eyes ignited. "Big mistake."

"Enough of that shit," warned Mad Dog. "I'll fire both of you fuckers. Spread out. Eyes on both sides of the river."

Rookie snapped free his hand. "Just get off my fuckin' back, got it?"

"I speak, you listen. You don't, and I will get you fired. Now move out!"

The oily water stretched off about a hundred meters to the opposite shore, and it was possible that the two guys were swimming warily across.

It was also possible that Mad Dog and his merry mutts had just let two million bucks slip through their paws.

Oh, the joy of mercenary work! Fuck!

At the least the rain had begun to taper off. Mad Dog used his night-vision lens, working his gaze along the river, studying both shorelines, trying to find something, anything. Those men didn't just vanish. Maybe they had stopped, were waiting it out, believing that Mad Dog and his men would eventually give up. No chance of that.

They were a plague. They were relentless.

Jaga watched as Savimbi finished burying the diamonds. They had chosen a spot near two small trees about three meters away from the water. He had urged his partner to hide the stash in case they were caught—

Because if that happened they would be questioned, but the men from Morstarr would be forced to release them without witnesses and evidence. If they got away, they could always come back for the diamonds later. Only they knew where the diamonds were hidden.

Also, if they were caught, and their captors suspected they had, in fact, hidden the diamonds, then he and Savimbi wouldn't be killed. Tortured maybe, but not killed— although he wondered how long they could hold out before they broke down and confessed. Then, of course, their lives would mean nothing.

"This place will look different during the day," Jaga reminded his friend.

Savimbi wiped his hands on his pants and smirked. "Don't worry. I'll remember."

"So will I. Okay, now. We'll lead them away from here. We should cross the river." Jaga started toward the glassy surface.

Savimbi made a face. "I cannot swim."

"You fool. Now we'll be caught."

With that, Jaga sprinted off, already placing himself at the next grouping of trees, hearing his fellow bandit rushing to catch up with him.

"We stay together," cried Savimbi.

Jaga sensed that they were already being punished for their crime and that his future would soon grow even darker. The knot in his stomach twisted tighter.

Wolfgang and Drac reached the dirt road about fifteen seconds ahead of the pickup truck carrying the men who might be Delta Force operators.

"Time 'em just right," Wolfgang told Drac.

"I'll try not to kill 'em, but it won't be easy!"

The truck bounced forward—

"Now!" hollered Wolfgang.

He and Drac lobbed a pair of fragmentation grenades directly into the truck's path, one right after the other. The average solider could throw an M67 about forty meters. They each reached fifty without a problem.

The idea was for the explosions to stop—not hit—the truck and force the guys outside. They'd think the fight was on.

Well, it would be, sort of.

The first grenades went off, twin, orange-white flashes that sent the pickup careening off the road and into a ditch—just as the second pair of grenades did their flash bang numbers.

The killing radius was only five meters, the casualty radius fifteen, but fragments could disperse as far as two hundred and thirty meters according to the nerds who recorded such things.

No doubt the truck had taken a beating.

"Wow, that was fuckin' cool," grunted Drac.

"Okay, they're getting out," Wolfgang said, lowering his binoculars. "Open up!"

Wolfgang fired wide with his carbine while Drac put his Stoner to work, tearing up the road a handful of meters away from the men.

It was a Hollywood bullshit battle at its best. All they needed was fuckin' Schwarzenegger to run around, holding a weapon the wrong way while he attacked the truck and kept his biceps rigid for the camera.

Yet it was a beautiful delaying tactic, so well conceived that Wolfgang assumed Jesus was about to come down from the clouds, shake his hand, and say, "Now that was a fuckin' attack!"

Yep, it was just beautiful. They had those boys pinned down behind their vehicle. Now it was time to level the playing field.

Wolfgang ran along the hillside, then dropped into a little ditch. He got the big girl ready as the men below returned fire, rounds thudding into wet clay just to his right.

"Hey, asshole on the Stoner," he called to Drac over the radio. "Flush 'em out. Get 'em away from the truck."

"Uh, I think I can arrange something like that."

Drac employed his weapon to deliver a sermon first written in the jungles of Vietnam. And that sermon, had, of course, been written with VC blood.

The two guys bolted away from the truck, working their way northward along the ditch.

"Drac, I love it when you do that," hollered Wolfgang.

And with a huge breath he brought up the big girl, took aim at the pickup's fuel tank.

And *boom* he let one round go.

His groin literally tingled, and his heart must have stopped.

He heard absolutely nothing for a split second, felt nothing, saw only a curtain of darkness.

Then the truck exploded in a blinding conflagration that sent the front wheels rising a full meter from the ground.

Wolfgang couldn't believe his own eyes, and he gasped as though he'd just rolled off one of those fine Russian divorcées he occasionally hooked up with via the Web.

Mad Dog was already yapping on the radio—what the fuck are you doing?—or some shit like that.

Sometimes the old dog just didn't get it. He was wrapped up too tightly in the business end of it all and needed to remember that the bottom line was to kick ass, get paid, and go home. Wolfgang was just getting that first part covered.

He crouched down, hauled his victorious butt across the hill, to where Drac was perched beside a tree and still letting 'em rip with the Stoner. He had probably gone through at least half of his 150-round drum.

"All right," Wolfgang hollered over the rattle of Drac's legendary weapon. "They'll get a fuckin' bead on you!"

The guys below had run out of ditch and were racing toward a hill opposite their burning pickup.

Drac hadn't heard shit. He was blissfully firing away, his pearly whites glistening with saliva.

"Hold fire, asshole!"

He did, then screamed, "Why? I ain't hit nothing yet!"

"Let's boogie!"

Drac winked and nodded, pushed back and away from the tree, turning the barrel of his smoking weapon skyward.

"If they're rebels we just slowed 'em down," Wolfgang said, still riding a wave of good feelings, good times.

"And if they're Delta Force, we've slowed 'em down and really pissed 'em off," Drac added.

Wolfgang gave a little snort. "They're pissed no matter who they are, you idiot!"

They jogged along the hill, parallel to the ditch and incoming gunfire.

"Waste of goddamn ammo if you ask me. When brass flies, people oughta die," cried Drac. "And hey, you going to answer him?"

Mad Dog was still howling over the radio.

Wolfgang reached a hill with tall, concealing grass and paused. "Okay, this looks good. You keep an eye on our buddies while I call the big guy. Blackhound One, this is Blackhound Seven, over."

Mad Dog repeatedly clenched his fist as he listened to Wolfgang's report. Then, nearly out of breath, he yelled, "I told you not to engage!"

"Goddamn it, we didn't! We just slowed 'em down. It was a necessary evil!"

"Well, then, fuck! Stay with them, you evil dumb fuck."

"Don't worry, we're on 'em!"

Uttering another string of curses whose combinations made no sense but did make him feel better, Mad Dog took off again. They were still combing the shoreline, he to the rear, with Sapper, Rookie, and Pope out front.

Bibby reported what he had seen from Wolfgang's location and said he was holding back in case their guys broke off to the west. No sign of them yet.

Oh why oh why hadn't Mad Dog taken on a simple training mission? They could've come to Angola to work with local police and the army. They could've been paid big bucks to teach flunkies how to fire guns instead of running across the jungle in search of possibilities.

Well, the big bucks wouldn't have added up to two million, that's for sure.

They just needed a goddamn break.

"Blackhound One, this is Blackhound Six," Rookie called. "I got 'em! I got 'em! They're running along the hills, heading east of the burning truck, over."

Had a prayer been answered? Time to find out.

Bender and Thorn were in "what the fuck" mode: firing first and asking questions later.

Rebels had obviously staked out the village. Maybe they'd heard about the diamond theft. Maybe they worked for Kisantu, maybe not. Didn't matter. They had some serious firepower and were laying it down with impunity. Bastards had the high ground, and Bender hated that shit with a passion.

Yet both he and his trusted companion knew that if those men were serious about killing them, they might've hit their marks much sooner. The automatic weapons fire was especially sloppy, and that was either intentional or the work of a rather poorly trained gunman. They were in Angola, after all, but Bender still had his doubts.

So it was no diamonds for them—but at least they still had their tour guides who would take them to Kisantu— providing he and Thorn reached the rally point alive.

And in the end, Kisantu was the real prize. Bring him down, and there would be no coup to finance with the stolen diamonds, right?

Aw, hell, they'd get some other asshole to replace him, and life—and the grisly deaths—would go on.

Sniffling and catching his breath, Bender keyed his mike. They hadn't bothered with radio call signs, and Dzoba was still calling on the radio, so it was high time he answered. "Dzoba, it's Bender. They've ceased fire. Hold your position and hold it tight."

"Roger that. What the fuck?"

"Yeah, ditto that. Now listen to me. We're gonna circle around, come in from behind you, try to lose these assholes. I know they're following."

"Gotcha. I'll be waiting."

Thorn gave Bender a hand signal: the next rise looked good. Move out! They did.

"Yo, Bender?" came Greene's voice through the headset. "Got news."

"And I got fuckin' guys on my back. Shit, man, what do you got?"

"I see two guys running. Could be the ones we were going to meet. There's a few more after 'em. I'm pretty sure it's a security team from Morstarr. I recognize the uniforms from our last intel dump, over."

"Can you intercept the guys before they get caught?"

"Roger that."

"Good! You tell 'em we came to pick them up, then you take 'em to the rally point, you hear me?"

"I hear you. I'm on it. I'll call when I'm close, out."

Bender thought a moment. Oh, Shit. Greene didn't speak fluent Portuguese. Ah, he probably knew enough words to get by.

Maybe. Bender hoped he knew how to say, "Hold your fire!"

Shit. Bender thought of voicing his concern to Thorn, and perhaps sending the man after Greene, but there was no sense in splitting them up further.

And no fucking time!

Besides, they were being chased themselves and couldn't head back to the rally point until they lost their shadows. Damn, he'd warned Thorn about a few fuck-ups, but he'd had no idea they'd be frolicking in the land of FUBAR lorded over by King FUBAR Maximus, who, of course, kept the land and the people Fucked Up Beyond All Recognition.

Pope finally caught up with Rookie and Sapper, both advancing at a real good clip. He couldn't see diddly beyond them.

"Where are they?" he shouted to Rookie.

"Just over the next hill!"

"They could've turned left," said Sapper. "I told you, Rook! They could've turned!"

"They didn't!"

"I think they did! I'm turning," Sapper cried, breaking off from the group.

"Rookie, you keep going. I'll head closer to the shore, in case they broke right!"

Pope splashed through a stream working its way down to the river, the water coming into his eyes. With a grimace, he leapt onto a small hump on the other side, blinked, and resumed his pace. He asked his sister what she thought of the whole mess, but she told him to shut the hell up, think less and run more. She was always the strong one.

He did have a plan if they happened to run into real Delta Force troopers. Instead of identifying themselves as independent operators, i.e., mercs, he'd tell them they were SEALs who'd been diverted off another mission. He had enough old SEAL tricks up his sleeve to get any asshole from Delta to believe anything—or at least he was cocky enough to think so. No one carried IDs of any kind, anyway, and Mr. Bibby could run some bogus intelligence through the right channels so that when the Delta guys checked up on them, they'd get confirmation. It'd be fun to fuck with them—verbally that was. Trading bullets was bad, and that goddamned warmonger Wolfgang had really put the cherry on this shit sundae.

But that guy would literally eat shit if you dared him. What had Pope expected?

"I don't see them," Sapper gasped into his mike.

"Me neither," answered Rookie.

"Shut up, assholes, and run!" Pope ordered.

A fit black man with a sharp jaw covered with stubble and the reddish scar of a gunshot wound on his neck had rushed toward Jaga and Savimbi, calling out to them. His Portuguese was bad, but that didn't mean he was an enemy. Kisantu often hired foreigners to help fight. There were Turks, a few Arabs, and even a guy from South Africa among the ranks.

With bulging eyes, the man gestured with a very fancy and expensive-looking rifle for them to come, that he was here to take them back to Kisantu.

"Well, you are very late!" cried Savimbi.

"Yes," Jaga said, then frowned at the man. "But the fire. The Morstarr people blew up your truck."

"How will we get away?" Savimbi added.

"Let's go!" the man cried, waving emphatically, then started away.

Jaga exchanged a wary look with Savimbi, but they joined their new "friend."

Gunfire tore into the hillside on their right, and Savimbi stopped, whirled, and returned fire, three-round bursts rattling even as their pursuers' fire closed in.

"No, you dumb fuck!" the man hollered in English. "Cease fire and let's move out!"

The stranger's English sounded quite natural, catching Jaga completely off guard. "Are you American?"

"Let's go," the man repeated, this time in Portuguese.

Jaga slowed. Would Kisantu hire Americans? Would his al Qaeda friends approve of such hires? Maybe the man wasn't an American. Still, that accent . . . Jaga had heard it when he'd visited Kinshasa and watched those Hollywood films.

"Jaga!"

He looked to Savimbi, who was leaving with the man. "No! Something's wrong!"

More gunfire ripped toward them.

A sharp pinch in his right arm.

Another pinch in his leg.

And suddenly Jaga found himself falling to the dirt, his rifle tumbling from his grip. Savimbi screamed his name, and he shouted back that he'd been hit.

Savimbi ran toward him.

Jaga extended his hand. "Help me!"

Instead, Savimbi raised his AK. "Sorry, my friend. You'll slow us down. And you can't tell them where the diamonds are . . ."

A violent chill raced down Jaga's spine. He looked to the rifle he had dropped, just a few feet away.

"But we were—"

Jaga never finished.

The man tore the rifle from Savimbi's grip, wrapped one arm around Savimbi's neck, then shouted for Jaga to come.

"I can't," Jaga cried. "I'm shot!"

Although Jaga could move, he wouldn't, and he sensed the frustration in the man's eyes.

The man had a decision to make.

Suddenly, he and Savimbi vanished over the hill, with Savimbi still shouting.

It all happened so fast that for a second Jaga thought he was hallucinating, that the shadows had come to life and choked his friend, the man who'd been about to kill him.

Savimbi released a final gurgling cry, then went silent. Had the man killed him?

Behind Jaga, the men from the mining company were closing in. He dragged himself up, grabbed his rifle, and hobbled toward the river, his arm and leg burning. His plan, though, was clear. He would swim across to safety. Then he would hide in the forest on the other side and return for the diamonds when night fell once again. It was all very simple. That his heart threatened to rip from his chest meant nothing.

*   *   *

Rookie thought he had injured one of the men, and as he rushed down the next slope, he mouthed the word, "Yes!"

A figure, barely discernable in the gloom, limped from behind a tree, heading straight for the river.

You want to swim? I don't think so, Rookie thought as he broke into a full-on sprint, determined to not only catch the guy but redeem himself for his fuckup.

No way would he ever admit to the others that he'd made a mistake. It had been too long since he'd been "in the shit" on a real op, and the excitement had over-whelmed him.

Could happen to anyone, really. You got itchy. You couldn't wait to engage. Patience wasn't a virtue; it was a pain in the ass.

But he'd already forgiven himself. He'd had to. You had to keep the operational tempo high, your confidence level soaring even higher. Believing wholeheartedly and without reservation that you were a great combatant was what really kept you alive.

Which was why Rookie knew he would capture the fleeing man. He just knew it.

And that steadfast belief would make it happen.

He was *The Man*. He owned the situation—

Until fucking Pope raced by him on a course much closer to their prey.

And suddenly Rookie realized that he wouldn't beat the man, that Mr. Baldy Bean would rob him of victory, of redemption, of the whole fucking ball of wax.

"I got one!" cried Pope.

"Where's the other guy?" asked Sapper.

"Well, he didn't turn," said Rookie, who shifted himself, away from Pope and toward a slight embankment, imagining that he'd spot the other guy racing off just on the rise.

But when he got there? Shit . . .

The universe hated him. But he hated it just as much.

All at once Pope threw down his weapon and threw himself into the air.

The scrawny black guy was just entering the water.

The guy looked back.

His jaw fell open.

And Pope came down on him like a pallet full of cinder blocks, like a fat man at a buffet suffering a heart attack, like a goddamned Navy SEAL proving to himself that he still had what it took.

Oh, he did, all right.

The dude collapsed with a heavy splash before he could lift his weapon. Pope's full weight brought him to the muddy bottom. With one hand locked around the back of the guy's neck, and the other reaching for the guy's weapon, Pope forced him down, into the water, half-drowning him until he had that AK in hand.

Then, as abruptly, he jumped back, still holding the guy's rifle. With his free hand he drew his pistol, trained it on the guy's head. You never trusted an enemy's weapon. Especially a wet one. No fuckin' way.

After dropping the AK behind him, he patted down the guy, searching for more weapons, for the diamonds. Nothing. And damn, he'd barely caught his breath. "Blackhound One, this is Blackhound Four. I've taken one runner alive. No rocks on him, over."

"You are Americans," the guy muttered in broken English. Then he touched his own cheek, referring to Pope's "special tan."

Pope bore his canines. "We're friends now, asshole. Bestest buddies. We'll even swap girlfriends, okay? You and me? We're gonna be famous!"

The guy just looked at him, water and mud dripping from his face. Then he winced, reached toward his arm.

"Aw, we hit you, huh? Don't worry. We got a doc. He'll fix you right up. But right now we got a lot to talk about, right?"

The guy uttered something in Portuguese, his tone sounding either sarcastic or resigned.

"Uh, sounds good," Pope said, then motioned with his pistol. "This way."

"No shoot?"

"No, dude. You'll spill your guts the other way."

Pope got back on the horn, called for Boo Boo, who bitched about having to walk so far but was on his way.

Wolfgang and Drac saw the one guy forcing the other guy toward the forest. The two fought a moment more, then the dude struggling gave in and followed, under gunpoint, of course.

"This is interesting," whispered Wolfgang before he signaled to Drac.

They kept close to the men, coming within twenty meters, careful not to get too close. Wolfgang was used to stalking people—not like a psycho but following on a mission. Mad Dog had trained him in the art of tailing, and he felt damned good about their progress thus far.

The other two guys with the expensive submachine guns had fled in the same direction.

Someone was throwing a party. Delta Force? Who knew?

But Wolfgang and Drac would crash it.

"Blackhound One, this is Blackhound Seven. We're pursuing two guys, possibly Delta, with two more guys heading after them. One guy was forced to go along. Honestly, I don't know what the fuck's going on. But we're still following, over."

"Roger, Seven. Stay on 'em and keep feeding me reports, over."

"You got it. Seven, out."

Drac suddenly froze, dropped to his knees, signaled for Wolfgang to do likewise.

The former combat controller lifted his binoculars, surveying the valley below, focusing on a point just west of the dirt road. Lightning flashed, tearing a jagged seam in the dark horizon.

Wolfgang came up beside Drac, flinching as a crack of thunder rumbled through the hill. "What do you got?"

"Looks like a rally point," said Drac. "Three guys already there. Two pairs en route."

"Okay." Wolfgang got his digital camera ready. Maybe they could shoot a few mug shots back to Bibby.

"Are we just going to take their picture or keep slowing them down?" asked Drac. " 'Cause they're a heartbeat away from going bye-bye."

Smacking his lips, Wolfgang began squeezing off shots, doing his best to zoom in on faces and realizing that Drac was right. They would need to keep following or distract those guys with another "simulated" firefight.

He called back to Bibby, told him he was sending back the pics. Look for 'em. The Brit acknowledged curtly, then Mad Dog offered his two cents. He wanted Bibby to get IDs on those guys ASAP. If they were Delta, that'd be a real challenge, but it wouldn't hurt to try.

Then Mad Dog ordered him and Drac to stay with the others. Tail 'em. Don't engage.

"They're moving already," said Drac.

Wolfgang opened a pouch on his ruck, tucked away the camera. "Let's go, Cap'n. Ain't nothing more fun than hunting men. Know who said that?"

"Patton?"

"Nope. George W. Bush."

"Are you sure?"

"Would I lie about something like that?"

Drac shrugged and trotted off. "I guess not."

Bender and Thorn kept close to the man who identified himself as Savimbi. He kept asking if they were Americans, and Thorn kept reassuring him that they were not, that they were new recruits who worked for Kisantu.

Thorn had told him that the first truck had broken down and that they'd been sent with the second truck, but it had been set on fire by the mining company men. Then he asked Savimbi about the diamonds—

And the man had just looked at him funny. "What diamonds?"

So they had held him, searched him, come up empty.

Dzoba had left the short driver's buddy, Kwezi, bound and gagged in the forest (he was just too much baggage), while they took along Roufai, gagged, his hands bound behind his back. As luck would have it, Savimbi did not know Roufai and asked why he was a prisoner. Thorn explained that Roufai worked for Kisantu but was a traitor who had tried to ambush them.

Then why keep him? Why not just kill him? Thorn had said that would be Kisantu's decision, not theirs. So

Roufai would come along—and Dzoba would pump him for information while Thorn kept Savimbi away from that conversation.

As lies went, it sounded pretty good. Bender liked it.

He didn't like moving on foot, though. He thought of the first truck, remembered Roufai describing the broken axle. No good.

He could call his commanders for help, see if they could chopper in a ride. That would take time, and a chopper might call a lot of attention. Maybe they could buy another truck at the next town, once they crossed the border.

They would head east now, toward Kamina in the Congo. Bender had reviewed the map on his PDA, noted the terrain. The first bitch would be crossing the river. They'd have to head a couple of klicks north where, according to the map, a narrow bridge had been erected for foot traffic. The only other bridge lay far south, but it had been blown up by rebels and was under repair.

"Why don't we ditch this guy, too," said Thorn, hustling up behind Bender.

"'Cause he's hidden the diamonds. He knows where they are."

"How do you know?"

"You see the look on his face." Bender put his hand on Thorn's chest, holding him back, away from Savimbi, who was following behind Greene and Dzoba. "Give him more room. He'll make a break. He doesn't want to leave. He's afraid his buddy will snatch them before he does."

"Okay. Amaze me with your fortune-telling."

"Just give him some time. And some room. We'll let him run. And we'll follow."

Bender keyed his mike and whispered ahead to Dzoba

and Greene to be ready for Savimbi to make his break. They were surprised by Bender's order to allow him to go, but he knew they'd catch on.

Mad Dog met up with Pope and their prisoner. "Wolf-gang and Drac are still on the other guys. I've called back Rookie and Sapper. I'll take this guy up to town, see what Doolittle can get out of him. He's called me like a hundred times already to get back there."

"All right."

"You go bring the truck around, rally the troops. When we got everybody we'll go follow Drac and Wolfgang. Bibby's tracking them on his map—two good beacons."

"You got it, Bossman." Pope jogged off, leaving Mad Dog with the bandit. He looked painfully young, obviously impressionable.

As they made the muddy hump back toward the village, Boo Boo hustled down from a hill to their right. "Hey, Zog. What do we got?"

Mad Dog cocked a thumb at the kid. "He's moving. He's breathing. Let's wait till we get up top."

"He *is* bleeding."

Mad Dog sighed. "He can wait."

The medic came around, putting the prisoner between them. "Long fuckin' night, eh?"

"That's the understatement of the year." Mad Dog broke into a double-time march, one that left Boo Boo and the prisoner a few yards behind.

Doolittle called again, telling Mad Dog to meet him outside the largest hut, the one facing the clearing. His voice cracked.

"What's wrong?"

"Just, please, come."

"On my way." Then he grunted, "What now?" He removed his ball cap, palmed sweat from his head, then called up Wolfgang, who was still on the enemy's tail. They were heading north, parallel to the river, possibly looking for a place to cross. *Shit,* Mad Dog thought. *We have to get moving.*

But when he reached the village, came around the back, then crossed to the main hut, he couldn't believe his eyes.

His old nemesis, James Moody, aka Jimmy Judas, scumbag spook, was standing there, his pistol trained on Doolittle's chest.

Mad Dog stopped dead in his tracks. "No. No way. This is *not* happening!"

Judas turned and grinned at Mad Dog. "Well, what do we have here? An old dog dressed up for Halloween. You look like an idiot, Hertzog."

Mad Dog realized his mouth was hanging open. "What are you doing here?"

"I should ask you. In fact, I will because you, sir, are in no position to interrogate anyone."

Judas's grin had been taught to him by Satan, and he had obviously been a quick study.

Chapter 7

••••••••••••••••••••••••••••••

Tongaso, Angola
Near Congo Border
0515 Hours Local Time

Mad Dog turned away from Judas, disgusted by the man's presence. However, that wasn't the only reason why he needed some room. He muttered quickly into his mike: "Boo Boo, take our guy around back. Hide in a hut."

"Gotcha."

He faced Judas and hardened his gaze. "Lower that fuckin' weapon."

"You're a comedian."

"Lower that fucking weapon!"

Judas's smile only widened. "Lower yours . . ."

It had been an instinct, really, like swatting a bug. Mad Dog had lifted his rifle at the sight of, well, a bug.

He raised his carbine a little higher. "No one will miss you. C'mon, asshole. You know it."

"You'll shoot me right here, with all these witnesses who know me as Uncle Jimmy?"

"Nah. I'll have one of my guys disarm you, then we'll haul you off into the jungle, scalp you Indian style, cut you up real bad, let you bleed to death. Give you time to think about it. Yeah, I think that's how it'll go."

Judas did a little gunslinger's twirl then holstered his piece. "You'd miss me." He showed his palms. "Good doggie. Don't bite."

At that, Doolittle's shoulders slumped. He spoke to the boy who had first tipped them off, sent the kid scurrying away.

"Why don't we sit down, have a Coke together?" asked Judas, wriggling his brows at the memory of the tainted drink Mad Dog and company had slipped him years ago.

"Sorry. I'm on the clock."

"I insist." Judas lifted his bearded chin at Doolittle. "Still working with him, huh? Fortunately, I never forget a face, even one covered in bad tanning lotion. Didn't they tell you that shit doesn't work?"

More villagers gathered around them, and one, an exceedingly dark-skinned man, issued questions to Doolittle in a demanding tone.

Judas gestured with his hands. "See, I've been here a while. They love Uncle Jimmy. They'll protect me."

Mad Dog snorted. "You bought that."

Pope came rumbling forward in the pickup truck and hopped out. "What's up?" He eyed Judas. "Nice beard. Very retro. Who're you? Jesus?"

"Anyone but." Judas twisted his smile, then cocked a brow at Mad Dog. "Took all your puppies along, huh?"

Mad Dog stepped closer, muscles tensing, the anger

sending tremors through his voice. "I'll ask the fucking questions."

"Calm down, Hertzog. You'll blow a nut."

"Why are you here?"

"Vacation. Can't find the Holiday Inn. The travel agent must've fucked up."

"You're wasting my time."

"Come on. It ain't hard, big dog. We're here for the same reason."

Abruptly, Wolfgang's voice buzzed through Mad Dog's earpiece. Still in pursuit. Bibby added that he had sent off Wolfgang's pics for analysis.

Then Rookie and Sapper hustled up, both frowning at Judas. Rookie opened his mouth, but Mad Dog silenced him with a hand and said, "Saddle up. We're leaving."

"You're not going anywhere till we talk," said Judas.

"Who are you?" Pope asked. "Hey, Bossman, who the fuck is this guy?"

"He's a spook," said Mad Dog, lowering his voice.

"And you're a fuckin' merc," retorted Judas. "I know Morstarr hired you. I know the whole fucking deal."

"What? Langley's trying to be proactive now? Sent you out to gather some HUMINT?"

Judas smirked. "Who knows? Maybe I just happened to be in the neighborhood."

"You're operating without portfolio. Be a shame if someone blew your cover, let the locals know there's an American spook running around without the consent of their government."

"Come on, Dog. Back to my hut. Just for a couple of minutes. We'll catch up on old times. And who knows, maybe we can help each other."

"I don't have time."

"Oh, for this, you do."

Mad Dog shifted away, threw his arm around Doolittle's shoulders and whispered, "You go find Boo Boo. He's with our runner. You talk to that guy. You know what I need."

"Yes, Sergeant."

Mad Dog shifted back. "Pope, you're with me. Judas, you got two minutes. Make that one minute and fifty-seven seconds . . ."

The man laughed, then ambled toward the huts, his back a little more hunched than Mad Dog remembered. They eventually ducked into a candlelit dump with rack and small table, along with a few rucks and some wet and warping wooden crates labeled UNICEF. He'd probably told the poor locals that he worked for them. "Hi, I'm Uncle Jimmy! I'm here to help!"

Asshole.

"Have a seat. You can post your man outside, if you're worried."

Mad Dog plopped into the chair. *What the fuck am I doing? I got one guy running free, I got men in the field giving chase to rebels or Delta Force troops, I got a prisoner to interrogate, and now I'm sitting down with the man I hate more than anyone on the planet? I am mad!*

But there was something strangely perverse, something important about talking to Judas, perhaps some need for closure or for putting to bed years' worth of guilt. After all, without Judas, Mad Dog wouldn't have had as much money to build his business. Scumbags like him sometimes served a purpose. And maybe the guy would share some information.

"All right, here's how this works," Mad Dog began. "You tell me what I want to know, and I listen."

Judas chuckled. "Absolutely."

Mad Dog stiffened. "Look, I tell the Angolan government about you, and suddenly you're booted out of the country. Your buddies back in Langley are embarrassed, and your mission's over. Fucking with my translator was a huge mistake. You could've laid low and let us mosey on by, you shitbird."

"I wanted to talk. I want to tell you I've been a big fan over the years. I know all about IPG and how you guys interfere in matters of national security."

"Bullshit. Why are you here? They worried about a little party in the Congo?"

"I told 'em they should worry more about you."

"Hey, man, when I write that letter of condolence to your family, I'll have to be honest and tell 'em you died a gruesome death because you were trying to help overthrow a government recognized by the U.S. and the U.N."

"Like I got a family to worry about? I'm just like you . . . fucked up. So fucked up that this is all we know. So don't give me that bullshit."

"Maybe I won't kill you. I'll just set you up. Sound familiar?"

"You stole my operating funds, fucked up my operation in A'stan. So I fucked with you," said Judas. "But you were done, anyway. Wanted out. The timing couldn't have been better. I did you a favor."

Mad Dog stood. "See ya."

Judas stammered. "Hey, uh, the diamonds will be used to fund a coup."

Mad Dog hoisted his brows. "Keep coughing."

"There's a guy named Kisantu who's been hitting villages up and down the border. He's tied to al Qaeda. They want him in as a puppet president. The diamonds will help pay the bill."

"That all you got?" Mad Dog asked, downplaying his reaction. Mr. Bibby had already gathered that intelligence. "You're boring me."

"Tell you how good I was. I second guessed these motherfuckers. Got here before they did. And I was going to let 'em lead me back to Kisantu before you and your assholes came along and screwed the pooch."

"So you're saying the two guys that were here have the stolen rocks?"

"I know they do. I've had the kids watching them. They saw one guy with a leather pouch. Rocks are inside. I pay them, and they don't lie to Uncle Jimmy."

"And you didn't steal them? Are you the same guy who pays off Afghan druglords with American tax dollars? You could've made a big score and told your buddies back in Langley that you came up empty. What the fuck's the matter with you?"

"It's a different world now, Hertzog. I'm already set for life. You know why I do this? These fuckers want to kill us because of who we are and the way we live. I got mine because of who I am and how I plan to live. Fuck ideology. It's me or them. I'm on anybody's side who thinks the same way."

Mad Dog reached the doorway and threw up his hands in disbelief. "Sounds real noble . . ."

"Hertzog, you know where those guys are, don't you? You're tracking them. Let's team up. One hand washes the other. Langley just sent me here to gather HUMINT, that's all. You feed me some. I let you recover the diamonds, collect your reward. I'm a hero back in Langley. We both want the same thing. If Kisantu gets a hold of those rocks, we're all fucked."

"What makes you think I'll give back the diamonds? I have friends in London. I can move 'em quick."

"You might steal my money, 'cause you fucking hate me, but you wouldn't do that. You're a merc, but you got honor 'cause you'll always be a goddamned marine. Kinda works against you, doesn't it?"

Mad Dog nearly choked on his own laughter. "Fuck you, Judas." He ducked out of the hut, still reeling from the spook's rap.

Judas started after him, but Pope put his broad chest and big gun between them. "Now, now, spooky. Sit down."

Outside, Mad Dog called Boo Boo, got the medic's location, and went to the hut, where he found their runner speaking with Doolittle. While Boo Boo continued to patch up the guy, Mad Dog interrupted his translator with a bug-eyed look.

"He says he's afraid to say anything."

"Tell him if he talks, we won't hurt him. But tell him if he doesn't, then we might. You tell him we know he had the diamonds, and if he works with us, we'll let him go, no questions asked."

Doolittle nodded. While that went on, Boo Boo explained that the man, who'd identified himself as Jaga, had only superficial gunshot wounds.

"Blackhound One, this is Seven, over," called Wolfgang.

Mad Dog turned up his radio. "Go ahead, Seven."

"Still in pursuit, heading north along the river. But they've spread out a lot. Weird. We'll keep following. Any IDs yet?"

"Negative. You'll hear when I do. We'll catch up with you, out."

Mad Dog closed his eyes, cleared his mind. Simple thing old Diaper Dan had taught him. When there's too much happening all at once, it's time to take a breath, see past all the bullshit, and focus on the end result, which, in this case, was finding the diamonds.

Jimmy Judas, that extreme asshole, had said he was positive that Jaga and his buddy had had the diamonds. So . . . either his buddy had them or they had hidden them.

Mad Dog and his mercs had been in close contact, giving them very little time to dispose of the diamonds. The trail was from the hut, through the jungle, to the river bank where they had captured Jaga.

Okay. The diamonds were either with the guy who got away, still back in the hut, or hidden near the river using a readily identifiable landmark.

What did they have out there, other than trees?

Trees . . .

Mad Dog called Rookie on the radio, told him to go back to the hut and ransack it for the diamonds. Damn, Mad Dog should've ordered that earlier, but he'd figured that if the guys had run, they'd probably taken the stash with them, and he'd needed every man.

He regarded Doolittle, who was waiting. "Sergeant, our friend wants to know why he should trust us."

"Why? Because we're nice guys."

The translator smirked. "He's worried that we'll kill him even if he does talk."

"Give me a second." Mad Dog slipped out of the hut.

He nodded and grinned as the memories flooded home. Old Dan had taught him a clever trick, one he'd used to gain the trust of a few POWs back in 'Nam. Now he would use it to gain this kid's trust.

Old Dan's ploy had been quite ingenious, and ever since then Mad Dog had made it a point to carry the tools necessary to re-create it. Better yet, the trick took only a few seconds to prepare.

He returned to the hut, reached into his holster, withdrew his MEU (SOC).45, removed the clip, then handed the pistol to a frowning Jaga. "Tell him he can hang on to that. Tell him he works for us now. I'll give him five thousand bucks if he takes us to the diamonds. After that, he can stay or take off . . ."

While Doolittle spoke, Jaga examined the pistol with widening eyes. The specially trained armorers at the Rifle Team Equipment (RTE) shop, Quantico, Virginia, who had hand-built the weapon had just won another fan. The kid ran an index finger over the barrel, tested the weight, then aimed it at Mad Dog, wearing a tentative grin.

"Hey, you're playing too nice," sang Boo Boo in an anxious tone. "We should get some zipper cuffs on this little fucker. Instead, you hand him a loaded weapon, then promise him money. What happened to old-fashioned torture?"

"We save that for the real assholes. This kid's just a tool. They used him, and they'll screw him over. He needs to realize that." Mad Dog gestured to Doolittle. "Is he in?"

No matter how incredibly secretive an organization was, and no matter how hard that organization tried to hide the identities of its personnel, there was often something in an individual's past, something as mundane as a driver's license photo or a relative's Web site where family pics were posted that would give him away.

Consequently, Bibby and his electronic cohorts had successfully identified one of the mystery combatants as Mr. Daniel Benson. Although they'd been unable to gather much about his military career, the pattern was clear, and the guy was no doubt a Delta Force operator. The other photos taken by Wolfgang had been too indistinct to confirm the IDs of Bender's accomplices, but it was safe to assume their records matched his. Add to that the intel from Big Booty and the weapons they carried, and you had confirmation.

Bibby, who'd maintained his position in the hills above the river, had just finished sharing the news with Mad Dog and was busy checking on the locator beacons carried by Wolfgang and Drac. He brought up the real-time map on his computer screen, then fell forward, his face crashing into the keyboard under the weight of a huge blow to the back of his neck. He literally saw stars.

First thought: machinegun. Where? To the left, right there in the grass.

Turn back. Who? Guy there. Black guy. AK in his hand. He hit me with the stock.

What the fuck was he saying?

Didn't matter. Instinct. Need weapon. What? Pistol?

First thing. Closest thing.

Bibby sprang back at the guy, releasing a bloodcurdling cry that sent the man shrieking in surprise. He was just bringing around his rifle, about to take aim.

But Bibby tripped him with one hand, while his other still held the laptop. Even as the guy dropped, Bibby was on him, slamming the laptop closed, then bringing the hard aluminum case down on the man's skull.

The rage inside Bibby would've shocked his colleagues. They'd never seen this button pushed, knew nothing of the violence in his past, hadn't lived with a man like his father.

Bibby beat his assailant over and over, as though with a brick, dark flesh swelling under his relentless, unforgiving, unimaginable hammering. The guy's skull begin to cave in, and he no longer struggled, was no longer conscious, possibly not even alive—but it was all unreal and swirling around Bibby, his own neck and head throbbing, drool dripping from his chin, the groans escaping his mouth with a life of their own.

And then he swore, kept bashing, kept swearing, until the computer finally bent like a pancake, its guts rattling, rattling, until he finally stopped, his arms now sore, like rubber and covered in blood. He blinked. Fingered his cheek. Bloody, too.

He fell back onto his rump, the shattered computer tumbling aside. No thoughts. Just breathing. Breathing. The air thick. Insects hummed. Shouts rose in the distance.

Oh, God. He'd just bludgeoned a man into unconsciousness or death with his laptop, a man who could very well be an American, a member of Delta Force. It was possible their team had left one behind.

In a sudden panic, Bibby fished through the man's pockets, found some money, not much. Found a ring, cheap, costume jewelry. No ruck. Just an AK.

Was he Delta? Could he be? Bibby kept telling himself no. No, no, no. He tore open the man's shirt, revealing a lean torso, not the well-muscled physique of a Delta operator. The guy was a local from Tongaso. Had to be. Came down when he'd heard the shots. Found Bibby. Figured he had a bad guy. Took a swing. Thought he'd bring one in alive. Didn't realize he was dealing with a deranged Brit.

Found out the hard way.

The laptop was gone. No matter. Only a complete fool would rely so heavily upon technology and not have a comprehensive plan that included encrypted, Web-based data back up, along with two more laptops, one back at Morstarr's camp, the other under the front seat of the pickup truck.

He checked the man's neck for a carotid pulse, found one. Weak. Thready.

Another thought: communication. Had his radio, mike, and earpiece been damaged. No sounds. He checked the volume. It had rolled down. He adjusted, heard another report coming from Wolfgang and Drac. Urgent:

One man was on the run, and the others were pursuing. They were all headed south, back toward Bibby's location.

Shit, if he had the map now, he could track their progress more efficiently, be ready for them.

Then Mad Dog was on the radio, saying that Pope, Rookie, and Sapper were coming down with the truck, while he wanted Boo Boo and him to stakeout the area along the river where Pope had nabbed their runner. They were bringing along the man who would take them to the diamonds. Excellent. They could be only moments away from collecting the stash and getting out of this godforsaken hellhole.

Bibby shoved his blood-stained laptop into his ruck, seized his machinegun—

Then summarily passed out.

Sure, they had their guns pointed at him, but Jaga still couldn't believe how much trust the mining team men had put in him, especially the leader, whom Doolittle called Sergeant.

They had given him medical attention, were willing to pay him a reward, and had handed him a weapon. They hadn't even bound him.

But could he really trust them? They wanted the diamonds. They would do or say anything to get them. But what other choice did he have?

He couldn't trust Savimbi. In his mind's eye he saw his friend standing over him with his rifle, just a second away from squeezing the trigger.

And would Savimbi go back for the diamonds? Would he really deliver them to Kisantu?

Everything Jaga had once stood for was crumbling before his eyes. How could this be happening?

He and Savimbi were revolutionaries. They were going to change their country! They would be great men whose deeds would be remembered and passed on from generation to generation. They would bring true freedom to their country and put an end to the atrocities. Kisantu has promised this. They had believed him. They would make it happen.

But now revolution was nothing more than a game of betrayal. His friend and brother in arms had turned against him. There was nothing left but self-preservation.

And the diamonds. The mining company men wouldn't kill him, so long as they thought he knew where the diamonds were hidden. That was power.

However, he couldn't move unless they said so.

If he brought them close to the diamonds, there was always the chance that he could snatch them and make a break.

And if he couldn't, if he was forced to return the dia-

monds to the company men, he would not rely upon their
trust. He would not work for them. He would still make
a break. To assume they would let him go afterward was
foolish. They would hold him, bring him back to the police as their prize.

So he now had a plan. Get close to the stash. Attempt
to steal it and make a break. If not, then give them the
diamonds and still run.

He pursed his lips, eyed the sergeant, and mustered up
a few words in English: "Okay. I help."

The moment that Savimbi had dashed off, Bender had
ordered Dzoba to hold back with Roufai. They needed
that little bandit Savimbi to lead them to Kisantu. The
driver was baggage to be sure, and they could torture
him for the information, but maybe he'd cave in once he
realized there was no escape.

And of course, American special forces operators
never, ever engaged in tactics of torture (read "information extraction") against undeserving enemies—

Only deserving ones . . .

For the moment, though, they needed to keep Roufai
out of harm's way, but that kept Dzoba out of the shit
and reduced him to prisoner guard. You took the good
with the bad.

So it was Bender, Thorn, and Greene tracking Savimbi, who was no fucking genius to be sure. He'd run
straight up and over the first few hills, not bothering to
skirt around the sides to be less visible. He was all about
speed. And he was all about heading south.

Funny though. The longer Savimbi ran, the more
Bender second-guessed himself.

Maybe the guy hadn't hid the diamonds. Maybe he

was just hightailing it away while simultaneously leading the team straight toward those rebels—who might or
might not be rebels.

They could be local law enforcement.

Could be the Congolese military, itself a hodgepodge
of former rebel militias.

Could be local townsfolk who had heavily armed
themselves and were mighty pissed off.

Could be the fuckin' Boy Scouts. Who knew? Shit.

Savimbi ducked behind a pair of heavily leaning trees
and suddenly jogged left, toward the riverbank, the water
beyond growing rough as a strong wind swept through.

"Thorn, he's turning down your side, over," Bender reported.

"I see the little fucker."

"Shit, Bender, I thought I saw movement way ahead.
Silhouettes, man. They're coming back!" said Greene.

"Geeky, come on over here, tighter to the water."

"Roger."

"You stick with me, now. I want suppressing fire if
they attempt to pin us down—but we gotta let our guy do
his thing."

"Okay, I'm on my way."

The pitch-black clouds had been gathering again, and
not a minute later, they broke open with a vengeance.

Perfect. They needed some cover. Mother Nature's
son was obviously a special forces operator. She looked
after her own.

Mad Dog and Boo Boo ran side by side, behind Jaga and
Doolittle.

Wolfgang reported that he and Drac were moving east
to flank the oncoming Deltas.

Moving wasn't the best way to put it.

Running their fucking asses off. Yeah, that was about right.

The man the Deltas were chasing had picked up a good lead, but those SF boys kept him in sight.

No way would those Delta boys lose him. They were just too damned sharp. They had allowed him to make a run.

Meaning what? Meaning they had a guy who knew where the diamonds were, too. They had the other guy.

Pope, who reported that he had "wrapped up" Jimmy Judas like a Christmas present (i.e., bound and gagged him), was bringing the rest of the boys around in the truck. He said he'd set up a perimeter along the road above the river. Once Mad Dog had the stash, he and the rest of the team should rally west, saddle up, and boogie oogie oogie.

"Beautiful, we'll meet you there," Mad Dog told him.

"He keeps looking back," called Boo Boo, gesturing with his head toward Jaga. "He ain't onboard."

"Best we got now."

"He's gonna shoot somebody."

"You think I'd let that happen?"

"Tell you the truth, I'm not sure. You didn't get that nickname for being sane."

"Hey, man. I swapped the firing pin. It's too short. He can't shoot shit."

"Nice. Very nice mind-fuck. Me of little faith is not quite as doomed as he thought."

"Don't get too cocky. You're still on the freeway to Hell. Slow lane for now."

Jaga was rattling off something to Doolittle, who

translated breathlessly into his mike. "It was dark, he says. Hard to remember exactly where. He can't find their footprints in the mud. Rain washed them away. But we have to keep going."

Another report came in from Wolfgang and Drac. Same shit. Three Deltas. One runner.

Pope saw them, too. In fact, from his vantage point, he'd be issuing the play-by-play color commentary until he leaned into his weapon himself. "Here they come. Guy's got about a hundred-yard lead. No more than that. And, hey, uh, has anyone heard from Blackhound Two?"

No, they hadn't. Goddamned strange. Wasn't like Bibby to keep to himself. He'd been checking in every couple of minutes; and they could use a report from his location about now.

Mad Dog called the man. Jogged a few more steps. No reply. "Blackhound Two, SITREP, over?"

Nothing. Damn. Had to be a comm problem. He couldn't be MIA. Not Bibby.

Drac was slowing down—and not because the Deltas were. He glanced sidelong at Wolfgang, eyes pleading.

"What the fuck, Air Force man?"

"I'm dying! This Stoner's a heavy bitch!"

"You'll be dead, you don't move your ass!"

Though they were harder to make out through all the rain, Wolfgang did see the one guy in the lead, running like a maniac . . . with three shadows closing behind him.

Landmarks. Mad Dog had said something about land-marks. Trees, he'd said. Well, bingo, there they were: some tall ones lying in the runner's path, along with two small ones, about twenty meters beyond.

"Hey, Blackhound One?" Pope called in a warning tone. "Deltas and their runner are headed straight for you. I mean straight for you, over."

Wolfgang realized that if he and Drac didn't pick up the pace, they'd be in no position to cut off the Deltas. Observation time was over. Bye-bye.

"Come on, you slow fuck!" he cried as he broke into a sprint. "You ain't that old!"

Drac found his war face, dug into his reserves, and put the goddamned pedal to the goddamned metal.

"Rock and roll, motherfucker!" Wolfgang howled.

"Yeah, man!"

Wolfgang was running on nitrous, as fast and furious as it got, the man with the bullets and the plan. A gun battle was in his future, and the future looked grand.

"Blackhound One, we're moving to cut them off, over."

"Don't engage, Seven."

With a snort, Wolfgang answered. "Roger that. Do not engage directly. I said we can cut them off. I'll lay down some fire ahead, over."

"Roger that. But watch our position! And report their fallback. You read me?"

"Don't worry!"

Nope, Mad Dog still hadn't left the Corps. He was a Force Recon squad leader barking out orders, and that's just the way Wolfgang preferred it. When the going got rough, Mad Dog showed his teeth.

"Holy shit, Wolfgang!" hollered Drac.

"What?"

"Up there, on the side of that hill. Looks like two bodies. You see 'em?"

"No!"

"Right up there, asshole! Look again!"

He did. Squinted. "Fuck yeah. I'll head up. You keep going."

"Uh, Blackhound Seven, this is Blackhound Four," called Pope. "I estimate contact between One's party and the Deltas in just a couple of minutes. If you're going to cut 'em off, do it now!"

"Roger that!"

Screw the bodies. They weren't going anywhere. It was time to get it on. "Yo, Drac! Set up on the next hill. Let's do this!"

They charged onward to their "raise fucking hell" positions, dropped to their knees and began to get set, with Wolfgang about ten or so meters farther south than Drac.

God, it was like being on top of a beautiful woman, knowing that at any second all that effort would pay off (at least for you), and it was the most beautiful thing in the world, the moment when you felt absolutely scared and absolutely powerful because you took the risk, made the leap, bought her the drink and smooth-talked her into the hay.

Make life. Take it.

And God once again came down from the clouds and spoke to Wolfgang, saying, this is what it's like to be me. Don't get used to it, asshole.

But for a few magical moments he would know.

"Drac, let 'em have it!"

Chapter 8

··

Were it not for all the clouds and rain, Rookie might've seen the sky wash over from a deep purple into a dark blue, then grow bluer, so blue that he would imagine himself standing inside one of his grandfather's paintings and looking up across that brushstroked sky.

And were it not for Mad Dog and Pope, Rookie might've been involved in some direct action, instead of crouching in position like an idiot who'd sneaked into a rock concert and was stealing a peek at the show while heavy-set women in security guard uniforms hunted him down.

He'd actually done that once, and it had taken those surly dykes over an hour to finally catch him.

But this was different. This was like sliding on a condom and being forced to watch.

He thought of opening fire, adding his weapons to Wolfgang's and Drac's, just to piss off Pope, knock him off his altar, remind him that he was just a grunt, just like anyone else. But Rookie reminded himself that he was here to earn a paycheck. Set the ego thing aside.

But that was damned hard when he was looking for some redemption, some way to show these guys that he was a consistent, first-class operator, that his error back in the village was an aberration. That, above all, they could count on him. Respect him. He knew the way of the warrior. It was in his blood. And he had proven that to his colleagues in the past. They didn't recruit Delta Force operators from your local bus stop . . .

Fortunately, Daniel "Bender" Benson, the Delta Force operator whom Bibby had identified, wasn't one of Rookie's closer friends. Sure, everybody knew everybody in Delta, but Rookie had been on his way out while Bender was on his way up. They'd trained together a few times before Rookie had left. He told Mad Dog that Bender had a solid reputation and excellent tactical skills—mercenaries beware. It was a small world, all right, which sucked if your name was Takahiro Masaki.

And you want to talk conflict of interests? Holy shit. Could Rookie be expected to fire upon American forces? Expected to fire upon Deltas—his former brothers?

Hell, they still were his brothers! Forever!

He wondered what he'd do if it came down to that. Mad Dog wouldn't give the order. No fucking way.

But if they were shooting at you with intent to kill, what were you supposed to do? Bend over? Run? Remove your skivvies and wave 'em atop your rifle?

Damn, encountering Americans in the field had been the last thing on Rookie's mind when he'd decided to join Mad Dog's team. He could deal with the insurgents and locals in every third world shit hole, but he wasn't sure he could engage the Deltas, even in self-defense. He was certain that if any of the others went head-to-head with Bender and his boys, they would lose, even Wolfgang, who it appeared could gun and run with the best of them. You don't fuck with Delta Force.

Okay, so he was biased. But the future didn't look bright. Nope. Not at all.

Rookie blinked again, kept staring through the thermal camera, as the gunfire booming from the hills caused the three Delta operators to scatter and the guy running ahead to leap forward and land flat on his gut.

Wolfgang followed up with a couple of grenades, blasting in succession, heaving mud and flashes that seemed fitting with all the rain.

It had to be painfully obvious to those boys down there that they were just being delayed, and because of that, Rookie figured they'd begin to suspect something. Real mining company guys would try to kill them, believing they were rebels or thugs.

Okay, so unintentional suspicion was a necessary evil in order to avoid a direct engagement, yet Rookie hoped Mad Dog had figured that into his tactical equations because as far as Rookie was concerned, there was a good chance that all of them would be literally crunched by the numbers.

"Okay, One, they stopped, fell back," said Wolfgang. "But fuck, they're returning fire!"

There it was. Rookie panned left with the thermal camera, saw the three muzzle flashes.

Had his heart stopped? It felt like it had.

"Seven, just keep 'em pinned down," Mad Dog ordered.

"Shit, I think they got *us* pinned down," replied Wolfgang, his voice barely discernable above the rattling of his weapon.

"They might need some help," shouted Pope from his position near the pickup. "Rookie! Put some fire behind them!"

After stashing his camera, Rookie took up his shotgun, sabot rounds loaded, and took aim.

He couldn't believe what he was doing, but his beliefs had nothing to do with it. He had made his decision to become a merc. Now he would eat it and shit it out. "Oh, God . . ." He opened fire.

Mad Dog and Boo Boo closed ranks with Doolittle and Jaga, who forged ahead toward trees whose limbs flapped violently in the wind.

Suddenly, gunfire sewed a path in the mud not two meters from Jaga, who broke to the right, toward the river. Despite his injuries, the little guy jogged at a good clip, and Mad Dog strained to keep up, hardly as spry.

Another wave of fire came in to the left, followed by an explosion: grenade!

Mad Dog and Boo Boo hit the deck, as did Doolittle. Shrapnel whistled through the air above them, though thankfully the blast had been far off to their left.

The explosion left flashes in Mad Dog's eyes, and it took a few seconds for his vision to clear while his ears kept ringing.

When he looked, he saw two things at once: Jaga diving into the water and Doolittle lying on his side, unmoving.

"He's making a run!"

Doolittle didn't get up. Was the translator hit?

"Boo Boo, check on him," cried Mad Dog, then he bolted to his feet and started down toward the riverbank, splashing through the mud and skidding as though on ice.

Jesus Christ, the kid had a big lead on him, and while Mad Dog focused all of his attention on the water, he shouldn't have. What did they say? Hindsight is twenty-twenty? Who the fuck knew? Fact was, he'd been caught with his drawers down.

He should have seen the first few rounds thumping near his boots. He had heard them all right.

At least he saw the next volley, which sent him once more onto his gut. "Goddamn it, Wolfgang, get them off my back! Our fuckin' buddy's making a run! He's in the water!"

"One, this is Four," called Pope. "You want me to take him out, over?"

"Negative, we need him! Hold your fire!"

"One, this is Nine," called Boo Boo. "Three's all right. Just took a bad step, over."

"Get the fuck up here!"

Mad Dog could barely lift his head. Automatic weapons fire tore into the small rise just above him.

He was muddy, soaked to the bone, fucking trapped.

Screw this shit.

He chanced another look up, eyes trained once more on the water. Was that a head, right there? Jaga coming up for air? It was too dark, and all that rain sweeping over the river made it nearly impossible to see.

But was that a head? Or was he seeing what he wanted to see, not what actually was? Christ . . .

Well, there it was. The Deltas had perfectly bad timing. But so did he. And now their man was getting away.

Had Jaga already snatched the diamonds? No, he couldn't have.

Could he?

Mad Dog slammed a fist into the mud. Fuck!

"One, this is Four, the guy running from the Deltas is back on his feet, heading toward you!"

Mad Dog propped up on his elbows, took aim, waited.

Bibby heard the voices in his ear, disembodied, coming at him through the darkness, as though carried on waves of vodka. He spun through the dirt a few moments, feeling wildly drunk, then sat up, blinked. It was pouring, and he'd been lying in a mud puddle. His weapon—there! He seized it, looked down toward the river.

Whoa. The world tipped on its axis again.

"He's almost on top of you!" Pope screamed.

What was happening? Mad Dog was in trouble. Bibby panned with his machine gun, saw a figure running south along the riverbank, while muzzles flashed like fireflies from points behind him.

"He's coming, One!" hollered Pope once more.

Bibby was about a hundred and fifty meters away from the guy. The Sterling was good out to two hundred. Surely at least one of the thirty-four rounds in the magazine jutting from the gun's left side would find its mark. He set his jaw, took aim, and opened fire—even as another wave of dizziness sent him leaning forward.

He paused after the first volley, the machine gun smoking, then shifted to his left as a few rounds chewed into the ground near the guy he had pummeled.

When he checked the hills again, he saw he had dropped the runner.

Still a crack shot, Bibby. Not bad.

"One, this is Four," announced Pope. "The Delta runner is down. I say again, the Delta runner is down. Someone shot him from up top! Wasn't us!"

Bibby's vision blurred so much that he had to crawl back behind the hill, blinking against the fuzz and rain, his head throbbing. His heart had, indeed, taken up residence between his ears. *Blast!*

Bender didn't realize he was cursing as he watched Savimbi fall under gunfire. And he didn't realize he was back on his feet and running toward the man until he was halfway there, the ground alive with a volatile mixture of incoming fire, rain, mud, and deceptively deep puddles.

Impulse. Action. Reaction. Adrenaline.

He threw himself forward, a machine programmed to do one thing, and it wasn't making love. He landed with a splash beside the guy, rolled him over, saw blood on his neck. Tore apart his shirt, buttons popping. Multiple gunshot wounds. The guy was gasping, bleeding out, his chest cavity taking on blood the way the *Titanic* took on water.

"Where are the fucking diamonds!" Bender demanded.

But the asshole didn't understand him. Bender needed Thorn or Dzoba to translate. No goddamned time!

"Where are they, you dumb fuck!"

Savimbi's head went limp.

"Bender, these guys are just suppressing us! I don't get it! This is fucked up!"

"No shit! Rally on Dzoba. Our fuckin' boy is dead. Let's move!"

"Okay, rallying back, out."

That puppy patrol of security guys had no idea what they had just done. No idea at all. Bender and company would have returned the diamonds. He would've done the right thing.

And now the goddamned diamonds could be anywhere. Greene had said that the other guy, a guy named Jaga, had been shot, which was why he'd been forced to leave him behind. He'd said the guy had probably been caught. But maybe Jaga didn't know where the diamonds were because the mining guys were still out there looking.

Bender got onto his hands and knees, grimacing over the musky, rotten smell that seemed everywhere in Angola. He bolted east toward the river, sensing gunfire tracking his steps. No, they didn't want to kill him.

For a second, he thought he saw someone dive into the waves before he darted left on a heading north to link up with the others.

He hazarded a look back. No shit. Someone was definitely in the water. He thought of turning around, but another spate of gunfire nixed the idea.

Damn, he and his boys had been so close. Should they just bolt and home in on Kisantu? Maybe not. Time to lay low, disappear, and try to discern just what the hell was happening. There was still a chance that the diamonds were out there, and maybe their disappearance would bring Kisantu to them.

Mad Dog had thrown down his ruck, abandoned his carbine and radio earpiece, and had toed off his boots before he had charged into the river. He figured the time it cost him to do that would be made up once he hit the waves.

As a marine, he'd done his share and then some of

swimming, but the river was pretty damned rough, the water cold, and when he got a mere fifty yards out, he realized he couldn't touch bottom and had completely lost sight of Jaga.

The son of a bitch had escaped.

Mad Dog floated there a few more moments, then decided he was better off swimming back than drowning. So he put his arms and legs to work. Shit, he'd have to spend more time in the pool when they got back home to Cebu Island.

Once he touched bottom, he trudged his way back to the riverbank, gunfire still cracking in the distance. He went immediately to his ruck, got his earpiece, got back on the horn, called Pope for a SITREP as he grabbed his carbine.

"Deltas are falling back. Like I said before, their runner is down. I don't know who shot him. They left him there. Wolfgang and Drac are still suppressing. Your situation, over?"

"We lost the guy!" Mad Dog screamed. "He jumped in the fucking river! Goddamned asshole did an Olympic breaststroke. What kind of shit luck is that?"

Behind him, Boo Boo came up, with Doolittle limping behind, their ball caps instantly IDing them as friendlies in all the gloom. Good thing. They hadn't used the radio or their clickers, and Mad Dog had been a heartbeat shy of shooting them.

"Lost him, huh?" asked Boo Boo.

"He's out there," said Mad Dog, turning toward the water.

Boo Boo sighed. "He get the rocks?"

"I don't know. I don't think he had time."

"Well, if he did, then he's long gone, and our little

foray is probably over—especially with fucking Delta Force running around. I'm here to make a buck putting on Band-Aids, not tangle with SF guys, *comprende?*"

Mad Dog shouldered his ruck, snatched up his carbine. "It ain't over till I say it's over." He keyed his mike. "Everybody except Seven and Eight get down here to the riverbank. Start digging around all these trees! Seven and Eight, you cease fire and stay with the Deltas. And hold up. Blackhound Four, you remain in position, eyes across the river."

"Surveillance in progress," Pope answered. "No sign of our little friend yet."

"Hey, Zog?" Boo Boo called. "You going to put on your fucking boots or barefoot it?"

Mad Dog scowled at the boots, then shot a last look at the river. "That little fucker didn't get the diamonds. No way. No how. He didn't have time. They're down here somewhere."

"There's a whole lot of mud down here, too."

"Sergeant?" called Doolittle. "I'm sorry."

"What're you talking about? Not your fault."

"If it's any consolation, I didn't see him stop. He just ran to the river."

"That's what I thought. Come on, let's dig. Boo Boo? We got the runner's body, plus Wolfgang says he's got maybe two more up top. Check 'em all out."

"I will. But my name ain't Jesus, and I don't think there's a one of 'em named Lazarus."

"Just let me know what we got."

"I'm on it, Zog. And hey, man, we may need to get out of Dodge and quick if these bodies keep piling up."

"Yeah, I hear that."

*　　*　　*

Wolfgang ceased firing and ran over to Drac's position, crouched down for a moment. "Did you shoot that fucking runner?" he asked. "You did, didn't you, asshole."

"Nope. I heard fire coming from the hill where I saw those bodies. Sounded like a sub. Who else was up there? Bibby?"

"I don't know. You stay on the Deltas. I'll check it out and catch up."

"Better call the boss and let him know."

While Drac sprinted off to keep the fleeing Deltas within visual range, Wolfgang gave the big guy a heads-up, then took a winding path back toward the hill, pounding over a little hogback near it—

And nearly ran right into Mr. Bibby, who was sitting in the mud, leaning over, rubbing the back of his head.

"Whoa, Bibby, what's up?"

The Brit just glanced vaguely at him, blinked slowly through the rain. "I've been whacked."

Wolfgang stared at the lean black man lying supine behind them. "Shit, you did some whacking, too. Is he dead?"

"No, unconscious. Massive head trauma. Would you mind helping me up?"

Wolfgang proffered his hand, dragged Bibby to his feet. "Hey, man, I gotta go link up with Drac. We're shadowing the Deltas. Mad Dog's up on the road. You can meet up there. You good to go?"

"I'm anything but good. But I can go."

"All right. See ya. Hey, wait. Did you shoot their runner down there?"

Bibby glanced down at his Sterling. "I might've."

"Shit, man that was the other guy who knows where the diamonds are. You whacked him, too."

"My mistake."

"You sure you're all right? You don't look so good."

"Just go, asshole." Bibby waved him off.

So he did, hauled light-speed ass over a series of three rolling hills, falling directly into Drac's path. The wiry guy was hunched over and trotting toward the next embankment, where he dropped to his knees, fished out his thermal camera from a side pocket on his ruck, then began scanning.

"Eight, I'm right behind you," Wolfgang stage-whispered into his mike, then dropped in beside the man.

"They're just off the road down there," said Drac, staring through the single eyepiece and making fine adjustments to the camera's zoom. "I see four guys, plus another guy. He looks like he may be bound. He never moves his arms."

Wolfgang had a peek for himself, the forest now painted a grainy black-and-white, with the men glowing bright white. "I wonder who he is."

"I'm, uh, to tell you the truth, I'm getting a headache thinking about this shit."

"They are, too. They don't know who the fuck we are, so maybe we're better off."

"Better off? You asshole. We're sitting in the fucking mud in Angola, we just lost the guy who knows where our big payoff is, and we're better off? What are you, a liberal?"

"I'm trying to keep up morale," Wolfgang snapped, his gaze riveted on the Deltas, who now gathered below a cluster of trees for a little powwow, two guys crouched in ready positions. They probably shit and drank coffee in ready positions, had sex in ready positions.

"Blackhound One, this is Blackhound Seven, over."

"Go ahead, Seven."

"We got the Deltas in sight. They're not moving. Will continue to observe and report, over."

"Roger that, Seven. No fucking luck here, out."

"Mad Dog's stressed out," said Drac.

"I'm stressed out."

"Bullshit. You love this. Fucking mayhem. Crazy shit. You're a warmonger. A pyro. Sick bastard."

Wolfgang grinned. "Okay. That's me."

Jaga crawled slowly out of the water and onto the riverbank, digging himself into the mud. He would cover himself entirely before finally leaving the bank. The mining company men had binoculars, and they would be trying to spot him. He would not make it easy.

All he had left was a pistol . . . and his life. There were no diamonds. There would be no revolution—

Unless he somehow got back to those two trees.

If he didn't, the others might find the stash. He had taken them very close to the spot. The odds might be in his favor for now, but time was not.

His wounds ached as he lay there, fighting for breath, trying to sense the opportunity to make his move, waiting for it to come in a whisper carried on the wind.

He wanted to hear Kisantu tell him when to go. Kisantu, who had placed both his palms on Jaga's shoulders and told him he was destined for great things, told him that he would play a major role in bringing peace to their nation, told him that he must come home with the diamonds in order to save his people. It was Kisantu whose vision would save them all.

Jaga needed to believe that was still true, despite Savimbi's actions.

His neck tingled. *Go now, brother.*

It was time.

He crawled forward, barely lifting his torso above the mud. He was an innocent turtle seeking refuge in the forest. No one would pay attention to him.

The rain swept in again, washing off some of the mud. He would have to move more quickly. Ahead lay a small embankment, and beyond it, the trees, a sanctuary where he could find cover and rest.

Holding his head a little higher, he moved another meter, then another.

He reached out, where just above his head lay some stones. Shots rang out, ricocheting off the rock, coming within inches of his hand. He froze. Took a breath.

Then sprang to his feet and ran.

Pope had spotted Jaga coming up out of the water, and he had decided to give the little man some pause.

But the son of a bitch had bolted. Mad Dog was screaming about the fire, but Pope was too busy trying to see where the little scumbag had fled.

He picked him up again, a thermal silhouette charging up a hill, tripping, falling, then crawling out of sight toward the trees beyond.

Gasping, Pope told Mad Dog that he had spotted Jaga and was still searching. In the meantime, Mad Dog wanted Rookie to bring the truck back to the village in case the Deltas decided to launch a counterstrike. After all, they had taken out Delta's wheels, so those operators were definitely in the market for a new ride, zero down, no payments ever . . .

Now, as a former Navy SEAL who had trained for and deployed on hundreds of varied and complicated covert operations, Pope had taught himself to be acutely aware of his surroundings and not make the mistake of focusing too much on one sense, like the images piped in through the thermal camera. He was an expert. Highly trained. Best of the best. Killer par excellance.

But he wasn't twenty-five anymore. And it was raining. And it was important for him to keep an eye on Jaga, try to get a bead on where he was headed.

And those Navy SEAL lessons had been taught a lifetime ago, or so it seemed.

Yet all of this was merely a lame excuse for allowing himself to remain so vulnerable.

Of course he didn't realize how vulnerable until someone reminded him—

By literally putting a knife to his throat. "Hey, there, scumbag. Guess who?"

Chapter 9

Bender rubbed his weary eyes, trying to stave off the stress and lack of sleep. The air was so thick that he could nearly taste it. He swore through his exhale. "All right, we've got an executive decision to make."

"It's a no-brainer," said Thorn, tipping his head toward Roufai. "We hang here. Savimbi was heading south along the river. He was either trying to escape or heading back toward his stash. It could be down there somewhere. We have to check it out."

"Yeah, I know, but it's getting real hot," said Bender.

"The mining guys are thinking the same thing as we are—those diamonds are around here, somewhere."

"You still think that's a security team from Morstarr?" asked Bender.

Thorn shrugged. "Well, their aim's been consistently bad, which I'm thinking is no surprise. The company shoves rifles into their hands and tells 'em to guard the mine."

"The intel we got indicates they were trained by a U.S. marine," said Bender. "I'm thinking if they wanted to shoot us, they would have. And I'm also thinking they're not all security guys. Nope."

"What are you thinking?" asked Thorn.

Bender grinned slightly. "Why, thank you for asking. I'm thinking we have some mercs in the mix, well armed, well trained, hired by the company to help out."

"Can we confirm that?" asked Thorn.

"We can try," answered Bender. "But for now, we walk on eggshells."

"I say we take up positions on the other side of the river, wait 'em out, see what they find, and in the meantime, see if we can ID them."

"Not on the other side of the river, but we'll stay, gather more intel," said Bender.

"We're more vulnerable here," argued Thorn. "But more distance would be good."

"Hey, I'm down with that, but we still got two problems," Dzoba began. "Roufai's little buddy is out there. Someone could find him. That's a loose end I don't like. And the more obvious one: how do we get out of here when the time comes? We ain't walking twenty klicks or whatever the hell it is back to Kisantu's place."

Bender's lip twisted. "No shit, we're not. Wheels are coming."

"You called for 'em?" asked Greene.

"No, he did." Bender gestured to Roufai.

"How?" Greene's frown deepened. "We confiscated all of their—"

"The replacement truck, the one he thought was ours . . . that's still coming."

Greene smiled. "No, shit. That'll work."

Bender looked to Thorn. "That's why we're staying on this side of the river. I want to set up an ambush along the road and intercept that truck before it reaches the village."

"Perfect," said Thorn. "Me and you on that. Dzoba hangs tight with Roufai, and Greene—"

"Heads back and continues reconning the river valley," Bender finished. "He keeps eyes on the mining guys or mercs or whoever they are. If they turn out to be locals, just employees of the company and we whack one, we could be talking international incident. Stranger things have happened. And like I said, eggshells for now."

"I just thought of something," said Dzoba, glowering at Roufai. "Maybe we don't need this fucking guy. The guys in the replacement truck will know where Kisantu is."

"Yeah," said Thorn. "But taking them out's easier than taking 'em alive."

Dzoba nodded. "We can't damage the truck, either."

"Oh, I'm sure you gangbangers will come up with something," said Bender. "Let's do this. I want everyone in place within fifteen minutes."

"Where should I hold?" asked Dzoba.

"Know what? You stick with us," said Bender. "That way we don't waste time once we got the truck."

Dzoba shrugged. "If it comes."

"Oh, it's coming."

"Why are you so sure?"

"We're talking about millions in diamonds. Kisantu is highly motivated."

"Yeah, but the terrain is fucked up. First truck broke down. There's nothing to say that the second one won't drop into a ditch and get stuck the same way."

"And you could slip in the bathtub and die. Come on, motherfucker. Kisantu rules his people with an iron fist. They don't get that truck here, they're dead. And they know it. The truck's coming. You worry way too much."

Dzoba gave a half shrug. "I'm trying to anticipate the variables."

"Anticipate my boot up your ass. Now let's move it!"

Bender wasn't in the habit of letting down his guard, given his profession. And now, given the variables Dzoba had so annoyingly pointed out, that guard would be held even higher. His team could very well be waiting around for a truck that would never show. They could very well be holding a man who only vaguely knew where Kisantu was located. And worse, Kisantu could be on the move.

Bender balled his hands into fists. Variables? Fuck 'em. He consulted his PDA, brought up a map of the region near the road. Oh, yeah. It was ambush alley. No question about that.

Bibby was leaning against a tree, feeling the lump on the back of his head.

Damn fool! You know better! Had he been working for Ricer and made a similar mistake, he would not have survived that man's wrath.

Ever since Bibby had begun toting the computer into the field, his attention had become divided . . . too divided. Staring at the computer screen slowly turned him into a techno zombie lobotomized by bits and bytes. There was no world, no people, no nuclear bomb exploding beneath his chair. Situational awareness? What was that?

He was a bloody junkie, all right, forever seeking the rush of acquiring data and allowing it to affect the team's mission. That rush—more precisely the release of dopamine in his brain—had resulted in someone whacking said brain.

It could be worse. He could be a computer gamer whose addiction caused him to lose his job or one who played for so long that he died of a heart attack. He'd read about those nuts, many of them from South Korea, where gamers often earned six-figure salaries and achieved celebrity status. Bibby swore to avoid that world.

At least until he retired. Then all bets were off.

Damn, the lump felt like it was growing, and he knew a thing or two about head trauma. He checked his ears for fluid, which would indicate a skull fracture, but it was hard to tell whether he was feeling fluid or just rain.

Someone was jogging toward him, coming down a hill to the west, then side-stepping along a muddy stream that had formed in the gulley. He saw a cap, sighed, relaxed his grip on the Sterling. A second squint revealed Boo Boo heading up. "Right here!" Bibby cried.

The medic reached him, his face creased by the climb and his requisite sour look. "I heard you call. Sit your ass down. Let me see that fucking noggin."

Bibby winced as much over his injury as the rude request, but he complied, grimaced again as the man stuck a light in his eyes. "Pupils look good."

"Maybe you should look again, now that you've blinded me."

Boo Boo seized one of Bibby's earlobes, tugged it hard while he shoved his light into Bibby's ear. "Your bedside manner is atrocious."

"Oh, I'm sorry, Mr. Bibby. You've confused me with someone who actually gives a fuck. I plug holes and tape up leaks, just like any other plumber. Okay. Let's see. No fluid in that one." He latched on to the other lobe, jabbed his light once more. "This one looks clear, too. You're as lucky as that bitch in Jersey who won the lottery twice in the same year."

"But not as rich." Bibby lifted a finger to one ear. "I checked for fluid myself."

"Leave that to the experts."

He snorted. "When can I meet them?"

"Fuck you. But really, you probably got a concussion, a mild one based on the swelling here. When I was in L.A. I treated lots of people who got pistol-whipped or whacked with baseball bats. This ain't shit. You got clipped at an angle, I bet, which was good. You didn't get the full brunt, otherwise he would've spilt your head open like a—"

"I get the picture."

"Yeah, but I'm sure a few of the other guys will be sad that you, uh, well, survived."

"Sapper and Wolfgang?"

Boo Boo returned the light to his med kit. "No love lost there?"

"I think not."

"So what happened? Guy came up behind you? Caught you with your pants down?"

Bibby averted his gaze. "Caught me with my face in the computer."

"Real warriors have a paper map in one hand and a firearm in the other."

"I wish it were that simple."

"It is. Try it sometime. Anyway, where's the guy who did this to you?"

Bibby rose shakily, grabbed the tree for support. "I'll show you."

"Why don't you point me in the right direction? I want you to get back to the truck and grab a seat. Stay off your feet for a while."

Bibby was about to roll his eyes, but even that might hurt. "Yes, doctor."

"Hey, man, I ain't no MD. Play golf with me once, and you'll figure that out."

Bibby nodded then pointed toward several more trees near the side of a sharply rising hill. "He's over there."

Pope didn't move a muscle.

Only one other time had he been in a similar situation, and in truth, that had been during an exercise. There was nothing simulated about this moment, nothing faked, no need to suspend his disbelief.

He wouldn't even swallow, and his breath grew shallower by the second.

Pope's attacker had his lips mere inches from the back of Pope's ear, had his knife pressed firmly on Pope's neck and a pistol jammed into Pope's shoulder blade, behind his heart. If Pope reached for one weapon, the other might spell his doom.

"Do you know who you're fucking with? We're the fucking C . . . I . . . A . . ."

"I thought you were just a D . . . I . . . C . . . K . . ."

"Let me say that again. The C . . . I . . . A . . . Not some fucking dirtbags in loincloths."

"Sometimes it's hard to tell."

"What the fuck? You don't think I have allies here? You don't think I can burn you for interfering with my investigation?"

"Like the bossman said, you got no portfolio. To burn us, you have to admit that."

"You're so naïve . . ."

"You going to cut me, shoot me, or kill me with bad breath?"

"Don't insult me, bitch. I know exactly who you are. I studied your group. I know all the players. Billy Pope. Navy SEAL? I shit on you, SEAL. I shit on you."

"I didn't know we had a stalker. Do you have fantasies about us? You got a shrine set up? You got pictures and candles and a jar of Vaseline nearby?"

"Your boss and I go way back. You have no fucking clue what you're talking about."

"I know you're a bad joke, man. Get the fuck off. I got work to do and no time for your shit." With that, Pope ignored the blade at his neck and lifted the camera lens to his eye, even though the spook's pistol jabbed a little harder.

"You call Hertzog right now. You tell him he's going to play ball with me."

"I'll call him, tell 'em I was right about carrying metal cuffs instead of the fucking zippers. But that's it. I'm dead before I'm someone's hostage."

"Don't test me. You and the rest of your merc buddies are the easiest people to kill in this entire country. No one gives a fuck about you. Unnamed American merc dies in Angola. Won't even make a newspaper. No one takes responsibility for you. You're on your own, buckaroo."

Pope closed his eyes, saw his sister smiling. But the smile evaporated, and she began to wave her index finger, no, no, no . . .

"I won't play," Pope answered, snapping open his eyes. "I won't."

He envisioned the smile on the spook's lips, envisioned the smile on his own—

Because he had just hit the camera's transmit button, sending sounds and images from the camera back to Bibby's laptop. The Brit had no doubt heard the conversation and was already warning Mad Dog.

"Call your boss."

"No."

"I'll kill you."

Pope's tone grew even more sarcastic. "Please, don't kill me. Oh, please . . ."

"Wait a minute. What's that light flashing on the camera? You fucking with me, SEAL?"

"That's the battery level. It's getting low. That's the warning light, you dumb ass."

"Look, you either call Hertzog right now or—"

"Why don't you call him? You want his number? What's the matter? You worried about roving minutes?"

"For a man who's got only seconds to live, you're a cocky motherfucker."

"Hey, meathead, I'm not afraid to die. I'm just afraid you'll be sloppy about it, like everything else you do."

"You're almost as funny as your boss."

"You know, I've studied guys like you, too. You probably wanted to be a SEAL or a Ranger but you didn't have the fucking balls for it." Pope's tone grew even nastier. "You sucked on your mama's nipple for too long, couldn't let go. Fucking pussies like you make me sick."

The spook's breathing increased dramatically, but for some reason he didn't reply. Then, finally, it dawned on him: "You're stalling me, you motherfucker!"

"They teach you to recognize that in the C . . . I . . . A . . . ?"

The channel crackled, then a report came in from Bibby, who had met up with Boo Boo, was okay, and was rallying back to the truck.

When Mad Dog asked him for the locations of the others, Bibby explained that his laptop had been trashed and that he needed to fire up the other one he had in the truck so he could pick up their beacons.

Pope's shoulders slumped. *My fuckin' luck.*

So the Brit wasn't listening to them. He hadn't alerted Mad Dog. No one knew that Pope was up there on the hill, being held by this hairy, smelly bastard.

Sure, Pope could call Mad Dog, tell him he was being held, do like the spook wanted.

But deep down, he was just too goddamned embarrassed to do that, too concerned that his screwup might get him fired from the team, not to mention how Rookie would rub his nose in it.

Still, would he allow his ego to result in his death? Wouldn't be the first time that had happened to a SEAL. Wouldn't be the last. You had to have hubris up the ying yang to do what they did.

The blade pressed a little harder. The spook was drawing blood. "Call Hertzog. Right now."

Up until that second, Pope truly doubted that the asshole would kill him. But now that he felt his neck growing wetter, the panic began to set in.

And he fucking hated that. His sister waved her finger again. No, it wasn't his time. Not yet. She would let him know.

"All right," he said, his voice cracking. "I'm going to reach around and key the mike. Slowly."

Rookie couldn't believe it.

Actually, he could. He just didn't want to.

But there it was. He had fucked up again.

Okay, as fuckups went, it wasn't a major deal, not something that would cost the team two million bucks, not something that endangered lives.

Yet no matter how you came at it, polished it, dressed it up in high heels and a thong and paraded it around, it still walked, talked, and quacked like a fuckup.

Were he not already on the boss's shit list, he wouldn't have made such a big deal about it.

But the fact was indisputable and condemning:

When he had gathered his gear before moving out, he had forgotten to pick up the thermal camera; the damned thing was still out there, lying in the wet grass.

If he didn't recover the camera, it and the data recorded on the memory card could fall into the wrong hands. Fingerprints could be run, traced, and that was bad, very bad. Plus Mad Dog would dock him the two grand or so it cost to replace it. Cheap bastard. And the way this cluster fuck was unfolding, Rookie would be lucky to collect his base pay, let alone a commission.

Time to bandage his sucking chest wound of a career. First things first.

Instead of bringing the truck back down the road, announcing his screwup to everyone, he took the keys and hustled off on foot. He thought he could be there and back within five minutes, and no one would be the wiser.

As he sprinted along the road, following in the truck's previous tracks, he happened to glance right, to where Pope had been positioned. Hopefully the big ogre had shifted forward enough to be out of sight.

But no, he hadn't. In fact, someone was behind him. Holy shit. Was that a beard? Yes, it was. Holy shit! That was the fucking spook. He was holding Pope!

Rookie suddenly froze in time, locked into a million-year second of indecision.

But then he broke free, started forward.

Stopped.

He couldn't just charge up. That might startle the guy. He'd kill Pope.

All right, so Rookie wouldn't bawl his eyes out if the big Navy fuck died, but he wouldn't take blame for that shit. Unh-huh. In fact, if he could save Pope, that could mean some serious redemption.

He took another step. Froze again.

Fuck! What do I do?

"Blackhound One, this is Blackhound Four," Pope called. "We got a little situation here, over."

For a moment Rookie thought of cutting in, letting Mad Dog know what was happening and telling him that he was behind Pope, ready to move in.

There was a code phrase they had, one that meant bad guys were listening: "Dumbo is flapping his ears." Then there was another that meant you were in proximity of an area and ready to attack: "The force is with me."

But if the spook was close enough to Pope's earpiece, he might overhear those, and, unlike some Middle Eastern terrorist who wouldn't know Luke Skywalker from a flying elephant, he'd know code—maybe not the exact nature of it, but he'd know something was up.

Rookie would lose the element of surprise.

Let them talk—he'd stay out of it—because a little conversation would make for a nice diversion while he skulked up and got some.

"Blackhound Four, what the fuck's going on, over?"

"Uh, yeah. Our friendly neighborhood spook has a . . . yeah, he's got a knife to my throat and a pistol in my back, over." Pope was a man of details, even in how he described being held, which was, of course, intentional so that anyone in the area would know exactly what danger he was in.

And yeah, he was fucked all right.

Rookie lost his breath. Two weapons? He would have to move in like a specter, gliding soundlessly over the mud to reach out and wrench away both of the spook's arms before he could inflict damage.

Possible? Absolutely, were the right forces applied, the planets properly aligned, the forces of good temporarily outweighing the forces of evil because the great Gods of Delta Mountain had come down to vanquish all assholes from the CIA.

It could happen. Not!

Shit. Double shit.

Rookie usually loved a challenge—but not when a spilt-second mistake could cost a fellow operator's life.

Then again, what was the alternative? Watch? The same goddamned thing could happen . . .

"Blackhound Four, I got no time for this shit," said Mad Dog, either taking it in stride or thinking Pope was bullshitting him.

"Blackhound One, I'm serious."

Another voice echoed in the background: "Yes, he is, Hertzog. I'm a fucking great white shark, and I got this SEAL in my mouth, and I am *so* hungry."

"Judas, what the fuck are you doing?"

"Oh, I have your attention?"

"I'm going to come up there—"

"And what? Fuck me up? You'd better watch your step. You might trip over your dead employee here."

"What do you want, you fucking limp dick piece of shit scrawny motherfucker? I'm going to kill you, you fuck!"

Mad Dog was slightly upset.

Rookie instinctively crouched down, shifted around some bushes to his right, then slowly, ever so goddamned slowly, moved up on the men, the sound of each footfall stealing his breath—until a rain band pushed through, whipping up the puddles and causing a welcome racket. He moved a little faster.

"Hertzog, we're all going to play nice together, otherwise I'm going to waste this man. As you said, I'm operating without portfolio—kind of like you. So we're both making up the rules as we go. You play nice, and maybe I will."

"Blackhound Four, this is One. I'm sorry, bro, but I don't negotiate with terrorists. If you can make your move and kill the motherfucker, do it. Otherwise, you're an acceptable loss, and he knows that. He's got nothing to lose, so he's just fucking with us. So you go ahead and kill him."

Ah, ha! Code phrase, and Rookie remembered it, all right. Mad Dog had told him, "If you ever get caught, and I tell you that you're an *acceptable loss*—I use those exact words—that means I'm coming for you myself."

"Hertzog!" the spook screamed. "I am as fucking serious as it gets right now!"

Rookie's boot came down into a puddle nearly a foot deep. He staggered, nearly fell, even as he drew within ten meters of the pair. God, had they heard him? He couldn't tell.

Okay, so Mad Dog was coming up, but he was still down on the riverbank. Too far.

Now Rookie thought of his breathing, of how he would remove the spook's hands. He considered just rushing up and jabbing his Remington into the back of the guy's head, that way Mad Dog could call the shots (literally or figuratively) when he arrived. "Let him go, or I'll blow your fucking brains across the river."

That'd be Rookie's line. It was his imagination; he was the director and star.

Nah, that wouldn't work. Just be another standoff, and Mad Dog would be pissed that he hadn't exploited his advantage.

In his heart of hearts, Rookie knew exactly what *must* be done. But he still wondered if it *could* be done.

He rehearsed the plan again: He had to swoop in, seize both wrists and pull with every fucking ounce of energy he had, pull so hard and so fast that the guy wouldn't have time to react, that he'd be so surprised that he'd fall back onto his ass, just as Rookie relieved him of the pistol, then the knife, leaving him lying there, shocked over what had happened, even still unaware that he didn't have the weapons, reaching up reflexively and jerking his head back at the sight of his empty hands.

And Rookie would be standing over him, backlit by the lighting, glossed in rain, his teeth shining before he held up the knife and pistol and muttered, "Gotcha, cocksucker. Now close your eyes. This might hurt."

That's what I'm talking about!

He saw it all happening again and again as he neared them, slowly setting down his shotgun, then flexing his fingers in preparation. His arms grew stiff. He blinked, made sure his vision was as clear as it could be. Every sense tingled with electricity.

He had never felt more powerful, more ready to act.

The spook's voice cracked, "Hertzog, I'm not fucking around!"

"Blackhound Four, you heard me," Mad Dog said. "Acceptable loss."

Rookie took a final breath. Held it. Two meters. One meter. Last step. His hands came down, and a guttural hiss escaped his lips.

Chapter 10

∙∙

Tongaso, Angola
Near Congo Border
0712 Hours Local Time

Wolfgang and Drac had been listening to the drama unfold on the radio while keeping close eyes on the Delta team. Drac had asked if they should go back, try to help Pope, but Wolfgang had shut down that idea. The big guy was on his own until Mad Dog got there. "Pope can handle it, trust me."

All right, so Wolfgang knew that was bullshit. He had tossed that out to make Drac and himself feel better.

And it didn't work. For either of them.

Like Drac, Wolfgang wanted to run back there and skin that asshole spook alive, but they'd never make it in time. And they couldn't lose sight of the Delta guys. So life at the moment was full of guilt . . . and full of shit.

He could barely concentrate on his surveillance, nearly all of his attention focused on his ears, on Mad Dog, who

had just ordered Pope to kill the spook. Unfuckinbeliev-
able.

Or maybe not.

That could be a stalling tactic. Wasn't there a code
phrase for that? Wolfgang really wasn't sure, and were
Pope's back pressed more firmly into the corner, there
was no doubt that he would react.

Had Mad Dog lost his mind? Not really. He had made
a tactical decision and was fully aware of the risks and
consequences. He had acted swiftly. And that's what
great leaders did. They had the brains and the balls to get
the job done. Of course, Wolfgang knew they could cover
up the spook's death. Bibby would be all over that.

But Wolfgang had to stop thinking, stop worrying. His
job lay out there, across the valley. The Deltas were on
the move, some taking a footpath out toward the road,
while another broke off, heading back toward the river.

Drac dashed over to Wolfgang's spot along the ridge,
was about to say something, when Wolfgang shushed
him, put a hand up to his earpiece. "Did you hear
that?"

"I didn't hear nothing."

"I think it's Pope. Sounded like he keyed his mike."

Drac pressed a finger on his own earpiece, his face
tightening into a knot. "I heard it."

Rookie wasn't sure how badly the spook had cut Pope
because all he saw was a flash of red on the blade as he
simultaneously wrenched both the spook's arms away
from Pope.

A second look scared him. Fuck! That was a lot of
blood!

At the same time, Pope, sensing what was happening,

threw himself forward, onto his gut, out of the line of fire—

And it was a good fucking thing he did.

Reflexively, the spook's trigger finger came down, and a round split the night, booming so loudly in Rookie's ear that the shock nearly made his grip falter.

But it didn't. He hung on to the skinny fuck for dear life, held so firmly that they'd have to pry his cold, dead hands off the bastard.

It was a challenge, though. The guy had the wrists of an anorexic, his metal clasp watch hanging loosely like a bracelet, his skin very wet.

However, all Rookie needed was another second to get his legs in motion, and he got that second, brought the bald asshole down to the ground, even as he twisted the knife arm around his back, applying so much pressure that he was a twitch away from breaking bones.

The spook cursed and moaned, fought with his gun arm, fired again, but now Pope had rolled back, was up on his knees, bringing both hands down onto the spook's pistol.

"That's all she wrote, scumbag," said Rookie, squeezing so hard that the spook dropped his knife. "Give it up, and I won't break your arm."

Pope ripped the pistol from the spook's hand, jammed it into the guy's temple as he clutched his own bloody neck and swallowed. "Hey, dickhead, do you know how much I want to pull this trigger?"

"Let him go," came a voice from behind them, a heavily accented voice.

Rookie craned his neck to spy four local men who were running forward, the business ends of their rifles wanting to do business with his flesh and Pope's.

"Did you fuckers think I came here alone?" asked the spook. "Did you really?"

Pope looked at Rookie, eyes emphatic. "Don't even fucking breathe."

"And I thought I was doing you a favor," Rookie muttered, then he faced the spook. "Better work more with your boys. They were late."

"Let him go!" The voice came from the tallest of the group, a would-be NBA star were it not for his malnourished body. His eyes grew wider, almost glowing in the half-light as he regarded the spook. "Uncle Jimmy? Where is my brother?"

"Your brother?" asked Rookie. "Dude, what the fuck are you talking about?"

Pope whipped his head around. "Rook, shut the fuck up . . ."

"Hey, Billy boy, these guys are amateurs," said Judas. "They'll fire at the drop of a hat. Let me go. I'll calm 'em down. You keep 'em hot, they'll pop."

"Uncle Jimmy! Where is my brother! Did one man here kill him? Tell me! Which man killed him!"

Rookie thought aloud: "Wait a minute. Bibby said he got hit by a guy up in the hills, said he was from the village. He's not dead, though."

"And you open your mouth again, *you're* dead," Pope said, removing the pistol from Judas's temple and aiming it at Rookie. "Let this asshole go. He's right. These dumb fucks will shoot us. And that'd be our luck."

"You trust him more than them?"

"I don't trust anybody right now—including you. Now do what I fucking say."

Rookie shook his head then abruptly released Judas's

arm. The man moaned again, slowly brought the arm around his torso, nursing it at the elbow. "I think you broke it anyway, you fuck."

"Bullshit."

"Whoa, whoa, whoa," cried Pope.

At that moment, the four locals closed in, weapons trained on all three of them.

"Okay," Pope said, turning an uneasy grin on Judas. "I think they're ready for you to calm them down."

Jaga lay on his back in the bushes, thoroughly hidden from anyone across the river. The rain was tapering off, and though cloudy, the sky was beginning to turn a bluish gray. He eyed the heavens from between the leaves, wondered what he would do next. He was wet, sticky, and a deep hunger knotted his stomach. The pistol given to him by the mining company leader dug into his side.

How long should he stay? Well, he could not move during the day. Could he remain there until nightfall? That was a very long time.

He thought of how nice it would be to sneak back to the village for something to eat, something to drink, for just a few rags to wipe his face and wounds. Did he need to torture himself anymore? Was he really a revolutionary?

Or was he just a young man who had been deceived by those who sought money and power, not freedom for his people?

He could just walk away. Head to the east. Cross the border. Disappear. Go to the coast and look for work.

But could he really? What if he were wrong? What if Kisantu could bring about change? If Jaga failed, then he would be responsible for more oppression, more atrocities. The blood of his people would be on his hands. He had always told himself that if he still had breath, then he still had fight.

The gunshots were long gone now. The fighting—or whatever it had been—was over.

Every part of his body ached, but yes . . . yes, indeed, he was still alive, and he had to find the strength to go on no matter how difficult his life had become. His father had once described him as more stubborn and more determined than anyone in their village.

Jaga needed to find that boy, whisper in his ear, tell him that under the cover of darkness he needed to cross the river again, snatch the diamonds, and slip back into waves as cunning and clever as a snake.

For now, though, Jaga would rest. Another hour, maybe two. Then he would shift about the hills, never staying too long in one spot until the hour came. He nodded to himself, backhanded the tears from his eyes.

The entire left side of the guy's face had swelled up like a pink-and-brown water balloon, and Boo Boo was damned sure he was looking at a major skull fracture.

"You are one fucked-up dude," he muttered to the unconscious man. And yes, the wannabe Rambo had fluid in his ears. Brain swelling could kill him if he wasn't rushed to a hospital.

And where was the nearest hospital? Correction, where was the nearest hospital with modern equipment? Who the fuck knew? Probably in Luanda. Maybe somewhere else in Africa.

Wow. Mr. Bibby had one hell of a greeting. Damn, you didn't piss him off. He'd beat the fucking shit out of you with whatever was lying around: a laptop, an empty jar of peanut butter, the next-door neighbor's Chihuahua . . .

And he'd beat this guy with the kind of rage found in drug users, betrayed spouses, and serial killers. Repeated blows. Probably dozens of them. *Die, you motherfucker! Die!*

Some scary shit. Definitely scary shit. He was the envy of disgruntled retail workers everywhere.

And consequently, his act had revealed more of his personality, which he always kept under wraps with the excuse that he was here to do a job, not make friends. Boo Boo respected that. He felt the same way. He didn't like getting too personal because he was usually the guy present when "a friend" would die.

So . . . Mr. Alastair Bibby had some serious issues. Did old Zog know? Probably not.

Boo Boo got on the horn, reported his findings to the big guy, who blew him off because the shit was still hitting the fan at Pope's location and he was almost there.

A terse report from Pope indicated that Boo Boo should begin immediate treatment of the local guy because his brother and three other guys were now holding all of them, including Judas, prisoner. If the guy died, that wouldn't bode well for them—kinda make negotiations a little more difficult, uh-huh.

And better yet, Mad Dog was about to join that particular and inviting mosh pit.

Boo Boo swore a few times, sighed a few times, broke open his med kit. His patient's GCS was very low, but he would start an IV anyway, Glasgow Coma Scale be damned. Boo Boo would go through the motions. Politics. Fuck 'em. Had the guy been eating a balanced diet and not been in such a sad state before he was injured, he

might have a fighting chance. Boo Boo figured his resis-
tance was low, his body's ability to mend itself severely
impeded. He had no eye, verbal, or motor response, so
he got a big score of 3 on that GCS.

Dead people routinely got 1s, 2s, and 3s. Dead people
or men forced to treat them.

And how were they supposed to move him? They had
no long backboard, no CV collar, no way to keep him
steady. He was a goner all right. Just a matter of time.

So much for friendly relations with the natives. Bibby
had stolen the guy's soul. Taking a picture would've
been easier.

Now Mad Dog and Pope had better practice their lines
of bullshit, 'cause they would have some serious "splain-
ing" to do once Mr. Bibby's victim embarked on the
short road to the pearly gates. Boo Boo hoped that would
happen soon—not that he wished death on the guy (he
didn't know this guy from a hole in the wall)—but because he still had one other body to check out, the guy
who'd been fleeing from the Delta operators.

As he charged over the hill, Mad Dog tugged free the pin
on his first grenade, lobbed it to his left, then relieved the
second grenade of its pin, lobbed it to the right.

Nothing like announcing your own arrival with a
couple of flash bangs and here's . . . Mad Dog!

Cue *Tonight Show* music.

He'd come out from behind the curtain, his carbine
blazing. No, he wasn't there to kill innocent tourists
who'd somehow acquired tickets to the show's taping.
He was just there to scare the living shit out of them.

The same went for Tongaso's homeboys and one

scumbag CIA agent who had accidentally remained alive in recent years.

The two explosions sent them hollering and diving to the mud. Strange men with painted faces were attacking again.

"All right!" Mad Dog screamed at the top of his lungs. "Nobody fucking move!"

Wasn't the most original statement, but given the circumstances, you had to sacrifice creativity for, well, getting those fuckers not to move.

He sprinted down the hill and right up to the group, repeating his words, his voice still dialed up to ten. Then he added, "Nobody raises a weapon. And I mean nobody!"

The four men gripped their rifles but were still on their bellies. Gazes followed Mad Dog as he went up to Judas, grabbed him by the collar, and dragged him to his feet. Rookie must've really hurt the spook's arm because he groaned when Mad Dog moved him.

Meanwhile, Pope and Rookie had drawn their pistols and aimed them at the four locals on the ground.

Damn, it was amazing how a couple of loud bangs could disorient and leave vulnerable untrained combatants. One second they had had the advantage, but in the next he did. The tables hadn't turned, the turds had; yes, they had turned their heads long enough to be distracted and disarmed.

"Pope? Rookie? Rifles," Mad Dog said, then he faced Judas, who kept that one hand tucked tightly under his hurt arm, and lowered his voice. "You're dead."

"So are you."

Mad Dog jabbed the muzzle of his carbine into Judas's chest. "I'm dead?"

"Look down."

He did, and right there, barely visible against the spook's chest, was the muzzle of a small pistol he had just removed from his armpit and had aimed at Mad Dog's own chest. The pistol had been there the entire time.

All right, props to the asshole. He was a clever old green bean, if an arrogant one. For almost an entire two seconds Mad Dog admired him, then he said, "You're kidding me."

"Work with me here. I'll give you these men. They'll help. You feed me the intel I need. That's all I'm asking. It's a win-win for everyone. I'm appealing to you as a fellow American. We're both in this cesspool together. Let's fix things together. Then we can say fuck you and leave."

"Come on, Judas. You don't play that game. You're setting me up again, aren't you? Still ain't over what happened back in the 'Stan? What? You're looking for some kind of closure here? Won't happen."

"I'm just here to gather HUMINT for my bosses. That's all."

"You volunteered for this shit when you found out I'd be here, didn't you? How'd you find out?"

Judas gave a loud snort. "This is all bullshit. Where's the kid you captured? Where are the rocks? You got 'em? Is this a done deal? I told you, I'm just a blue-collar hunter, just like you. And FYI, I already got my revenge. You ain't a marine. So we're even. And we are on the same side."

"Are you going through Prozac withdrawal? What the fuck?"

"I probably am. I just think we can make it easier on

each other. Don't let your arrogance get in the way. I have some information you want."

"Information? I doubt it. You sell bullshit. That's all the inventory you got."

"Not this time."

"Look, asshole, all I need to know is one thing: where those fucking idiots hid that rough. Once I know that and recover that stash, I'm out of here. Game over. Job done. Miller Time. Adios, motherfuckers. Unless you got that, you got nothing."

"So you don't have the guy or the rough . . ."

Mad Dog swore. He'd been accused of opening his big mouth more than a few times. Shit, even as a kid he could never keep a secret. *Dumbass!*

"You know, I didn't want to resort to this, but I just knew it'd be necessary," Judas began. "And yeah, I knew you were coming here. I got myself assigned to this fucking dump."

"You're a psycho, Dude. Obsessed. Fucked up."

"No, I'm not. I thought we could have a little fun together, but I also assumed you'd need some extra motivation. I thought, money? Nah, you got a lot. I need something better."

"What're you talking about? Extra motivation? Is that what the CIA calls blackmail? Works for you, huh?"

"Whatever you want to call it. I just knew I'd have to do something . . . I don't know . . . you might call it unethical . . . I don't know . . . too harsh . . . too cruel."

The spook was really getting off on the moment, and the more animated he became, the more Mad Dog wanted to splatter his gray matter across the wet clay.

"Uncle Jimmy? We will not be held any longer," cried the tallest guy, still on his gut. "We will fight now!"

"Calm down, Friday. They're going to set us all free!"

"Friday?" asked Rookie, raising his chin at the leader. "That's your name?"

"No," the guy said. "He calls me that."

"From *Robinson Crusoe*," said Judas. "Local savage."

Rookie frowned, probably had never even heard of the book.

"All right, no more of this shit!" screamed Mad Dog. "Rookie? Pope? Get these guys on their feet. March 'em back to the village, along with this asshole." He cocked a thumb at Judas.

"I'm not done with you, Hertzog," snapped the spook, now waving his pistol.

"Oh, yeah, you are."

"I have Dan."

Mad Dog craned his head sharply. "What did you say?"

Judas raised his brows. "I have Dan. The old man you take care of, the old man you love so much? I have him—actually, a few of my colleagues do."

"Bullshit!" Mad Dog gripped his carbine with both hands, aiming directly for Judas's heart. "You're fucking with me!"

"Yeah, I am. I really am. Big time. And if you don't believe me, call your little British wanker. I'll give him the Web site address."

"Drop your weapon. *Now!*"

"You don't want that address?"

"Drop your weapon!"

Judas tossed the pistol matter-of-factly at Mad Dog's feet. "Poor old Dan. He was a great solider—but now he's going to die in excruciating pain if you don't do what I say . . . exactly what I say."

Mad Dog moved in, jabbed the muzzle of his carbine into Judas's chest. "Fuck you!"

"Oh, you got the gun, but I hold all the fuckin' cards, you stupid fucking jarhead."

Mad Dog dropped his rifle, grabbed Judas by the throat, drew back a fist, about to pummel the man. He'd beat the guy into a bloody pulp first, then he'd kill him.

"Bossman, don't!" cried Pope. "Let Bibby check it out. Let him check it out!"

Bibby sat in the pickup truck, resting his sore neck on the poorly padded seat. Where were the engineers from BMW when you needed them?

He winced and focused his attention on the glowing screen. Yes, he had halfheartedly fired up the laptop but was still rebelling against technology because technology had not been very kind to him. Not at all.

However, Mad Dog needed to know for certain that Dan had been kidnapped, and Bibby was, in fact, able to pull up the Web site and view the webcam images of the old man, gagged and tied in a nondescript room on Cebu Island, at least according to a very forthcoming Judas. It was doubtful that Judas and his cronies could employ a double, and Bibby made certain to zoom in on the tattoos on the old man's forearms, which would help to positively ID him. Still, Judas and his fellow frogs in the CIA could have engaged in an elaborate hoax to trick Mad Dog into believing that old Dan was a prisoner. But Bibby didn't believe that. Mad Dog did employ a team of local security guards to help watch over the dog pound estate, but that puppy patrol could've been infiltrated by a few determined agents or local rebels hired by Judas. Why hadn't they called to alert Mr. Hertzog?

Or maybe they had. Bibby checked his voice mail, where a message from their chief of security confirmed it all: old Dan was missing. Bibby sighed. He could've checked the voice mail first, but at least now he had what he needed.

In a resigned tone he informed Mad Dog that he had seen images of Dan being held prisoner, that they seemed legitimate, and that the security chief had called to say that Dan was missing.

"What's happening?" asked Doolittle, whom Bibby had asked to stand guard near the truck while he was on the computer (no more techno fuckups!)

"It seems Mad Dog's old acquaintance from the CIA wants to work with us, and he has old Dan, which means he has Mad Dog, which in turn means—"

"He has all of us," said Doolittle. "Do you think the sergeant will sacrifice Dan?"

Bibby snickered. "Not for two million. Not for a hundred million."

"He is a mercenary. He's not supposed to have a conscience."

"You know him better than I do."

Doolittle smiled weakly. "Yes, he's a good man. And that is what leaves him vulnerable."

"Yes, but I think I like it better this way."

"Even if we have to work with the CIA?"

"I've worked for worse people, trust me."

Boo Boo's current patient had a faint but steady pulse and weak respiration. Fluids were being administered—and wasted. But he was doing his job. He figured he could take a quick jog down the hill and check on the other dead guy. At least that man wouldn't be a tease. He was dead meat.

What surprised Boo Boo was not the young man's body, which bore quite a few entry wounds, but the image he saw across the river. He had made a casual glance for no reason in particular, just a turn of the head.

Sapper was coming out of the water, dragging himself onto the shoreline. Boo Boo didn't remember hearing Mad Dog order the man across the river. Everyone was to remain on this side to help search for the diamonds.

Maybe the engineer was trying to show some initiative by going after Jaga. Maybe he had been ordered to search for the man and Boo Boo had missed the radio call. Nevertheless, Sapper's appearance was odd enough to warrant a SITREP.

"Blackhound Five, this is Blackhound Nine, over."

After a long pause, the Mr. Blow Shit Up finally answered. "Go ahead, Two."

"I see you across the river, over."

"Roger that."

"SITREP, over."

Boo Boo had no business asking for a situation report; he was only the goddamned medic, but what the fuck, if Sapper was being insubordinate and could screw up the mission, then Mad Dog ought to know about it. Boo Boo wasn't a kiss ass or stool pigeon, but he sure as hell wanted to get paid, and if Sapper's little field research could affect Boo Boo's paycheck, well, there was the bottom line.

"Fuck you, over," answered Sapper.

And to hell with radio protocol. "Hey, cocksucker,

what the fuck you doing over there? You looking for
him, over?"

Sapper wasn't saying. A second call yielded more of
the same: static.

So fuck him. Boo Boo called Mad Dog, told him Sapper was across the river and wouldn't answer his call.
Mad Dog had been listening, called Sapper himself. No
response.

In the meantime, Boo Boo finished examining the
body, searching pockets and such, and noting the mud
beneath the guy's fingernails. It was possible that he had
buried the rough somewhere nearby, and he might have
done so recently, judging from those nails. Boo Boo
wasn't a forensic expert, but he'd watched enough TV to
be reminded to check the hands. He was about to share
that finding with old Zog, when the man called to say
that he, Pope, Rookie, and Judas's party were heading
back to the village. Doolittle would head to the hills to
help Boo Boo transport the injured local. Wolfgang and
Drac would stay with the Deltas. Sapper would issue a
SITREP immediately.

Which, of course, he didn't.

Boo Boo acknowledged Mad Dog's order, and as he
started back for Mr. Bibby's victim, he informed Mad
Dog of his findings. Mad Dog acknowledged and told
him to hurry up. Boo Boo picked up the pace, but by
the time he made it back to the man, the inevitable had
occurred. "Blackhound One, this is Nine. The injured
guy over here has expired. I say again, he has expired."

A click sounded twice. Someone keying a mike.
"Fuck!"

It was Mad Dog, who was in desperate need of a smiley sticker on his lapel.

Mad Dog, Pope, and Rookie were still holding Judas and his four cronies at gunpoint, but the spook was hardly bothered by that. He marched back toward the village like a real estate agent who had just purchased Angola, and Mad Dog couldn't help but curse him.

Yet if he let Judas get to him, he'd be letting the man win. So he took long, deep breaths, tried to clear his head, tried to analyze the situation as thoroughly as he could:

Jaga was somewhere across the river, possibly gone, but it seemed likely that he hadn't recovered the diamonds.

The diamonds might be hidden somewhere near the river, and Jaga's partner had the dirty fingernails to support that.

Judas apparently had Dan and wanted to force Mad Dog to work with him.

The Delta operators had not left, were staking out the road, and had sent one back to the river, presumably for a recon.

Sapper was not answering calls and might be MIA. Shit, maybe he'd found the diamonds and bolted.

Bibby had bludgeoned a local who had just died.

And Mad Dog had a huge fucking migraine, and for the moment, he had only one thing on his mind: his friend Dan. "I assume that if anything happens to you, your colleagues will kill Dan," he told Judas.

The spook chuckled. "Absolutely. Old Dan is your motivation and my life insurance. I bet the old fucker never knew how important he'd become to your little job."

"And you're telling me you went through all this trouble just to get me and my team to help you? You're that incompetent? And you're that fucking naïve to think you can rid the world of dictators and terrorism?"

"Oh, I love that shit. I'll never get 'em all, but I love trying. And like I said, I've been around. I'm set for life, but there is a small debt you owe, and that'll need to be paid. I'll even cut you slack on the interest. I think you know the amount: it begins with four and ends with million. And it's the exact amount you stole from the warlord I paid off. That was my fucking money!"

"Bullshit."

"You'll have your boy Bibby transfer that to my own Swiss account. We'll take care of that right away."

Mad Dog was a half-second from collapse. The job in Angola wasn't just Fucked Up Beyond All Recognition; it was about to ruin his life.

"That money belonged to the taxpayers! And you used it to pay off drug pushers and line your own fucking pockets! It was never yours. You're living in a fucking fantasy world!"

"Don't get technical, Hertzog. You stole it, too, and now Dan's life depends on it. You either pay up or plan a funeral."

"So it's all about the money."

"No, actually, it's about hurting you." Judas stopped, turned back and glared down at Mad Dog. "Does it hurt yet?"

"I don't know. You tell me."

Mad Dog lifted his elbows, bringing his rifle stock to bear. He jabbed the spook in the chest so hard that he might've cracked a rib. Judas went crashing onto his ass, drawing a fit of screaming from his cronies.

"There's only so much shit I can take," Mad Dog cried above the others. "I want to talk to Dan right now!"

Chapter 11

....

Tongaso, Angola
Near Congo Border
0742 Hours Local Time

Bender stood in the bushes while Thorn rushed into the road and began waving his hands. An engine growled in the distance, became louder, but the truck was still hidden in the morning fog.

The irony was, Bender had just unzipped and was letting go a hot, steamy one with good arc when the call had come in that their ride was rattling down the road. After a good tug and zip, he was ready—

And just in time. The truck settled into a squeaky halt, and one man wearing brown, nondescript fatigues jumped down from the cab, rifle in one hand, while two others hopped out of a flatbed covered by a tattered tarpaulin.

While Thorn approached the driver, whose two men moved in behind him, Bender sprinted off and smiled.

They were all looking at Thorn, who wasn't even wearing a thong.

Dumbasses.

As Thorn began a verbal song and dance, his Portuguese building toward a crescendo, the name Kisantu echoing, Bender and Dzoba slipped up behind the two men.

There was an air of practiced efficiency that kept Bender calm, that reminded him that both he and Dzoba were going to take lives because the mission demanded it and because these men would ultimately bring evil to the United States of America. There might be some regret much later on in life, but not now. He and Dzoba were unstoppable gods wielding hard pieces of metal designed to do two things: pick chunks of meat from your teeth . . . and kill men.

They had, of course, already flossed.

Bender thrust his knife home, felt the pop, like sausage on a barbecue, heard the man's last exhalation, heard Dzoba's victim gasp.

The commotion caused the driver to spin back, and two things must have occurred to him at once: 1) someone was removing the rifle from his hands and 2) someone was thrusting a knife into his back, the blade quickly penetrating his heart.

The pain must have accompanied the horror of knowing he had seconds to live. He gasped, uttered something incomprehensible, then dropped in a heap to join his comrades.

Thorn was so amped up that he paced before the bodies, the knife jutting from his fist, his eyes threatening to explode in their sockets. He was a panther, and someone had slipped crack cocaine into his meal. "Dead fuckers! That's what I'm talking about! You fuck with Uncle Sam, and you ain't going home. Ever! Hooah! Adios, motherfuckers!"

Bender pulsed with the same near-orgasmic energy, but as a man with more experience, he had learned to control the rush, come down from it much more quickly. You had to—especially in a combat environment. Ironically, you were most vulnerable when you thought you had just kicked ass. There was often some clever asshole who had watched the whole thing and was aching to cut short your victory celebration.

With a quick wave of his hands, gesturing for Thorn to ease down, Bender said, "All right, get the bodies back into the truck and let's drive into the woods." He scooped up the man he had just killed and began hauling him toward the flatbed.

"Yo, Bender, it's Greene," came the man's voice through Bender's headset. "Something weird's going on. Not sure what the hell they're doing."

Bender groaned as he slung the dead man over his shoulders, then nearly lost his balance as he threw the guy onto the flatbed. "All right, what?"

"The mining guys or mercs have moved back toward the village, but there's one guy on the other side of the river. I don't see Savimbi's partner anywhere. Think he got away. But I saw another guy, real tall guy, beard, Caucasian. Don't know who he is, but the mining guys hauled him away like he was a prisoner, over."

"Let me phone home, see if anyone else is supposed to be operating around here. Maybe that guy is UNICEF or Red Cross or a missionary, who the fuck knows. Just keep an eye along that riverbank, out."

"He's right, you know," said Thorn, slapping a palm on Bender's shoulder. "This place is weird."

"Not weird. I would refer to it as a diverse community of rebels, thugs, and other assorted motherfuckers. But the bottom line is this: I want those diamonds. I want Kisantu. Dude, I want it all."

"Can't fault a man with ambition."

Bender grinned then hustled for the cab. They would stash the bodies in the woods, establish their perimeter, and take a much needed break while Greene fed them the news, and stock market and weather reports. Just another day in the jungle. Too bad the coffee wouldn't be hot.

Wolfgang rolled back and signaled for Drac to come over. Stoner in hand, breath mostly gone, Drac sank to his knees on Wolfgang's side of the hill and dug an index finger into one nostril.

"How'd the Deltas know that truck was coming?" asked Wolfgang.

Drac didn't react; he was too busy digging for gold and inspecting his progress.

"What do you think? They pulled up some satellite video? And who were those guys in the truck? You think they work for Kisantu? Come to pick up Jaga and the other guy?"

Drac shrugged, dug deeper.

"Dude, that's gross."

"Can't help it. You ever get one that's so deep it drives you nuts? I can't get it out."

Wolfgang made an ugly face then keyed his mike. He issued his report to Mad Dog, who returned a terse, "Roger that, stay with them."

Meanwhile, Pope called and asked Wolfgang to switch to another secure channel, where they could speak privately. "What's up, Bro?" Wolfgang asked.

"The spook's got Dan."

"What?"

"He sent some assholes to kidnap Dan. I'm guessing he hired some fucking rebels, maybe Abu Sayyaf, maybe even some scumbag al Qaeda jackoffs, so that if it goes south, they take the fall, not him."

"You're shitting me."

"Wish I were. I think bossman's going to lose it, and between you and me, I don't want Bibby running this show if it comes down to that. I'll be taking over. And don't give me any fucking shit."

"The bossman won't lose it, so forget your big dreams of playing God."

Drac lowered his binoculars and grabbed Wolfgang's arm. "There's a guy down there." He pointed toward the riverbank. "Right there. Delta . . ."

"Hey, numb nuts, I gotta go," Wolfgang said. Then he grabbed Drac's binocs and looked himself. "Yeah, that's one of 'em. He's picked out a nice little spot overlooking the entire bank and all the trees. He stays there, and we can't move without being seen."

"So we take him out?" Drac asked in disbelief.

"Well, we can go down there, try to capture him alive, or we can just leave him there and put on a little show."

"What do you mean?"

"I don't know what I mean. I'm thinking out loud, asshole."

"I could lay down some fire, distract him, while you move in. But you'd better call the boss first."

"Fuck that. He's got the spook to deal with right now. We're on our own."

"Maybe you should call back Pope?"

"Fuck him."

"Uh, not much of a team player, are you Wolfy?"

Wolfgang shook his head. "Shit . . . what're we going to do about this fuck?" He zoomed in with the binoculars on yet another man zooming in with his binoculars.

One of the mining managers had called Bibby to say that Kidman had just arrived on site and was demanding an update on their progress.

Meanwhile, Mad Dog, Rookie, Pope, the spook, and three locals were crowding around the truck, and the spook was demanding that Mad Dog transfer four million dollars from one of IPG's accounts into his own. Mad Dog was denying his request and repeatedly demanding to speak directly with Dan. The spook said the webcam images were real-time and should be enough. While they continued to square off like pit bulls circling each other, Bibby attempted to speak calmly and professionally with Morstarr's CEO:

"Yes, Mr. Kidman. We believe that Mr. Palansky's death was the result of a traitor on your security team. A man named Mbandi may very well have killed him. We also believe, and I have the phone records to confirm this, that someone at your office in Luanda is in contact with rebel forces in the Congo and may have arranged for the theft of your diamonds."

"Mr. Bibby your intelligence doesn't surprise me. There's someone I've suspected for a while now. I'll follow up on my end if you'd be willing to supply me with copies of those records. Can you do that, mate? Also, how far along are you?"

In Basic Sales 101 they taught you that it was best to keep the customer in a positive frame of mind. Thus Bibby offered a very encouraging report: they were in Tongaso and were very close to recovering the diamonds. Kidman was impressed, admitting that he didn't have high hopes for the recovery.

Bibby then made arrangements to email those phone records directly to Kidman, who said he would remain at the mining camp for the rest of the day and looked forward to the next update. In the meantime, he would take steps to see if he could handle his "internal problem" himself—which was just fine by Bibby. The team didn't need any more work or surprises.

Bibby got off the phone and regarded Mad Dog, who was leaning against the truck, looking about as haggard as Bibby had ever seen him. "What do you want me to do?"

Just then, Doolittle and Boo Boo descended the ridge and came onto the road, carrying the man whom Bibby had killed. Mad Dog shouted and waved them off toward the village, but it was too late. The tallest of the three men who were accompanying Judas became hysterical and charged forward.

"Friday!" cried Judas. "Come back here!"

Doolittle and Boo Boo dropped the body, grabbed their rifles, and stepped back as the tall guy named Friday collapsed before the body, sobbing and screaming.

"You've made a lot of friends here, haven't you?" Judas asked Mad Dog. "Oh, they just love ya."

"Call your buddies. I want to talk to Dan. If he's all right, then I'll transfer the money."

"Sure you will. Then you'll have your British geek

make it disappear from my account. I know how it works, Hertzog."

Mad Dog looked to Bibby, who most certainly had that in mind. But Bibby also had a few other ideas that he believed Judas would not anticipate. "Mr. Moody, I can assure you that once the funds are transferred, they will remain in your account, and you will be able to verify that via satellite phone, computer, whatever method you choose."

"How will I know ·you've released Dan?" Mad Dog asked.

"You can watch it on the Web. And at that point I *will* let you speak with him."

"Then let's do this now. Right now," said Mad Dog. He came toward the truck and lowered his voice. "A straight transfer. Nothing funny about it. Do you understand?"

Bibby nodded, though his mouth dropped. They were just handing over four million dollars. Mad Dog was too afraid to play any games. He was willing to pay anything to save Dan's life. And he was willing to work with the spook.

Maybe he thought there wasn't time to call Cebu and start an island-wide search.

But then he mouthed the words, "I want Dan found. And I want Uncle Jimmy ruined."

Ah, yes, Bibby thought. No need for further explanation. Bibby would demonstrate the length and breadth of his computer skills. And suddenly, technology wasn't quite as evil.

Pope was hating life, but it wouldn't be the first time, no, sir. It seemed the natives weren't just restless; at any moment, they'd be out for blood, and all he, Rookie, Boo Boo, and Doolittle could do was cover them, hope they didn't flip out, but if they did, he told the others to defend themselves. Mad Dog always supported that.

But the moment was getting even more tense, with the locals shouting at them now. Pope grimaced and shot a look toward Mad Dog. "Come on, Bossman, let's boogie. We should be down by the river, looking for the rocks."

Mad Dog waved him silent. He, Bibby, and Judas were fixated on Bibby's computer screen.

So Pope keyed his mike and called for Sapper again.

Waste of time.

What was that asshole doing? He'd gone AWOL all right. Maybe he was a rat fuck who'd been working for the CIA all along, tipping off Judas. Maybe he was a goddamned terrorist himself. But how the hell would he have concealed that all this time? Mad Dog routinely ran exhaustive background checks on them. Handshakes and smiles were never enough. In their business, trust was a rare commodity, earned over long periods of time. But even then, when large sums of money were involved, any dog could turn on you at any time.

"Still not answering?" asked Rookie with a snort. "I guess since he's on your fire team, that makes you responsible. That reflects badly on you."

"Shut up," Pope snapped. "Blackhound Five, I know you hear this, and if you don't respond right now, I'm going to—"

"Like he cares?" Rookie interrupted. "He probably found the rocks and took off."

Pope shook his head and grinned crookedly. He had to believe that Sapper knew exactly what he was doing, and what he was doing would help the team. He couldn't lose faith, but at any moment he'd be on a rescue mission to find his.

Jaga had drifted off to sleep, his body so battered and abused that it needed recovery and would not take no for an answer. There was no more fighting.

He lay there in the bushes, the tension seeping away from his muscles. He dreamed of his return to Kisantu with the diamonds, dreamed of the celebration and the great feast and the beautiful women. The fires carried the sweet scent of roasted pig throughout the camp, and the soft, cool waters of a bath trickled over his shoulders and head, washing away the caked blood and sweat. A fine woman disrobed before him, cupped her breasts, drove one of her nipples into his mouth while placing his palm on her rump. She breathed long and hard into his ear, whispered that she had been waiting for him.

But then she grabbed his shirt, suddenly wrenched him from the ground, whirled him around and took one of his arms, pulled it behind his back until the fires ignited. He screamed, opened his eyes—

And realized someone had just pulled him from the bushes and taken his pistol.

"All right, little homey," came a low, thick voice in English. "Easy now. Easy. We're going for a little swim across the river."

Jaga glanced down at the pistol held to his chest, at the hand holding it, a naturally black hand. His attacker had not disguised his skin like the other men who worked for the mining company. Jaga had encountered this man before, had heard one of the others call him "Sapper."

* * *

So he wanted to save the day, but if he tipped off the other guys, they'd rob him of the glory, especially Pope, that greedy bastard. And so it had gone down like this: Sapper had caught a glimpse of Jaga on the opposite riverbank and had had a good idea of where the guy might be hiding. Share that with the others? Bullshit. He played ghost and slipped off on his own to get the job done. Team player? Sometimes. But not when it came to this shit. He knew he could find the little guy if he wasn't hauling along baggage, namely another merc. And yo, it worked. Should he call Papa Dog?

Not yet. Make him sweat.

Sapper was going to go one better. He'd earn some serious respect, the kind that their new boy Rookie only dreamed of. He would get Jaga across the river, then he and the boy would recover the diamonds. Then he and the boy would head up to the village. Game over. Sapper bags a bonus. Hell, he'd even recovered the pistol Mad Dog had given the kid. Sure, Sapper had heard that the pistol didn't work, but little homey didn't know that.

The hard part was getting Jaga to understand what he wanted. He shoved him forward, and they started up the hill, bound for the riverbank. "We swim," Sapper said, wishing he could demonstrate with his hands. But those hands were busy, holding a pistol and a wrist.

Knowing a few words in Portuguese would have helped. Mad Dog had told them to study up before they had left, but the language book and CD had given Sapper a headache. Leave that crap to Doolittle.

And pretty soon, as they came down the next hill, nearing the muddier ground along the river, Jaga knew exactly what Sapper had in mind. Boy, did the little fucker struggle to break free. But Sapper probably weighed twice as much as the man. Jaga was a mouse on his hind legs, trying to topple a brick wall. They reached the riverbank.

Then Sapper released him, aimed at the bandit's head. "Let's go. Swim." He gestured with the weapon.

A chill ripped across Sapper's neck, reminding him that they could be spotted. The guy needed to move. Now!

Jaga glanced to his right, his left, as though looking for an opening to bolt.

Sapper's teeth came together. "Go!"

The bandit was visibly trembling, and Sapper could almost hear the rumbling fear inside the guy's head.

Abruptly, he faced the river, then with legs appearing as heavy as cast iron, he trudged into the murky water.

Wolfgang lay his binoculars on the grass, then held his breath. He was about to give Drac the signal to open fire. Wolfgang had reasoned that trying to capture the Delta guy fell somewhere between stupid and suicidal, though it leaned more to the right.

So they would try to get him on the move, force him farther east into a shitty location where he couldn't see as much of the valley, keep him pinned down via occasional fire so that the team could return to the bank to search for the diamonds—when Mad Dog finished playing with the spook.

Although Wolfgang had told Drac that they were on their own, he was feeling a little guilty about that, and he knew that once they fired, Mad Dog would want a report, anyway—and by then he'd be too busy, and it'd be too late.

He keyed his mike. "Blackhound One, this is Seven.

We're going to lay down some fire so we can force one Delta operator east, away from the bank. We need to keep the search area clear for observation, standby."

Wolfgang looked to Drac, who had just set down his binoculars and was wide-eyed, wagging his head, and pointing emphatically toward the river.

What the fuck? Wolfgang grabbed his binoculars, and holy shit, there they were, two men swimming toward the bank.

The image was indistinct at first, just silhouettes, figures, nothing specific until he zoomed in, saw a ball cap, a beefy black face, noted the scrawny guy in the lead.

Sapper and Jaga.

Holy shit and holy shit.

Wolfgang's voice trembled with excitement. "Blackhound One, this is Seven. Holding fire. Looks like Five has caught our runner, Jaga. They're swimming across the river now, coming toward the bank. Repeat, Five has caught our runner, over."

Drac charged over, plopped onto the hillside beside Wolfgang, his breathing hard, his stutter kicking in equally hard. "Sapper's got him. But, uh, that, uh that Delta guy's going to, uh, fuck it all up. We gotta take him out!"

"We can't do that!"

"Then we have to do something! Distract him like we thought. Something."

"I don't know if Sapper's listening right now. Our diversion might help the little guy escape again."

"Fuck!"

"But you know what?" Wolfgang added. "We gotta take a shot. Get ready on your Stoner my friend. We're moving up to make big fire and big boom. Ready?"

Drac nodded vigorously. "What the hell. Should you call Mad Dog?"

Wolfgang smiled. "You're always asking that. I should. But he'll figure it out."

They exchanged another nod, then rushed over the hill and came barreling down toward the Delta guy's position, just as Jaga and Sapper were nearing the riverbank.

Wolfgang had a grenade in each hand. He had fire in his heart. He wanted to drum fists on his chest and howl.

Too bad he didn't have a camera. He could film the whole thing, show it to chicks when he was trying to impress them into bed. Some of the more venturesome types would really get off on this.

Wolfgang let the grenades fly.

Yes, that Delta Force operator would be safe from shrapnel, but the flashing and banging would be loud enough to send him into high gear and get him madder than when he watched Chuck Norris's inaccurate Hollywood betrayal of his unit and the operators who staffed it.

Boom! Boom!

Well, those were technical terms to describe both explosions and sex, so Wolfgang's thoughts really hadn't strayed too far from the task at hand.

And neither had Drac's. Those booms were his cue. And the rat-tat-tat of his Stoner was Wolfgang's cue to stop, drop down to one knee, raise his sniper rifle and fire at the tree nearest Mr. Delta.

Even Thor himself would've winced at the sound of Wolfgang's rifle. Thor himself would've thrown down his hammer and demanded an RT–20 for himself.

Consequently (and with no surprise), the tree exploded, pieces hurtling in all directions, even as the Delta guy darted off, firing wildly up the hill, clearly unsure of his attackers' positions.

"On the deck!" cried Wolfgang, and together they dropped onto their guts, out of sight, a wall of mud and grass above them, the Delta guy on the other side, still firing.

Wolfgang waited another three, maybe four seconds, then he said, "Okay, to the river, now!"

They took off, just as the Delta guy ceased firing. Wolfgang knew that if he and Drac could come around, putting themselves into the guy's original position, they'd have him partially cut off from Sapper and Jaga. What now scared him, though, was that they had lost sight of the Delta guy, which could nix the plan. And worse, losing sight of anyone with that kind of training could be exceedingly lethal.

The second Mad Dog heard that Sapper had caught Jaga, he ordered Pope, Rookie, and Boo Boo down to the river to assist. There was no way in hell they'd let that bandit escape again. One fuckup was embarrassing enough.

And wasn't Sapper's timing just grand? Mad Dog was in the middle of trying to free Dan and ruin Judas. Part of him wanted to stay, while the other part wanted to rush down there and nab Jaga himself, then whack Sapper with a big stick for acting on his own (just before he kissed him, of course). What the hell was the matter with that guy?

For the moment, Mad Dog stood there by the truck, literally trembling, while Doolittle covered Friday and the other two locals, Mad Dog keeping the spook at bay with his carbine. He imagined what he'd do to Judas if something happened to Dan. That old man was all Mad Dog had. And fucking Judas had known that.

But what he didn't know was that while Mad Dog clung fiercely to his personal honor, he had decided that if push came to shove, everyone was expendable: Judas, the Deltas, the locals, members of his own team . . . All laws would be broken: military, international, you name 'em, because when it came down to it, nothing mattered if he couldn't save Dan. Nothing at all. The line had been crossed.

"What's going on?" Judas demanded, distant gunfire punctuating his words.

"Things are happening fast," said Mad Dog in the exaggerated tone of an escaped mental patient. "I hope you can reach your friends back in Cebu."

"All right, Mr. Moody," called Bibby from the truck. "The money has been transferred. However, if you fail to release Dan within the next eight hours, I have several communiqués on time release, and a couple of programs that will pose some interesting problems for you, particularly with your government credit card. If Dan dies, or if I do, there will be no way to stop them."

"Oh, fuck you, you pretentious Brit."

"No, I believe we'll be the ones doing the fucking, thank you. Are you familiar with any of the kiddie porn sites online? And are you familiar with the new international terrorist watch database?" Bibby didn't give Judas time to answer, he kept firing away. "And perhaps you are aware of a certain network in the Middle East that likes to expose U.S. spies. Your cover is a uniquely valuable asset that I suppose you want to protect. Again, if Dan's not released in eight hours, the consequences for your career will be dire. But then again I suppose, too, that you would not survive such a double cross."

Judas chuckled, his face growing flush. "If that money disappears . . ." His gaze darted from the truck to the hills, and abruptly, he shifted away from the threat, tugging nervously on his beard. "And hey, do you think any of that threatens me? I've been doing this for a long time, Governor. Do you know how many times I've heard that?"

Bibby was an expert at the smug smile. He demonstrated.

But the spook was too self-absorbed to notice. "Do you realize how inadequate those databases are? I've used them for years, and they've failed me nearly every time. Besides, my colleagues would know someone set me up, especially when it comes to your pathetic kiddie porn threat." Judas frowned at Mad Dog. "You can't do better than this?"

"Nice bluff, asshole. We got you by the balls. And if you want me to do better, I'll shoot you in the head, dismember you, burn the body parts, burn the village, kill all the witnesses, then go home and smoke a cigar. So fuck you very much, you fucking nerd."

Judas gave a little snort, averted his gaze.

Mad Dog noted another slight nod from Bibby, and he read that as a sign that a rescue operation had already been ordered. Mad Dog's strong connections with the Philippine army were paying off, and a team of commandoes, assisted by Mad Dog's security team, would quickly assemble to find Dan.

Now in theory, they wouldn't need to scour the entire island because old Dan was wearing a Swiss Army officer's watch containing a personal locator beacon, though Mad Dog had purchased it for an entirely different reason.

There was an incident the previous year when Dan's blood sugar had fallen to dangerously low levels, causing him to become confused and wander off the estate. It had taken Mad Dog nearly ten hours to find the man, and Dan had nearly slipped into a coma. Talk about a heart-pounder.

Thus, the beacon was a simple insurance policy. Mad Dog had purchased them for his team and figured he'd throw one Dan's way. Good decision, though it was hard to tell in the webcam video whether he was wearing the watch or not, but their security chief back home said they had just picked up a signal. Judas probably hadn't lied about Dan still being on Cebu; the old man was some serious baggage, and moving him too far would be a real pain in the ass.

Mad Dog smiled to himself. Dan was probably giving his kidnappers hell. By now they wanted to kill themselves after listening to him bitch and moan so much.

Judas, who seemed to grow more calm, thought a moment, rubbed his sore ribs, then said, "I want to verify the transfer on my own computer. It's back in my hut."

"Then let's go," said Mad Dog. "You'll verify, then you'll order Dan released."

Judas just looked at Mad Dog, then turned and started away. "No one trusts anyone," he called back. "Not a good way to do business."

"Business? You call this business?"

The spook didn't answer.

"You want all of us to go?" asked Doolittle.

Mad Dog regarded the translator and nodded. Then another volley of gunfire drove him to go on the radio. "Blackhound Four, this is One. SITREP, over!"

*   *   *

Pope stood in shock as the truck came thundering down the hill, nearly running over Wolfgang and Drac, who each dove to one side, as though they'd been running directly in front of the old heap. It was like a goddamned movie, so surreal that it took Pope a couple more seconds to raise his submachine gun.

One of the Deltas was hanging out of the passenger's side window, firing at Wolfgang and Drac—or more precisely, firing at the dirt alongside them. That shooter had a bead on both men. Pope answered the shooter's fire, rounds ripping along the bottom of the truck's door. Another salvo directed at the front tire missed big time. Shit.

Meanwhile, Sapper was near two trees, and Jaga had just scooped up something from the mud. It had to be the diamonds—but even as Sapper was about to reach for them, a man rushed up behind him. Another Delta? Pope wasn't sure. He kept dividing his attention between the oncoming truck and Sapper. The truck was headed right for him, even as Rookie and Boo Boo fired warning salvos parallel to its path.

Another look to Sapper.

Was that him, running toward the truck with Jaga? No, it wasn't. It was one of the Delta operators, and there, over near the tree, was Sapper lying flat on his back.

Pope started jogging to his left, out of the truck's path, even as he screamed on the radio, "Blackhound One, our runner is getting away with the stash! He's heading for a truck full of Delta guys. We need our ride down here ASAP!"

"Let me shoot them!" cried Rookie from somewhere behind Pope. "I got a clean fucking shot!"

"No!" hollered Pope.

"I'm taking fire from the Deltas!" cried Rookie.

"Hold yours for now, asshole! Boo Boo, check on Sapper!"

The medic suddenly raced across the hillside, opening fire on Jaga and the other guy as they approached the truck. It was just covering fire, stitching very wide, but enough to drive Jaga and the Delta guy away from the truck.

"Rookie?" Pope called.

No answer. He tried the radio. Nothing.

Pope spun around, ran back toward where Rookie had been positioned, along a deep cut in the hill. He figured the two of them would take out the truck's wheels if he could get Rookie back up top. Gunfire woke in his footsteps.

He reached the crest of the hill, ready to drop down into the cut. A glimpse ahead robbed his breath.

Rookie was slumped forward, his rifle pinned beneath him. "Rookie, you dumb fuck!"

Pope leaped down, nearly collided with the man. He rolled him over. Too many gunshot wounds to count. One to the head. Bloody face. Hands still quivering. Jesus, God, the Delta guys had got him.

An engine roared somewhere up on the road. That was the pickup coming down.

A shudder tore through Pope as he put his ear to Rookie's lips, trying to hear or feel any breath signs.

And suddenly Pope was back on that beach, listening to his mom scream about watching after his fire team, his men.

Jesus Christ, Rookie!

The guy had simply obeyed orders. Pope's orders.

Somewhere on the other side of the hill, a door

slammed on the Delta operators' truck, and the engine revved. They'd be history in a few seconds.

Pope needed to stop them, but he couldn't help himself. He couldn't move. He could barely key his mike:

"Blackhound One, this is Four. We got men down. Five and Six are down! I say again, we have men down!"

Chapter 12

....

Bender was driving the truck and shouting at Dzoba, who had been hanging out the window and returning fire on the mining guys. "You hit him! He's down!"

"I didn't mean to," cried Dzoba.

"You killed him, you asshole!"

"Fuck 'em! They don't know who we are!"

Bender banged a fist on the steering wheel. "Well, if they ever find out, we got a big fucking problem, don't we?"

Greene and Jaga had just hopped in back and slammed the tailgate shut. Thorn and Jaga were bouncing Portuguese off each other. Greene was screaming that they had the diamonds in hand and should exit fucking yesterday. He had held up a fist containing a leather pouch that assumedly held the diamonds. Bender was no diamond expert, and he wasn't sure that even examining the rocks would prove anything. They could be carrying fakes, but Jaga had been willing to risk his life for them, and that had to be enough for now—at least enough to get them back to Kisantu.

Roufai was in the truck, too, saying about as much as your average gagged man.

"Just head north up the river," said Dzoba, still hanging out of the window. "There's another truck back there! They're coming! Move it!"

Jaga didn't trust these men, even though the one they called Thorn had assured him that they were taking the diamonds back to Kisantu. Thorn said that Roufai was a traitor whom Kisantu would deal with later. All Jaga knew for certain was that he was getting away from Morstarr's security people and that these men, whoever they really were, wanted to do likewise. So for the moment, they were allies.

The moment did not last long.

Greene suddenly grabbed Jaga's wrists and bound them behind his back with a pair of heavy steel handcuffs.

"What are you doing?" Jaga demanded.

"It's okay," said Thorn. "We'll let you go when we reach Kisantu. But for now, we want you to stay with us. It's for your own good."

"Who are you? You don't work for Kisantu."

"Yes, we do. We work for him and his friends. But we are very cautious."

Jaga doubted that. But what did it matter? He was now their prisoner, and they had the diamonds. He closed his eyes and hung his head as the truck bounced and weaved forward.

Thorn put a hand on his shoulder. "Don't worry. We won't hurt you. You'll be okay."

"No, I will be dead. Soon."

Thorn glanced away.

"Will you kill Kisantu when you find him? Because I want you to know that killing him will not stop the revolution. The war will come no matter what you do."

Boo Boo helped Sapper sit up. The Delta guy had given him a good whack on the side of the head, otherwise he was all right. That made two mercs with head trauma. Boo Boo sighed. They came in threes. One more merc to go.

"So you're alive, asshole," he told Sapper, quickly examining the man's eyes and ears. All clear. "I need to go check on Rookie."

Grunting that he was most certainly too old for this marathon shit, Boo Boo hightailed his weary ass across the hills toward where Pope was waving.

Just behind the former SEAL, Bibby was rumbling down the hill in their pickup truck, with Mad Dog in the passenger's seat, and, lo and behold, Doolittle and Jimmy Judas in the back. Why Mad Dog had allowed the spook to ride along was beyond Boo Boo . . . Better to just go with the goddamned flow.

He was fighting for breath by the time he reached Pope, who stood over Rookie. Pope's eyes were wide and bloodshot. "I told him to hold fire."

"Aw, fuck." Boo Boo dropped to his knees. Rookie's neck felt cold. No pulse. He had bled out fast.

"Let's get him up." Pope seized one of Rookie's arms, then his hip. Boo Boo helped Pope lift their fallen comrade onto his shoulders.

They turned to the truck as it slid down the hill, Bibby braking hard and kicking up thick waves of mud.

"Get in!" cried Mad Dog.

"He's gone, Bossman," Pope said. "Rookie's gone."

Mad Dog closed his eyes and cursed as Pope and Boo Boo hustled around to the back of the truck, where Doolittle was waiting to help receive Rookie's body.

"What the fuck are you doing here?" Pope asked Judas.

The spook twisted his lip, baring a crooked tooth. "I'm bumming a ride. Fuck you."

"Sapper's over there," Boo Boo said, pointing toward the trees for Bibby's benefit. "But we have to hurry. They got a good lead on us."

"No shit!" hollered Pope.

"I liked him," said Doolittle, shaking his head in disbelief, his gaze fixed on Rookie. "He was cocky, but deep down, honorable, you know? Like maybe his ancestors."

Boo Boo hopped into the truck, then Wolfgang and Drac crammed in behind him, both visibly stunned by Rookie's corpse though they didn't comment beyond a few expletives.

Bibby floored it and fishtailed, throwing everyone sideways before he regained control.

Despite the potholes and ruts that continued to toss him, Boo Boo leaned over Rookie's body and forced the eyelids shut. He put his hand on the man's forehead and said a prayer for his soul.

No, Boo Boo wasn't much of a churchgoer, and he didn't seek out the Lord very much. Shit, he wasn't even sure if Rookie was a Christian himself. But it felt like the right thing to do. Rookie was the first man the team had ever lost, and it had been a long time since Boo Boo had been confronted by the dead. He could've waited longer. A whole lot longer.

"Lost one, huh?" asked Judas.

Boo Boo withdrew a poncho from his ruck, then began wrapping it over Rookie as a sign of respect and to keep down the distraction. When he was finished, he eyed Judas and said, "You're a fucking idiot, you know that?"

Judas's gaze went skyward as he snorted. "You should've let my boys back in the village take him. No need to be riding with a corpse."

"You'd best shut up," said Pope. "Otherwise *we'll* be riding with two."

"Oh, yeah, SEAL? I die, so does old Dan. Your boss wants me alive more than you. So you'd better get used to me. I'm the star of this show."

"Get in!" Mad Dog ordered Sapper.

"Hey, I'm sorry," cried the man, still rubbing his shoulder. "I had the guy, and he got the stash! It was right there . . . right there!" He extended his palm to demonstrate.

"Just get in the fucking truck! I'll tear you a new asshole later!"

The big guy swaggered to the back, where Pope extended a mighty arm and hauled him aboard.

"They're heading north up the river," said Bibby, throwing them back in gear. "Probably toward shallow water. According to our map, there aren't any bridges suitable for vehicles north of this area, just one footbridge a couple of klicks up."

"Maps lie—especially those old ones from the DoD," said Mad Dog.

"I know, but I checked the map against the satellite photos. The bridge to the south that could've supported us was blown up. You can see the debris. That truck's probably from the Congo as well, and it got here somehow. There's got to be low-water crossing somewhere."

"All right, we'll look for it. Just don't lose them." Mad Dog winced over the words. His nerves were talking for him, shit.

And worse, his heart was sinking fast to the floorboard. They had actually lost a man, the new guy, of course. You either bought it as the FNG (Fucking New Guy) or the veteran on his last mission. Call it the irony of the universe, Murphy's Law, or whatever you wanted.

Rookie was a good man, cocky enough to make him a great operator. Now Mad Dog felt as hollow as he had on the day Eddy and Doc had died, like some invisible hand was squeezing his gut, forcing the air out of his lungs, killing him slowly, allowing him enough time to remember that he was responsible for each man, merc or not, and that he and he alone must accept and bear the loss—not Pope, who was already blaming himself.

He glanced back at the others through the open rear window, stained by a light rain. Sapper was getting the heads-up on Rookie's death from Pope. Both men were blinking hard, trying to stave off the emotions.

And there was Mr. James Moody. Jimmy Judas. Uncle Jimmy.

Son of a bitch.

The prick hadn't had time to verify the transfer, so he'd demanded to come with them after the diamonds. He said he wanted to ensure that the rocks were returned, too. And he'd have his cronies kill Dan if he didn't get his way. Mad Dog had no time to argue with the idiot. Judas was outnumbered, anyway, so fuck him, let him come along.

The truth was, the second Mad Dog knew that Dan was safe, he'd have Bibby withdraw that money from Judas's account, although Bibby had said a hack like that might take some time and that Judas could freeze the account while Bibby was working. If that happened, Bibby's withdrawal could very well be detected despite him trying to disguise it as one of the more common bank scams like "phishing." Mad Dog didn't pretend to understand the particulars involved—so long as he got his money back. Bibby swore he could do it, and the Brit rarely made promises about anything, let alone four million bucks.

And now it was hardball time. A man was dead. Dan had been kidnapped. Four million plus another two was up for grabs.

But would Mad Dog really play that hard? Could he ever give the order to fire on the Delta operators with the intent to kill?

Was everyone really expendable?

He cursed aloud.

Bibby glanced at him. "Are you okay, Mr. Hertzog?"

"Shut the fuck up and drive."

The Brit returned a glower, then concentrated on the riverbank ahead.

Half a minute ticked by, the whining protests of the engine and rattling suspension the only noises.

"Hey, I'm just . . . there's too much shit going down," Mad Dog suddenly said. He softened his voice. "I need to clear my head."

"You will. And I'm sorry about Rookie. Bloody fuck-ing shame."

"He knew the drill. Maybe he was coming up to take a shot. Maybe that's what got him killed." Mad Dog's voice had gone cold, but he couldn't escape the suffocat-ing pain. He withdrew the laptop computer from beneath the seat and opened it. "I want to pull up the maps and photos. Maybe I can find something. That low-water crossing, who knows."

"Maybe you should drive."

"You got the head trauma. You get the least demand-ing task right now."

"Is that how you rationalized it? I suggest you take a look at these roads. And by the way, it's raining again."

"Most people in the U.S. drive like they got head trauma. Just move it." Mad Dog inputted the computer's password, then watched the screen ripple to life. He glanced at Bibby, who looked deep in thought. "Hey, I know that look, the one I don't like. Talk to me."

"You really want to hear this?"

"Talk!"

"Well, the way I see it, Delta now has the diamonds, and they might have a lead on Kisantu's whereabouts. We can only hope their mission is to stop the diamond transfer and take out Kisantu, both of which would ben-efit the United States—and us. So technically speaking, they might be allies."

"Allies? They just killed Rookie."

"But they don't know who we are—or at least they think we work for Morstarr," Bibby countered.

"So we have to stop them before they reach Kisantu."

"They'll use the diamonds as bait, draw him in, take him out."

"And there goes our fee."

Mad Dog sighed loudly. "Anything else from Big Booty?"

"She says Kisantu has about forty men, so we'd be slightly outnumbered, though not outwitted."

"I'm not witty, and I'm no math guy. It's all giving me a headache."

Bibby cocked a brow. "That makes two of us."

Kisantu Base Camp
Jungle Somewhere West of Kamina
The Congo
0920 Hours Local Time

Mboma Kisantu wound up, ready to pitch the cell phone across the tent.

Then he stopped himself. No. Would a great leader let his temper get the best of him?

He squeezed the phone, took a deep breath.

The men he had sent in the second truck had not contacted him. He had given them specific orders to call once they picked up their cargo. Calls to them had gone unanswered.

Kisantu lowered his arm, took a deep breath, willed himself to relax. He would address this problem with his intellect, not his temper.

He got on his radio, ordered his team of three scouts to move farther west, toward the border, expanding their reconnaissance. They knew this region well and often fled across the border when the army swept the area, searching for them. If the truck did return, they would catch its approach. Nothing would slip by them. Kisantu had handpicked those three. Their skills, however, hardly calmed him. He kept thinking about that truck, kept reaching the same conclusion:

Jaga and Savimbi had already been caught—even before the first truck had broken down. Kisantu had sent the men in that second truck into a trap. They, too, were not returning.

And worse, if they were tortured, then they might give up his location, so he had already told his men to begin packing. They would move again, come nightfall.

Kisantu would turn thirty in the current year, and he firmly believed that it was his year to shine. God wanted him to lead his people to freedom. All he needed was a strong army to seize back control of their nation. Those diamonds represented the money to do that. It was the future. It was everything.

The satellite phone rang, startling him. He checked the display, then swallowed hard before answering.

His friends in al Qaeda had little patience, and he feared how they might react to yet another delay. They assumed he was already on his way back with the diamonds in hand.

When he told them that he had yet to hear from his men, they ordered him back to the river. He was to take his two remaining trucks to Tongaso himself and find out what had happened.

He should not return without the diamonds.

The man on the other end implied that if he did, they would find another man to assume his leadership. Kisantu swore to them that he would have the diamonds, that he would lead his people to freedom.

Abu Sayyaf Safe House
Cebu, the Philippines
1620 Hours Local Time

They had cuffed Dan's ankles and wrists, but at least they hadn't drawn his arms behind his back. The old wooden chair was uncomfortable as hell, and that goddamned computer with its little camera attached hummed and rattled like it was on its last legs. But it didn't whir as loudly as the fan near the cracked window. That piece of crap should be put out of its misery, along with the rest of the goddamned shack.

The one guy, whom Dan had nicknamed Shitforbrains, was a little chimpanzee with slightly less hair and more narrow eyes. Dan's other captor, "Artfag," was a taller guy with an Adam's apple jutting from his stubbly neck like a little pecker. He wore narrow, purple-framed glasses like he was some light-loafered artist from New York City instead of a fucking scumbag thug who'd been hired to kidnap him.

Dan might be a half-senile bastard whose short-term memory wasn't so good—or was it? He couldn't remember . . . But he knew some shit must be going down in Angola, and that the stench had finally reached him. They were blackmailing the kid, no doubt, and had waited until the nest was nearly empty. Michael had a soft heart, damn it, and he'd probably bargain with the assholes, even though he shouldn't.

Shitforbrains and Artfag spoke in Tagalog, the Filipino national language, but they occasionally switched to broken English to take calls.

A few times Dan thought he recognized Arabic, too, which suggested that these two fucks might be members of Abu Sayyaf, the local rebel group in the Philippines that had direct ties to al Qaeda.

Over the years Abu Sayyaf had become notorious for their kidnappings and murders, and they'd been exceedingly difficult to wipe out, even after several of their leaders were caught or killed. There was always some other schmuck with delusions of grandeur who would take charge of those poor kids and pay them much more than they'd receive for legitimate work—not unlike the lure of dealing drugs in the inner cities of the U.S.

IPG often helped the Philippine army better deal with the rebels by providing ordnance and intelligence, though the Filipinos took great pride in addressing the problem themselves. Michael had to be very careful not to overstep his bounds with them; their egos were tremendous.

Dan shifted his ass on the chair for the nth time. Okay, so it wouldn't be too long now. He was missing, and help would be on the way, thanks to the beacon Michael had forced him to wear, though his wrist was now bare. However, the beacon was exactly where it needed to be.

Dan's new friends had looked at his watch when they'd first captured him, and Shitforbrains had decided that he liked it, so there it was, dangling loosely from his hairy wrist. The dumb fuck occasionally played with it, too, wearing a silly grin, like he had gas.

Joke was on him, of course. He had painted a target on his back, and Dan imagined a giant missile hurtling down from the heavens, homing in on him and impacting with a magnificent blast.

When the dust settled, there'd be a huge crater, and sitting on its rim would be the scorched watch . . . still ticking, of course.

Jungle North of Tongaso
Near Congo Border, Angola
0925 Hours Local Time

Dzoba wasn't finding shit, and Bender was a half second away from blowing both nuts. "Come on, asshole!"

"I'm looking! Too many obstructions. Hard to tell the depth," the man cried.

Bender called back on the radio to Thorn, who'd been trying to get more information from Roufai about how he had crossed over the river.

The man had finally broken down, said there was an area of low water and gravel where a truck could pass. It would be easier if Roufai were up front with them, but Bender couldn't waste the time to stop. The other truck carrying the mining guys or mercs was still tailing.

"I'll have him keep an eye out back," Thorn said. "Maybe he'll see something."

"Are there any landmarks?"

After a moment, Thorn said there weren't, but that you could see the low water quite obviously.

"You hear that?" Bender asked Dzoba. "Come on. Pay attention."

"Oh, I am. Those guys in the truck are closing on us!"

Wolfgang steadied himself for a shot. If he could take out a rear tire on the Delta truck, he'd be a hero in the next minute. His hero status would last another minute, then he'd return to being just another mercenary asshole with a love for weaponry and long-limbed lesbians. All-American guy.

He had elbows propped on the roof of the truck's cab, and had enlisted Drac and Sapper to hold him steady as he peered through the open iron sights installed on his G36c carbine's Picatinny rail, which was manufactured by those good folks in New Jersey who liked shooting shit as much as he did.

Could he get a bead on that tire, about a hundred yards ahead of them?

Not with all the damned rain coming down now. And not with the friggin' Brit driving like a drunken redneck out for a weekend of offroading.

On the outside chance that he could hit something else, like the fuel tank—maybe rupture it without blowing those guys to Kingdom Come—Wolfgang tried for the wheel, saw it shift out of his sight, but he fired anyway.

His senses told him everything was right. The weapon vibrated, and the gunpowder clung tightly to his nostrils, smelling like a T-bone hot off the grill. Hell, he could even taste it.

Except his eyes were telling him that the rest of his senses were full of shit. He hadn't hit a thing. The truck rumbled on, unaffected by some winking, soaking-wet asshole with bad aim.

Sure, he might have had better luck with his RT–20, but then he would most certainly have blown that truck into another time zone and launched its inhabitants into orbit.

"Let me try," said Pope. "Come on, Wolfgang!"

"You can't see shit," snapped Wolfgang. "Forget it, man. We're still out of range."

"Blackhound team, this is Blackhound One," called Mad Dog. "I see your fire has had no effect. Hold fire until we come within better range, out."

"What'd I tell ya?" Wolfgang asked.

Suddenly, incoming pinged off the rails and echoed

ahead—just as Mr. Bibby veered sharply to the left, taking them up a small embankment, the truck listing hard to the right.

"Everybody get down!" hollered Pope. Then he was screaming to Mad Dog that the Deltas were returning fire.

"Stay down, they won't keep it up," said Mad Dog. "They're letting us know they don't like our bullets."

"Oh, yeah?" grunted Wolfgang. He dragged himself past Doolittle, hung himself over the rail, fighting against gravity, and let loose with a pair of wild salvos that he hoped returned the message.

Pope went ape shit, screaming for him to cease fire.

"What?" asked Wolfgang, squeezing off his third volley. "I can't hear you!"

Kisantu rode in the lead truck, and as they came up and over a steep hill, the engine roaring under the boot of Jonas, his confidant and boyhood friend, Kisantu stuck his head out the window, into the heavy rain, and watched in horror as the second truck began sliding back, into a deep mud puddle at the base of the hill.

"Stop the truck!" he ordered.

"Let me get up top first." Jonas gunned the engine once more, reached the crest of the hill, then braked suddenly as a few of the men on the flatbed began shouting that the truck below was kicking up mud, digging deeper into the puddle.

Kisantu jumped out and rushed down to the second truck, whose driver, Carlito, was not prone to making such mistakes. Kisantu had fought alongside the man many times in the past year, considered him both courageous and reliable. "You should have taken this hill on an angle," he shouted, his voice nearly lost in the engine sounds and thumping of rain.

"I know! But the rain is washing it all out!"

Kisantu crossed to the tailgate and regarded the men huddled beneath the tarpaulin. "Get the planks and rope!"

Two men leapt from the flatbed, while two more handed them long wooden planks already scored by rubber and used to help free the tires from muddy holes.

"Faster!" Kisantu cried, his voice cracking in frustration. "Attach the rope!"

With good timing, a little luck, and a sufficient supply of alcohol, most plans could survive at least their first moments of life. After that, you'd need better timing, a shitload of luck, and top shelf merely to make things happen.

Mad Dog was 0 for 3.

What he did have, however, was a burning desire to prove to himself that even a job as screwed up as the current one was still salvageable. He had to play it out; he owed that to Jack and to Rookie.

He tried calling back to his security chief in Cebu, but he couldn't get the call through. Interference from the storm, who knew? The maps hadn't helped locate a low-water crossing, but Mad Dog figured that now Delta team would help them find it. Mr. Bibby was doing a damned fine job keeping them out of the mud, though he was blinking hard behind his narrow-rimmed glasses. Twice Mad Dog asked if he was all right, and twice he had snapped, "Yes, damn it!"

Wolfgang had finally ceased firing, and while Mad Dog was glad for that, he couldn't deny that having a monster like Wolfgang on his team was necessary, even important. He'd cut the guy's leash when the time came.

And he was one werewolf who laughed at silver bullets.

In the meantime, they kept the Delta operators within their sights. Mad Dog leaned forward, gleaning what he could from his binoculars. There were a few guys inside the covered flatbed, whose rear flaps occasionally swung open. Two of the men Mad Dog assumed were Delta Force; the other two were definitely locals, and yet a closer inspection revealed that one guy was, in fact, Jaga, his hands bound behind his back, just like the other guy, whom Mad Dog did not recognize.

All right, where were the diamonds? They could very well be with one of the two Delta operators sitting in the back. Sapper had said they were inside a leather pouch. So how were they supposed to "recover" the gems from some of the most highly trained, lethal men in the world? Appeal to their greed? Mad Dog doubted that would work.

God, it was hard to concentrate when his thoughts were torn between the moment and what was happening back on Cebu. Too many questions. But old Dan . . . he just had to hang in there. And the commandoes . . . they just couldn't fuck up. *God, please, no, don't let them do something stupid.*

A tremendous boom resounded ahead, hurling mud and debris across their windshield—

And Mr. Bibby swore and cut the wheel hard, even as shrapnel drummed across the truck's side.

"What the fuck was that? Grenade?" cried Mad Dog.

"I think so!"

Bender hadn't seen Dzoba pull the grenade from his vest, but he'd heard it, all right. "What the fuck are you doing?"

"Don't worry! Just slowing them down!"

"Dude, you're already on my shit list."

"We can't let 'em catch up to us. What're we going to do? Tell 'em, hi, we're SpecOps, sorry to bother you?" Dzoba tugged free another grenade. "Don't worry, I'll force 'em off the road, get 'em stuck."

"Hey, Bender," cried Thorn over the radio. "Our guy says the crossing's coming up!"

"He's going to toss another grenade!" hollered Mad Dog.

Mr. Bibby was already anticipating big boom number two. He steered them off the path and between a few rows of bushes as the grenade exploded harmlessly in their dissipating exhaust fumes. Then he rolled right, the truck bouncing hard until they got back onto the path, spun out, then straightened.

But now they were bound for a massive puddle spanning the entire path and growing by the second. Waves to the left revealed where the Delta guys had passed through, so Bibby followed their lead.

Water rushed up into door cracks and began leaking into the cab as they plowed on through, Bibby shouting that the engine could stall at any second.

The engine coughed, shook hard, and then . . . fuckin' A it didn't stall! Bibby revved up, guided them up and onto the path.

And there, only fifty or so yards ahead, were the Delta guys, sweeping closer to the trees dotting the riverbank, rain bands partially obscuring their truck and shaking the tarpaulin over their flatbed. The driver was veering madly between puddles and ruts, then he suddenly cut the wheel right, as though turning a ninety-degree corner.

"The crossing has to be down there," said Mr. Bibby—

Just as a brilliant flash shone ahead, followed by a crack and boom.

Mr. Bibby tugged the steering wheel, and the truck suddenly lurched to the left, breaking into a three-sixty spin, even as the explosion continued to rise.

And then they began slipping down an embankment that washed out toward the riverbank. Bibby had lost all control of the truck.

They were carried along by torrents of rainwater and mud, swept down the embankment sideways, the truck coming up on two tires for a second, coming down, hitting a rut, coming up again, just as Pope and Wolfgang screamed for everyone to bail out.

A pair of seconds later, the truck rolled onto its side, the window nearest Mad Dog smashing loudly, safety glass blasting into his face.

Mr. Bibby was still swearing, and the truck was still sliding, waves of mud now washing over Mad Dog as he reached up, grabbed the rearview mirror for support. It broke off in his hand, but then, without warning, the truck crashed into something, a tree probably, and came to a jarring halt.

The first thing that occurred to Mad Dog was that there was mud in his mouth. The second was that the engine was still idling. And the third was that Mr. Bibby was, yes, still swearing.

Mad Dog coughed and spat, then craned his head at the Brit, who hung suspended by his seatbelt like a mud-caked marionette, his glasses hanging crooked.

"Are you all right, Mr. Hertzog?"

Mad Dog slowly lifted an arm, wiped his mouth, and said, "Nice fucking driving."

Voices sounded from outside, Pope and Wolfgang. They were coming to help free them.

And out of nowhere, Mad Dog began chuckling, his gaze going distant. "You think you got me, Murphy? Huh? Fuck you. We're still in the game!"

Chapter 13

....

Low Water Crossing
Jungle North of Tongaso
Near Congo Border, Angola
0948 Hours Local Time

Kisantu and his men had just freed the truck when they heard the explosions in the distance.

Immediately after, one of his scouts called on the radio to report two vehicles headed their way: a pickup truck pursuing a much larger, Russian-made utility truck, the one that belonged to the second team.

Suddenly, the fact that his men had failed to communicate was unimportant. They were coming home—but for their sake, they had best have the diamonds.

Kisantu had taken his cue from his friends in al Qaeda, who routinely beheaded prisoners and incompetent members alike.

Yes, he was in the business of increasing his numbers and firepower, but each failure was treated swiftly and brutally. There were no exceptions.

He hustled back to his truck. A second radio report indicated that the pickup had slid off the road and tumbled down an embankment near the river. His scouts reported seeing men in the back but lost them. They weren't sure if there were any survivors.

"Take us down to the crossing," he ordered Jonas. "We can meet them there."

After peering at the rearview mirror, Jonas threw the truck in gear, just as the second truck came up beside them. Together they set out, leaving deep trenches behind. The rain now came down in sheets, the wind buffeting them.

Kisantu resisted the temptation to call back his friends to report the good news. He would wait until the diamonds were in his hands.

"The weather is getting worse," groaned Jonas. "No trucks will pass here today."

"But we're so close. Just beyond the hills. We can pass here and reach the river. We can do it!"

Jonas shrugged, took them down another small hill and onto a path spanned here and there by huge puddles whose depths remained unknown. He braked hard.

Kisantu glared at him. "What are you doing? Find us a path!"

After a long breath, Jonas applied a bit more gas, then guided them along the edge of the first puddle. "So why didn't they call?" he asked.

Kisantu saw through the man. He was trying to make conversation, trying to take Kisantu's mind off the road. He was an expert at keeping Kisantu levelheaded, at reminding him of his responsibilities to the men.

Kisantu threw up his hands. "Maybe they couldn't get through."

"There were three of them, all with phones and a radio. The scouts have no problems . . ."

Yes, that was odd. He frowned and nodded.

"We must be careful, my friend." Jonas pursed his lips in thought. "Very careful."

Bibby seized the door handle before unbuckling his seat belt, then he set one boot on Mad Dog's hip, the other on part of the seat. He unclasped the buckle and began rolling down the window. Before he finished, Pope was there, latching onto his wrists and hauling him out.

Next came Mad Dog, who resembled some strange, muddy bush creature, all eyes and cusswords. That they were alive was a small miracle. Sure, the bruises would reveal themselves later, but they'd walk away from it all. Even Bibby's computer was still running.

The truck, however, was a definite casualty.

"We all okay?" asked Mad Dog.

"Beat-up to shit," said Boo Boo, blinking rain from his eyes. "But we're all here. Even him." The medic turned a sour look on Judas, who stood nearby rubbing his chest in the spot where Mad Dog said he had struck him. The old wound had been aggravated. Good. Just then, the black clouds rumbled, as though announcing Lucifer himself.

"That's the problem with you Brits," said Judas. "You can't stay on the road, and even when you are, you're driving on the wrong side."

Before Bibby could retort, Doolittle intervened to say that Rookie's body had been ejected from the truck and was lying on the side of the hill. Mad Dog ordered him and Boo Boo to bring it back, then join them.

"What the fuck? We're still going after them?" asked Judas.

"The fuck we are," answered Mad Dog. "We ain't working CIA hours here. But if you want to stay, that's fine. I'll cuff you to Rookie."

"The corpse?"

"Yeah, don't want you to skip off without keeping up your end of the bargain."

"I'm going."

"Then you're with me, never out of my sight. Never. Do you read me?"

"Roger that, asshole. I want my weapon back."

"That piece of shit? Here, use this," said Sapper, who came forward carrying the pistol Mad Dog had given to Jaga, the one with the "special" firing pin. Sapper winked at Mad Dog and said, "I've been meaning to get it back to you, sorry."

"No, that's all right," Mad Dog said.

Judas examined the pistol. "Very nice piece." He slipped the weapon into his empty hip holster. "We're all still Americans. And you need me alive. You should *really* remember that."

Bibby's satellite phone rang. He shifted over to the pickup and leaned down, away from the blowing rain. It was their security chief back in Cebu. He wanted to speak directly with Mad Dog. "Mr. Hertzog! Cebu's calling!"

Mad Dog made a face, then jogged over. "More good news?" he asked. "I don't know if I can stand any more."

He put his back to Judas, then took the call. "Tell me you found him."

Abu Sayyaf Safe House
Cebu, the Philippines
1655 Hours Local Time

Dan had been kidnapped by Abu Sayyaf terrorists and holed up in some godforsaken rat hole while they blackmailed the kid.

However, he was still alive, and he would use whatever he had left, namely his mouth, to fight them until the end.

Artfag turned away from the window and lit up another cigarette.

"Hey, dickhead? Can you at least open the window?" asked Dan.

"Shut up, old man!"

Dan glanced longingly at the glass. Holy shit! Was he seeing things? He blinked. No, he wasn't.

A man wearing a black balaclava, only his eyes exposed, lifted his head, took a peek inside the window, saw Dan, and put an index finger to his lips. Then he sank back into nothingness, a ghost who still might be a product of Dan's imagination. He wanted so badly to be rescued that anything was possible.

No, goddamn it, he had seen the man. He had!

He glanced at Artfag, who whirled to face the window. Had he seen something? Or had he been looking at Dan and seen Dan's reaction to something outside?

Shitforbrains was back on the computer, a second window just behind him.

The front door lay opposite Dan's chair, not more than twenty feet away.

He took a deep breath.

Was he too old for this shit? Hell no! He was as excited as the day he had sweet-talked his nurse into bed. Would his heart explode? It could.

He set his feet firmly on the floor, pushed up on the chair, testing his weight. Any second now.

Any second.

Five excruciating minutes passed. At least five, Dan thought. Maybe ten! Christ, what were they waiting for?

Maybe they had decided it was too dangerous. Nah, that wasn't like them. They were cocky enough to believe they could rescue one little old man.

And then, just as he was hanging his head, his eyes involuntarily closing from the wear and tear of waiting, the front door smashed off its hinges, hit the floor with a considerable thud—

While two men came crashing through the windows, pieces of wooden frame and glass were hurtling end over end and clattering everywhere.

Shouts from inside. From outside. From inside Dan's own head: *holy fuck!* Total chaos.

Beautiful.

Old or not, cuffed or not, Dan could still take a cue. He gave himself a huge shove backward, knocking the chair up onto two legs.

And, boom, he collapsed onto his back, then he gave another shove, forcing himself onto his side, figuring he should be out of the line of fire.

He gasped as the AK–47s popped, answered immediately by the ear-shattering report of carbines fired at close range.

Reflexively, he pulled at his cuffs, feeling totally useless. The gunfire had triggered his marine's instincts, the training, all of it ingrained, coursing through his body like blood. In his head he drew his sidearm and returned fire, found the next target, and fired.

The most dangerous thing in the world is a marine and his rifle . . .

Threat, respond. Threat, respond. No sorting through the bullshit. He was a jarhead, goddamn it! Squared away, cradle to rack to grave.

But all he could do was lie there, reminding himself of the obvious crap and trembling with the desire to attack.

More boots shuffled. More glass flew. Men shouted, their voices muffled by their masks. Artfag barked something in Tagolog. Three pops.

A carbine answered. An AK posed another question, and two carbines answered it.

Yet another shout—

Dan turned his head, locked gazes with Shitforbrains, who was just turning with his AK, the weapon aimed directly at Dan.

Even as the asshole fired, bullets tore through his chest, sending him back, crashing across his computer desk, the monitor and keyboard plummeting to the floor.

Artfag's scream to his buddy was cut off by two sharp rounds from a carbine.

As those shots echoed, a sharp pain tore through Dan's chest, a pain so cutting that he could hardly breathe.

Cocksucker got me, he thought before the pain finally overcame him . . . and then . . . nothing.

Low Water Crossing
Jungle North of Tongaso
Near Congo Border, Angola
1001 Hours Local Time

Mad Dog and his men followed the riverbank toward the crossing, keeping tight to the dense brush about twenty yards back. The river at that place wove through much thicker jungle, which made the trek a bit unnerving, not that any of them would reveal that. Between the rain and the heavy brush, everyone had good cover—bad guys included.

Pope and Sapper took point, while Wolfgang, Boo Boo, and Drac headed west, seeing if they could hook around to establish positions on the north side of the crossing. Mad Dog, Bibby, Doolittle, and Judas would draw up on the crossing and establish positions on the east side as they continued their advance.

Mad Dog wished doom on the Delta team, willing their truck to get stuck, and in that regard, the weather was truly welcome. Perhaps that low water wouldn't be so low after all. They might sink as they attempted to ford the river, and their engine would become flooded.

However, that truck would need to sink at least three feet, maybe more, since the Russkies had designed the thing for rough terrain. Better to wish for a long, muddy furrow crossing their path, one that would trap them like quicksand, their wheels spinning them into a deeper pit.

"Blackhound One, this is Four," called Pope. "I have the Delta truck in sight, but get this: we got two more trucks coming down on the opposite bank. Could be the homeys from the Congo, over."

Mad Dog was about to respond, when Bibby, who was

still jogging behind Judas but had just answered his satellite phone, interrupted, his voice low: "One, this is Two. Report from Cebu. They have Dan. But he's been shot. They're rushing him to the hospital, over. Repeat, we have Dan, but he has been shot, over."

It was hard not to choke up. It was hard not to stop right there, say, "Fuck this!" and abandon the whole goddamned job.

It was hard just to breathe.

But Mad Dog forged on, kept telling himself that he was all right, in charge, able to lead no matter what happened. When guys died in combat, you didn't linger on it. You moved on; there was always time later to mourn. Too much time. "Roger that, Two. Tell them to keep us updated. Go duck out somewhere, take Blackhound Three with you, and start your transfer hack now. I want that money back. We'll go on without you, over."

"Uh, One, we have a problem. He's a very clever spook. Looks like he's done this before and anticipated these kinds of hacks. He's got a real bitch of a firewall set up, and I've already been trying to crack it. Doesn't look good, over."

"You promised me . . ." Mad Dog warned.

"I know. I'll duck out and keep trying. I just didn't expect this. Not from him, anyway."

Mad Dog heard Judas call after Bibby and Doolittle, neither of whom responded. The spook, who was just a few steps behind Mad Dog, hustled up and said, "Where are they going?"

Although he raised his carbine, Mad Dog repressed the urge to turn it on Judas. Yes, they had Dan, all right, but they still didn't have the money back. If Bibby couldn't get it, they needed Judas to return it.

But the asshole would never do that. Not unless—

Shots blasted through the brush, striking a few of the trees behind them, bark splintering. "Blackhounds, I'm taking fire on my position," cried Mad Dog as he hit the mud.

Judas crawled up next to him. "I need a fucking rifle."

"You need to shut up."

More rounds razored overhead, and Mad Dog eyed the trees ahead, trying to pinpoint the shooters' locations. Yep, there had to be more than one. Sounded like three.

"I die, Dan dies. I want a fucking rifle!"

"Stay down. Try not to get killed." Mad Dog crawled forward toward a little hump, then suddenly rose and slung lead in the shooters' direction.

He paused, ducked again. "Okay, move up!" he ordered Judas.

The spook elbowed his way forward, keeping his useless pistol high above the mud.

Three more shots popped and whipped through the brush, kicking the spook into a frantic crawl, like an injured grasshopper, all lanky and uncoordinated.

Bender had pulled the truck up to the water's edge and had stopped. He took a long hard look at the guy getting out of the lead truck, parked on the opposite bank, and even through the windshield wipers and the torrential rain, he knew he was staring at Mboma Kisantu himself. He had studied the intel photos very closely as part of his mission preparation. They all had.

"That's him," cried Dzoba.

"Dropped himself in our laps," said Bender.

Kisantu was waving frantically for them to come forward across the submerged gravel that spanned the river, where he stood only forty or so meters away. The man behind the wheel of his truck was borderline hysterical, shouting and motioning for him to get back in the cab.

A second truck pulled up next to Kisantu's and at least a dozen armed men poured out of the back, half heading north up the river, the rest spreading themselves along the southern part of the crossing.

For a moment, Bender thought he heard shots in the distance. Wait a minute . . . he had.

And so had Kisantu. He stopped waving and ran back toward his truck.

"Do you have him?" Bender asked Dzoba, who was rolling down his window.

"I will in a second." Dzoba lifted his weapon.

At that, the men along the river bank opened fire, muzzles flashing like Christmas lights in the gloom, mud puddles suddenly miniature geysers erupting around the truck.

"I lost him!" shouted Dzoba. "Fuck, we're taking fire! Too many of 'em! Get us out of here!"

Bender flinched, shrank reflexively in his seat. He stomped on the clutch, threw the truck in reverse, and floored it, backing away from the crossing.

Pope and Sapper had donned their balaclavas while nearing the back of the Delta operators' truck. Pope had seen why the Delta team had stopped: two more trucks were on the other side, and dozens of combatants had hopped down and begun searching for good points of cover. They were poorly trained, because once they assumed their positions, most of them were still visible, crouched beside a tree or popping up from behind an embankment. But they had moved like they had a purpose, and it was evident that most could point and shoot, a definite deterrent.

Despite all the new company, Pope and Sapper were about to surprise the guys inside the Delta truck when the shots had rung out—

And the damned truck had begun to back up.

He had motioned for Sapper to ease gently but quickly onto the tailgate, and he had done likewise. They now hung on each side of the vehicle, clutching metal canopy rails with one hand, their submachine guns held fast in the other.

The tarpaulin flaps were still closed, but they began to flap as the truck turned and caught the wind, then the driver really hit the gas, nearly knocking Sapper from his perch. Pope widened his eyes, and the guy nodded that he was all right.

Incoming fire tore the shit out of the path, even punched a few holes high in the tarpaulin. Pope felt like a paper target swaying in the storm.

Meanwhile, the two trucks roared forward and began crossing the river, their front tires quickly swallowed, waves washing up over their hoods. Then Pope lost them, the ride growing too rough, the jungle too thick.

He just breathed, blinked hard, looked to the tailgate, to Sapper, then closed his eyes for just a second:

Cheryl, I need you now . . .

Pope drew in a very long breath, then gave Sapper the signal.

The big engineer's eyes were bloodshot, and he was soaked to the marrow let alone the bones, but he, like Pope, was good to go.

Nothing could stop them.

But something did. A hand parted one tent flap, and

one of the Delta operators peered straight out. Pope held up his hand for Sapper to hold.

Then he nodded, suddenly reached in and grabbed the guy by the wrist, yanked him out of the truck and tossed him onto the mud. He cursed and hit chestfirst with a hard thud, his machinegun snapping from his grip.

As he slowly rolled over, Pope and Sapper swung themselves onto the flatbed, boots first, guns at the ready, Pope dropkicking someone all the way to the back.

More gunfire from the river must have distracted the men shooting at Mad Dog and Judas, because as those rounds boomed, the jungle around them fell silent, save for rain splattering on the puddles and thumping off thousands of fronds.

"Blackhound One, this is Seven," called Wolfgang. "Delta team took heavy fire and has just pulled out. Four and Five were hanging on the back of the truck and were moving north, but I've lost them now, over."

Shit, the Deltas were bugging out with the diamonds, but at least Pope and Sapper were still with them. They just had to go head-to-head with those incredibly proficient operators, relieve them of the rocks, and take off, no shots fired. A proverbial walk in the park.

Mad Dog vowed to give each a shiny new nickel if they could pull it off. Being chief wiseass had its perks . . .

Wolfgang continued: "Two trucks trying to cross the river now. Looks like the lead truck has stalled out. I'm pretty sure the guy up there is Kisantu. If he's not, he's his twin brother, over."

"Roger that, Seven. Engage those guys. Keep 'em pinned down for as long as you can, over."

"So we're good to shoot 'em?"

"Well, they want to kill you, asshole! Fire!"

Mad Dog got up on his hands and knees, even as he heard Wolfgang, Boo Boo, and Drac bring sudden hell to the river valley. He looked to Judas. "We're moving out again."

The spook rose cautiously, backhanded rain from his brow. "Where?"

"To the crossing—so we can take out Kisantu."

"Bullshit."

Yes, it was. But Mad Dog wanted to keep the asshole guessing.

Bibby was, once again, so engrossed in his computer screen that he didn't hear the commotion behind him.

Well, he had actually heard it, but he didn't turn back until it was all over.

A rebel wearing olive drab fatigues lay on the ground, moaning softly and rubbing the back of his neck as Doolittle lowered his Galil, whose stock had just come down on the unsuspecting fool.

"Jesus, man, why didn't you shoot him?" asked Bibby.

"I just reacted," confessed the translator, who confiscated the man's AK.

"Next time shoot."

"I will."

Doolittle sloughed off his ruck and dug through a side pocket to produce a plastic zipper cuff. He forced the rebel to sit up, then bound the man's hands behind his back. That finished, the translator raised his chin at Bibby. "How's it going?"

"Not good. I think we've lost four million dollars. And if we don't recover the diamonds, we'll be six million in the hole. Shit!"

"Do you want me to call the sergeant?"

"Why do you keep calling him that?"

"That's who he is."

"No, he's a merc, just like you and me."

"To be a great leader, he needs a conscience."

Bibby gave a little snort, keyed his mike. "Blackhound One, this is Two, over."

After delicately filling in Mad Dog on his progress, or lack thereof, and letting him know that they had taken one of the rebels prisoner, Mad Dog requested that they move forward with the prisoner and meet him along the path near the riverbank.

"He wants us to take him?" Doolittle asked, tipping his head toward the rebel.

"That's what he said." Bibby closed the laptop, shoved it in his ruck. "Off we go."

Pope shoved his submachine gun squarely in the Delta operator's face. The guy was arguably the meanest-looking black dude he had ever seen, and thank god Pope had exploited the element of surprise. To a point. The guy had his expensive weapon, a German-made HK no doubt, pointed at Pope's chest.

Meanwhile, Sapper had Jaga and one other guy covered—like that mattered.

"We just want the rocks," said Pope.

The Delta operator smiled. "Who the fuck are you? You work for Morstarr? Or are you just another merc? And by the way, nice tan."

Jaga was screaming in Portuguese and pointing at Sapper. The little fucker obviously recognized him, balaclava notwithstanding. Then he looked at the operator, and, in English said, "Thorn, it's him! From the mining company."

"Hand over the rocks, and we're out of here."

The Delta operator began chuckling.

Pope drove his gun's muzzle in the operator's forehead and growled, "What's so fucking funny?"

"You . . ."

"Give us the fucking rocks!" shouted Sapper.

"Shut up!" ordered Pope. "The rocks, motherfucker! *Now!*"

"So which one of Uncle Sam's cousins trained you? SEALs? Force Recon? Air Force, probably, huh?"

Suddenly, the truck slowed, brakes squeaking.

"Hurry up," Sapper warned.

"The rocks! Last chance!" hollered Pope. "Come on. At least we'll give 'em back to the company that owns 'em. You think your bosses will do that?"

The Delta operator smiled again. "You want the rocks? You'd better go get 'em, you dumbass. You just threw them off the truck."

Pope looked at Sapper, all red eyes and probably mouthing an "Oh, fuck" beneath his mask.

As was Pope.

And then, in the next second, he was airborne, with Sapper right behind him, hurtling through the rain, the ground coming up too fast. He hit and rolled, as did Sapper, the Delta guy cackling behind them.

The truck had come to a full stop and was turning around, with one operator hanging from the passenger's-side window. He opened fire, spraying the mud in front of Sapper and Pope.

They scrambled to their feet, and Pope took point, leading them down and off the path, into the thick brush. His legs were on fire, his breath nearly gone. Trees blurred by, and the rain threatened to blind him—

But then, just off to his right, he saw a figure limping along the path: the guy they had thrown off. He was hurt, vulnerable.

"Right there," Pope cried to Sapper.

They cut through the shrubs and high grass, neared the path, turned, came up behind the limping man.

Pope leaped forward and tackled the guy.

But the truck was just roaring up. He had only a few seconds to disarm and search the man. Not enough time.

But Sapper was there, already digging through the Delta guy's pockets while Pope pinned him facefirst to the mud.

Gunfire boomed from the truck, rounds tearing into the puddles not a meter from his head.

The operator wasn't wearing a ruck, just his fatigues and boots. There wasn't much to search. Sapper was panting, cursing, then finally said, "He doesn't have 'em!"

"Bullshit!"

"I'm telling you!"

"Fuck!" cried Pope as he released the guy, snatched up the man's weapon, then tore ass back into the bush, with Sapper in tow, the other Deltas firing behind them.

"Hey, asshole," Sapper called as they continued to run. "Just fucking with you. I got 'em! Really! I looked inside, and they look like diamonds to me!" He held up a small leather pouch and gasped through a shit-eating grin.

Pope wanted to shoot the big fuck. Instead, he led the man on, tried to catch his breath as he keyed his mike. "Blackhound One, this is Four. We got 'em. I say again, we have the diamonds!"

Chapter 14

••••••••••••••••••••••••••••••

Low Water Crossing
Jungle North of Tongaso
Near Congo Border, Angola
1008 Hours Local Time

"**B**lackhound Four, this is One. Say again, over."

Which part of "we have the diamonds" did Mad Dog not understand? Well, the whole damned thing. After all, they were in Angola, where the best laid plans of mercenaries went straight to Hell.

Pope's voice grew more terse as he repeated that they had the rocks, then added, "We took 'em right off a Delta guy, and he's still okay. No shots fired."

Half shocked, half ready to swing a fist in the air and scream, *"Yes!,"* Mad Dog asked Pope to make sure that the pouch contained the diamonds and not something else. Pope sounded insulted by the request and said that while he and Sapper weren't gem experts the rocks appeared genuine.

That would be the real kicker, wouldn't it? All this

work to rescue fake diamonds. Would Kisantu really be that clever? Plant a couple of guys with fakes in Tongaso? Maybe he wouldn't, but if there was an inside man at Morstarr, he could pull off a switch, send Morstarr and its hired mercs on a wild-goose chase while the real thugs fled into the Congo.

But as far as Mad Dog was concerned, he and his men had recovered the rough; it wasn't his problem if the rocks turned out to be fakes. He'd argue that point to Kidman when the time came. It was a weak argument. Shit. He'd have to come up with something better. But he didn't want to think about that right now.

There was another four million to worry about.

Doolittle and Bibby came jogging up the path with the prisoner between them. Mad Dog used a clicker to gain Bibby's attention, and they turned off the path and into the brush, where Mad Dog and Judas sat on their haunches.

The spook was staring intently through the binoculars Mad Dog had loaned him, observing the two trucks still stuck at the low-water crossing and the dozen or so rebels trying to free them as they squinted against the driving winds and rain.

"Take off his cuffs," Mad Dog ordered Doolittle as he cocked a thumb toward the rebel. "And Mr. Bibby? Get back on your computer. And oh, yeah, I want you to call Kidman. Tell him to meet us in Tongaso. Tell him to bring two trucks. We'll need transport back to the mining camp."

"You got it."

"Sergeant, you're letting him go?" Doolittle asked, glancing to the rebel.

"Yes."

Judas turned away from his binoculars. "Hertzog, what the hell are you doing now?"

Mad Dog ignored the spook, regarded Doolittle, and raised his voice for the spook's benefit. "Tell our friend that he's about to become a hero. Tell him he's just captured an American CIA agent, and he's going to deliver him to Kisantu."

While Doolittle translated, Mad Dog withdrew a zipper cuff from his ruck and waved over the wide-eyed Judas. "Time to pay the piper."

"Oh, really?" Judas looked incredulous.

Mad Dog extended a hand. "Your weapon."

"Fuck you." Judas raised the pistol. "You have lost it, haven't you?"

"Yup."

"Mikey, Mikey, Mikey. Pay attention. I die, so does Dan."

"We have Dan. He was shot. He might die. But we have him, and you'd better hope he lives. Now I want my money back."

"So you're deaf and blind. I'm looking at a pistol pointed at your head. What do you see? A white flag?"

"I see an idiot who trusts his enemy's weapon. You *never* trust your enemy's weapon."

Judas turned the pistol away, took aim at a tree, pulled the trigger. Click. Firing pin too short. CIA agent fucked. He threw the pistol at Mad Dog's feet and appeared ready to run. "You'll have to kill me."

"No, I'll leave that to Kisantu. You know, after we got Dan back I thought of putting a gun to your head. But a quick death? That's no real threat. Not to men like us, right? But turning you over to him . . . ah, ha, now that's real fun. Yeah, he'd play the torture game, but he'd hold off killing you because he'd think you're worth something—till he finds out you're just a piece of shit. Maybe he'd dump you on his friends, you know, those funny men in black turbans? They'd cut your head off, show it all on the Web. Or you could give me my fucking money."

"I'm ready to make the transfer when you are," Bibby told the spook. "Just need your user name and password."

"I give you those, you'll clean out my account."

"There's the difference between you and me. I'll only take what's mine."

Judas laughed. "Don't give me that shit! You ripped off the money in the first place."

"It was never yours. And, in a way, we're giving it back to the people."

"You're groping, Hertzog."

"Doesn't matter. You got five seconds to make a decision. And maybe it is worth four mil to get you off my back."

Yes, Mr. James Moody, dedicated employee of the CIA's operations directorate, seemed to age right there, his long beard looking a little grayer, his eyes beginning to vanish behind the deep furrows of skin. Hell, he might just implode.

"Okay. I get you in, you make the transfer, but then I walk away."

"You have my word."

Judas opened his mouth, and then, for a moment, the bush grew strangely silent.

Mad Dog's neck tingled. *Oh, no.*

AK–47 rounds scissored through the brush, the popping somewhere in the distance and growing louder. A loud snap came from the tree trunk not a meter from Mad Dog's shoulder.

At once Judas ducked, turned, and bolted away—

As did the rebel, whom Doolittle had under guard.

"Oh, Jesus Christ," grunted Bibby, slapping his laptop closed. "Shoot him!"

"I'm trying!" The translator took the shot. Cursed.

"Bibby? Doolittle? Rally back to the truck! I'll be back with him!" cried Mad Dog. He broke into a sprint toward the riverbank, falling hard into Judas's path.

The bad guys were somewhere off to his left, maybe fifty meters, maybe a hundred. Just too hard to tell with all the wind and rain. Their aim sucked. But they had no problem wasting ammo. A lucky shot could be in their future.

"Judas! Don't do it!" cried Mad Dog. "Don't be an asshole!"

Of course, Mad Dog was asking the impossible.

Bender's frustration had worked its way into his hands. He maintained a white-knuckled grip on the steering wheel. That was understandable. They had been this-close to returning the diamonds and taking out Kisantu. Now the diamonds were in the hands of some asshole mercenaries, and the madman was still on the loose.

"There, I see 'em," cried Dzoba. "Turn to the right!"

Bender didn't see jack, but he trusted Dzoba, swung the wheel hard, and took them down a pot-holed path between trees, the truck fishtailing in the mud.

"Turn again, there!" Dzoba pointed through the windshield.

"What the fuck?" hollered Bender.

"To the left! Wait, no! Oh, my God!" Dzoba shoved

himself out the window and brought his rifle around. He opened fire—

And Bender still could not see a goddamned thing.

Until a man darted out of the bushes about ten meters ahead of the truck. He was one of Kisantu's men, and he brought himself to full height while shouldering his Rocket-Propelled Grenade.

Bender was shouting above the rattling of Dzoba's rifle, and even as he cut the wheel hard to the left, he thought he saw the RPG flash.

When he faced forward, he realized the truck was barreling straight for a tree. He turned the wheel again.

But it was no good. The RPG must have hit the side of the truck—because the next thing Bender knew an explosion ripped through the cab and he was hurtling through the windshield. It felt as though a thousand pins had struck his body as he crashed into the mud, flat on his back.

The stench of gasoline and burning rubber and something sickly sweet came in a smoke cloud, and when he raised his head, he saw nothing ahead but a wall of flames.

When he looked down, he saw that his legs were gone. So was his left arm. His right arm was bloody and mangled, but he could move it, so he reached into his breast pocket, withdrew his stogie, and shoved it into his mouth.

He tried calling out to his men, but his voice was low and broken, lost in the rush of flames. They were probably dead already.

God damn it!

No, he wouldn't feel sorry for himself.

It is what it is.

But shit, he wished he could check his watch, attached to his missing limb.

How long would it take to die?

Slowly, the world grew dim around the edges. Not long now. Not long.

Wolfgang, Drac, and Boo Boo huddled in the shrubs just north of the crossing, where the river took a sharp turn to the east, affording them an excellent view of the crossing site. Unfortunately, Wolfgang didn't like what he was seeing at the moment: too many bad guys, and he didn't like what he was hearing either: radio silence. Mad Dog wasn't answering his calls. And Wolfgang had been calling to report that Kisantu and his men had abandoned their trucks and were moving fast across the river.

Drac continued giving those chuckleheads lead poisoning, while Boo Boo created more work for Kisantu's medics with his compact submachine gun.

Wolfgang, on the other hand, was all about that perfect bead on Kisantu himself, figuring his sniper rifle would separate the man into a dozen pieces, all of which would arc over the lake like bleeding water birds. What an image. What a fact. Damn it, where was the guy? Still in the truck? Wolfgang wasn't sure. He had lost him. What the hell kind of sniper was he? Self-taught to be sure, and damned sloppy now.

"Fuck," sang Drac between volleys. "A lot of 'em are still getting across!"

Flyboy was right. Among those falling lifeless into the water there were others who surged forward, reached the riverbank, and charged onward toward where Mad Dog and the others had rallied along the path.

"Well, that's it, man," called Boo Boo as the last trio

of men vanished, leaving behind about fifteen or twenty wounded or dead rebels floating in the river.

A familiar hissing sound had Wolfgang whipping his head around. Yeah, those rebels had found themselves some cover, all right, cover they could exploit to remain still, set up, and launch their RPGs.

"Incoming!" Wolfgang shouted. "RPG!"

All three hauled extreme ass and dove behind the hill to their right, just as an RPG turned the shrubs into a ball of bright orange, the boom thundering so loudly that Wolfgang could feel it in his bones.

A second explosion closer to their left heaved a massive cloud of mud and fire that rained down on them, Wolfgang thanking God that he ducked again, just in time, and that they were so soaked that the flames had nothing to ignite.

With his ears ringing loudly, his nose crinkling at the rotting stench of the jungle made more pungent by the explosions, he gave Drac and Boo Boo the high sign. Then he led them down, across the hills, deciding that at this point it was time to go bye-bye and rally on the truck to help Pope and Sapper, those glorymongering bastards.

Yep, the team would meet back at a vehicle that would take them absolutely nowhere. And they were being hunted by a force over four times as large.

Wolfgang chuckled aloud, reminding himself of just how crazy he was, already seeing himself at some bar, telling some big-titted bitch all about it. If she were naïve enough, he could make her believe that he had single-handedly saved the entire team. And if she were horny enough, his exploits would have her legs on his shoulders by midnight.

That's exactly what I'm talking about!

In fact, the rush was so intense now that he thought he could fly over the treetops and land like a Huey beside the truck. He vaulted over a puddle, hearing Boo Boo and Drac scream for him to slow down.

Kisantu and Jonas were two of the first men to cross the river and press on into the jungle. Yet even as they did, the questions haunted Kisantu:

Why had the second team suddenly fled north in the truck before delivering the diamonds?

Why would they still not answer his calls?

Jonas believed that their men had been killed, and Kisantu now agreed. Then what was going on? Who had the truck? The diamonds? It was maddening to consider.

For now, they couldn't confirm anything. There was no way to pursue the second team's truck with their vehicles stalled in the river.

Meanwhile, he and the rest of his men would deal with the others along the riverbank, men dressed in mining company security uniforms. Kisantu had received firm instructions not to leave any witnesses to their activities, and Kisantu knew that if he failed his "friends" in this regard, they would not be forgiving. Not at all.

As he and Jonas moved stealthily between the trees, Kisantu saw a flash of green ahead, off to the left.

"Over there!" he told Jonas.

A tall, bearded figure in nondescript khakis—a white man to be sure—ran wildly through the jungle, glancing over his shoulder.

Jonas was about to fire, but Kisantu told him no, that this one they should try to take alive.

Another mystery. Was this man a member of the Red Cross or some other humanitarian agency? Or was he, more likely, an American spy or military special forces operator?

Kisantu broke into a fierce sprint, came up behind the man, dropped his rifle, then took a flying leap toward his prey.

Judas had been about twenty meters ahead of Mad Dog. Twenty meters. About sixty feet. Not very far at all.

So when Mad Dog saw that the spook had just been tackled by one of the rebels and knocked to the ground, he reacted instinctively, diving off to the side, hitting the deck, rolling, and coming back up to avoid being caught himself.

Jesus God, he'd need a month off after this job. He'd beaten the old body half to death. With sore ribs and a throbbing shoulder, he dug out his binoculars to get a better look at the rebel screaming at Judas.

At the same time another man jogged up to the them, carrying two rifles. The guy who had tackled Judas turned, and Mad Dog recognized the man from the intelligence photos Bibby had shown the team.

Oh, shit!

There it was: Judas had become Kisantu's prisoner after all. But that wasn't the goddamned plan. The threat was supposed to cause Judas to fold, give up his user name and password, and get Mad Dog his money.

God, if those idiots decided to kill Judas, the four million would never be recovered, unless Mad Dog was listed as a beneficiary in the spook's last will and testament.

The odds of that? Four million to one, naturally.

Okay. Mad Dog could call for help, but he wasn't sure his men would arrive in time, wasn't sure of his own GPS coordinates and would have to wait for that data first.

Forget that shit. He'd just give 'em a SITREP. "Blackhound team, this is One. Kisantu has Judas. Moving to intercept, out."

A message like that ought to have raised some brows.

Damn it. Here he was, looking at two bad guys (three, really) one of them a major player in the region. Shit, if he killed Kisantu, he'd be doing it for free when an assassination job like that went for at least a million, maybe more depending upon the circumstances, terrain, a whole slew of risk factors.

So it was a pro bono job just to save his own ass, his own money. And the booby prize? Uncle Jimmy Judas. Great.

As Kisantu forced Judas back onto his feet, Mad Dog checked his carbine, then bolted toward the men before he had anymore second thoughts. Fuck it. Just go. See what happens.

They turned toward him.

In a tone so calm that he even surprised himself, he said, "How you doing, fellas?"

Then he shot the first guy in the head, blood splattering everywhere.

Kisantu's rifle rang out as Mad Dog turned, put three rounds in that motherfucker's head—

But not before the stinging pain ripped through his legs, causing him to crumple as his finger went slack on the trigger.

And Judas stood there, watching it all, mouth half-open.

Kisantu and his partner lay there, dead. Mad Dog sat up, screaming inwardly against the pain. He'd taken one round in the right calf, the other a little higher, his left hip. Fuck, he hoped the asshole hadn't hit an artery.

Judas just looked at him, eyes on fire.

Shouts from rebels resounded from somewhere over the hills. They were coming.

Mad Dog grimaced, forced himself forward, onto his knees, dragged one foot up, tried to stand.

Couldn't.

Another shout. Very close. Gunfire. Three rounds.

Judas looked to the hills, then back at Mad Dog.

"Call him!" hollered Sapper. "Tell 'em we can't hold these guys for much longer!"

After catching a glimpse of the Delta Force truck exploding behind them, Pope and Sapper had reported to Mad Dog, then had rallied back to their own truck. They were now taking fire from the oncoming rebels, maybe a dozen in all who paused, fired, then advanced, two coming within fifty meters and popping up from behind a slight berm.

After pitching a couple of grenades at those bastards, Pope got on the radio, called Mad Dog, got no reply.

But just then a massive shit storm of fire tore at the enemy, and only a second later, Wolfgang called to say that he, Drac, and Boo Boo were playing cavalry, come to save the goddamned day.

"Just get your asses over here," Pope told him. "If One doesn't get back, we'll have to move without him."

Pope had stashed the diamonds inside his ruck, right next to his sister's Barbie doll. Diamonds were, after all, a girl's best friend, even a plastic one.

So what now? Pope knew that Mad Dog would want him to go on no matter what. They had discussed what to do if the big dog went down, knew the plan, same for every job, and Pope had always nodded.

But you didn't leave men behind, mercenary or not. So Pope decided that he would give his ruck to Wolfgang and send the rest of the team back to Tongaso. He alone would go after Mad Dog—if it came down to that. Sure, the bossman would be pissed. Better alive and pissed than dead.

After a particularly vicious volley of fire, Sapper cursed and screamed, "A little help over here!"

Pope swore himself, then chucked another grenade. "Eat shit and die," he ordered the enemy.

"Blackhound Four, this is Two," called Mr. Bibby. "We're coming in from the northwest, look for us, over."

"Roger that. Hurry up, out!"

In just a few minutes everyone except Mad Dog would be present, and Pope would give the order. He didn't care what Bibby thought. The Brit might be second in command according to Mad Dog, but Pope knew what was best. He'd put his SEAL skills and intuition up against the Brit's training any day. If Bibby knew what was good for the team, then he'd go along.

Pope returned fire at some knucklehead trying to get a bead on him, then keyed his mike. "Blackhound One, this is Four, over." *C'mon, Bossman. Give me a sign.*

Rounds thumped into the mud a couple of meters ahead, driving Pope onto his belly. He answered with half a clip, grinding his teeth over the rebels' tenacity. "Give up, you dumb assholes. Go home." He keyed his mike, called Mad Dog again. And again.

Sapper started bitching and moaning. Pope told him to

shut up and hold his position. Enraged, Sapper began unloading grenades, pulling pins and letting them fly like he was a cop on the Fourth of July who had confiscated the entire neighborhood's illegal fireworks so he could shoot them off in his own backyard.

Pope shook his head at the maniac, fired another few rounds, then got back on the radio. "Blackhound One, this is Four, SITREP, over."

Chapter 15

....

Low Water Crossing
Jungle North of Tongaso
Near Congo Border, Angola
1031 Hours Local Time

The explosions coming from the south, where they had flipped the pickup truck, along with the repeated calls from Pope, gave Mad Dog even more motivation to stand. He screamed aloud as he finally rose, his knees buckling.

Why hadn't Judas left already? Didn't matter. God, he couldn't bring himself to ask for help.

He took a step, his legs seemingly gone. Down he went, swearing all the way.

"All right, scumbag," the spook said, then suddenly came around and, with surprising strength, hauled Mad Dog up. It took a moment's more struggle, but the spook lifted Mad Dog across his shoulders, then began carrying him toward the truck site.

"This makes us even," said Judas. "I keep the four million."

"Okay," Mad Dog lied. Then he reached around, struggled a second against Judas's grip, and managed to key his mike. He spoke through clenched teeth: "Blackhound team, this is One. Judas and I are coming in, just north of your position, over." His legs felt like they'd been dipped in kerosene, the match lit . . . and whoosh!

"Roger that," came Pope's excited voice. "Be advised we have about twelve meatheads directly east of our location, over."

Mad Dog relayed the information to Judas, who said, "Great, you heavy bastard."

"I got big bones. Just move your ass, nerd. Otherwise they'll shoot it out from under me."

"Screw you, Hertzog."

"You do, and you'll never go back to women."

The spook just groaned as he lost his footing, slipped into a puddle, recovered (thank God), and shifted farther up a small hill, weaving between a couple of trees and a few scattered bushes.

As they came down the other side, Mad Dog forced his head up, wished he hadn't.

Pinpricks of light shone from just near the overturned pickup, followed by an explosion off to the left, probably RPG fire. About fifty yards away, strung out along the tree line, were the rebels, their rifles popping and winking under long, dark clouds. He and Judas were bound for the gauntlet of fire.

"Don't move, jarhead," instructed Judas. "You make a good shield."

"Just run, you fucker."

"Call your knuckleheads. Let 'em know."

"Yeah." Mad Dog got back on the radio. "Blackhound team, we're coming in now!"

With that, the god of war came to Angola.

Mad Dog's men unloaded everything they had, the sound of all that firepower simply awe-inspiring.

Bibby was on his Sterling, gritting his teeth and blasting those rebel bastards to bloody hell.

Doolittle kept the rounds coming with his Galil—no need to translate his intentions.

Sapper was letting them have it with his carbine and finding the exact moment in which to engage his M203 grenade launcher to add some pyrotechnics and flying body parts to the whole extravaganza.

Boo Boo, while not carrying the biggest weapon like Navy corpsmen did, was probably gripping his MP5 with one hand, lobbing grenades with the other—and still proving that the best form of combat medicine was a massive, unadulterated display of superior firepower.

Pope was hosing down the trees with his submachine gun, pausing to throw a curve or breaking ball that would do a whole lot more than strike out batters. Twin booms shook the ground.

Drac was giving the rebels a little history lesson about weapons made famous in the Vietnam War. You could almost see Mick Jagger pouting, hear him wailing as Drac kept time, his Stoner glowing and smoking like an expertly rolled joint. *Peace, man!*

More grenades exploded between the ceaseless barrage of lead, punctuated again by Wolfgang's big sniper rifle. Though Mad Dog couldn't hear the guy growling, he knew he was. You couldn't keep a good warmonger down.

But then again there was Rookie, whose ghost was watching over the entire scene, perhaps longing to take part, and maybe, just maybe, protecting them somehow, putting in a good word upstairs for some fellow brothers.

And if he didn't, there was always Jack, good old Jack, who didn't deserve to buy it in this shit hole. Good old Jack, who was gung ho till the end, a marine's marine—a man who needed to be remembered.

"There they are," someone hollered. Sounded like Pope, but Mad Dog couldn't be sure.

The rain had tapered off for a few minutes, but the sky opened up once more, adding that racket to all the gunfire. Mad Dog's legs were throbbing now, the imaginary knives poking every time Judas jostled him.

Abruptly, he was on the ground, rolling off the spook's back and looking straight up into a face: yes, Pope's.

"Jesus Christ, Bossman. Boo Boo, get the fuck over here! Bossman's been hit!"

"Tell somebody to get Rookie's body," Mad Dog ordered Pope. "We ain't waiting here."

"Boo Boo has to look at you first."

"Fuck that. I'll live. Handcuff Judas to the truck. Leave him here."

Hands seized his wrists and forced him up. The hands belonged to Judas. "Double cross again?"

"No."

"Bullshit!"

"Kisantu had you. I took him out. I took out his buddy. Otherwise, you'd be eating lunch with them and al Qaeda."

"And because I dragged you back here, we're even—and you still want your money?"

"Very good. And even with Kisantu gone, these rebel fuckers will still take you back to the Congo as their prize. So you give Bibby what he needs, otherwise you're staying here."

"Fuck the money, Bossman," said Pope. "We'll make it up on another job. I say we leave this piece of shit."

Judas lifted his voice: "This piece of shit just saved your boss!"

Mad Dog took a deep breath. God, even that hurt. "All right, Pope. You win. Cuff him to the truck. Forget the money."

Boo Boo had just arrived and was already cutting open Mad Dog's pants to inspect the wounds.

In the meantime, while the others still held the rebels at bay, Pope shoved his machinegun in Judas's chest and ordered him to move. The spook refused.

"Bossman, can I shoot him?"

Mad Dog winced as Boo Boo applied gentle pressure to his leg. What had Pope said? The pain was excruciating. "Whatever you say, Pope. Do what's best."

"Did you hear that?" Pope asked Judas.

"Hertzog, you can't kill me. I've already taken steps to ensure that if I die, you get the blame. You don't want to test me on this one."

"Move out! Otherwise, you're dead," cried Pope.

An RPG suddenly whistled in, Doolittle and Sapper screaming for everyone to get down.

The explosion lifted behind them, igniting a stand of trees for a few seconds before the rain turned the flames into hissing smoke. While that light vanished, Judas apparently saw his: the bright, flickering light emanating from the fires of Hell, where a platoon of marines with glowing red eyes were waiting for him.

"All right, Hertzog. You get me out of here, and I'll give you the money back."

"Oh, I think we can hold these rebel assholes for a couple more minutes." Mad Dog got back on the radio, told Bibby to boot up and meet them by the truck. "Boo Boo, can you get me there?"

"Shit, Zog, we have to carry you back to Tongaso. You're a liability now. I say we cuff you to the truck, too."

Before Mad Dog could answer the wiseass, Boo Boo was hauling him across his back, doing a much more professional job of the fireman's carry than Judas had.

And off they went, toward the truck, with Mad Dog calling out to Judas, "You give Bibby the name and pass-word right now."

The spook closed his eyes for a moment, but then they snapped open as a sudden wave of incoming fire sent everyone to the ground except Boo Boo.

"Drop me," Mad Dog hollered.

"Shit, it was hard enough getting you up. I ain't put-ting you down. Besides, those assholes couldn't hit the broad side of a fat lady."

"What about a stubborn medic carrying his stubborn boss?"

"Well, the boss makes a good target. They could prob-ably hit him pretty easy."

It hurt to smile, but Mad Dog did, anyway. Boo Boo broke into a half jog, splashing through shallow puddles and nearing the hill where the pickup truck lay within a river of clay washing down from the ridge. Mad Dog al-ways insisted that everyone do lots of hard PT and weight training so they could, among other things, haul his fat ass out of the fight.

Boo Boo lowered himself to one knee, then eased Mad Dog down from his shoulders. Biting his lip against the pain, Mad Dog rolled over and sat up as Boo Boo returned to treating the wounds. The bullet was still in Mad Dog's calf, but the other one had entered and exited. Boo Boo didn't believe any of the major arteries had been struck, but they'd need to get Mad Dog to a hospital to be sure. He did, however, believe he could remove the bullet on the spot.

Behind them Bibby had placed his laptop on his ruck and was typing furiously, despite the rain. "Okay, I'm ready!"

"Get back up there, hold them off," Mad Dog told Pope as he came forward with Judas. Mad Dog withdrew his .45, the one with the correct firing pin. "I got the spook."

"Okay, but not for long. We're going to shift north, then come back around to throw 'em off."

"Good. Get going. Uncle Jimmy? Get over here."

"Hertzog, I changed my mind. I'm keeping the money."

"User name. Password."

"Adios, motherfucker."

"You don't think I'll shoot you?"

"I'm willing to take that risk."

Mad Dog smiled broadly. "No, you're not."

Judas turned away. Took three steps before Bibby called out, "Oh, Mr. Moody? Your user name is JamesR, all one word with a capital R, and your password is Spooky 9947."

Judas froze.

"I've made a sizable withdrawal, left the minimum hundred grand and transferred sixteen million into one of IPG's accounts," Bibby went on. "Your bank will blame this on fraud. You, unfortunately, will be out all of that money unless you follow our instructions to the letter. Once we're safely back in Tongaso, I will return the money to your account, sans our four million. At that time, we'll all be square. If you don't believe me, you can check for yourself on your own computer, once we get back to the village."

"I don't believe you."

"I don't care." Bibby lifted his head to Mad Dog. "Mr. Hertzog, you can kill him with impunity now. We have Dan. We have our money. Hell, we have his money, too."

There was something not quite right in Bibby's tone. Mad Dog wasn't sure what it was, but he'd have to ask the Brit about it later, in private. If they survived.

"All right, you heard him, Jimmy boy. You're either coming with us to get your money back, or you're staying here to die broke. I'm thinking this is a no-brainer."

Judas roared, and somewhere within that scream was the word Fuck, drawn out so much that it was almost unintelligible.

Mad Dog winked at Bibby. "He's coming."

A second later, Mad Dog roared himself as Boo Boo dug deep into his calf and removed the bullet.

What do you know about the dialectics contained within the Aesopian language relative to the Marxist-Leninist theory?

Mr. Bibby was trying to answer that question, or, more precisely, predict what Mr. James Moody's answer was to that question.

It was a bizarre question, no doubt, culled from some academic text or exam or some legal proceeding—

But obtaining its answer was vital.

In truth, Bibby had hacked into the spook's account, and he had been able to view the account's balance, but he still was not able to make the transfer without the answer to that security question, which was part of a secondary software package Judas used for added protection. Even the bank geeks themselves were unaware that Judas had modified his account in such cunning ways, the bastard.

Damn, if Bibby outright asked Judas, the guy would catch on. The remark had to be carefully constructed to elicit the answer while not revealing Bibby's ignorance.

And worse, Bibby needed to hack in and make the transfer before they got back to Tongaso. It would all need to happen while they were running through the jungle, trying to flee from the rebels, in a torrential downpour.

Yet a strange little miracle did occur. Seven local men from Tongaso, including Friday, whose brother Bibby had beaten to death with his laptop, came sidestepping and sliding down the hill, AKs in hand. Initially Bibby thought they would shoot him and the rest of the team as they were preparing to leave.

But Doolittle spoke quickly with them. Kisantu's name came up several times, and suddenly they began holding off the rebels, allowing the rest of the team to fall back. Judas added something about paying all of them handsome bonuses.

So reinforcements had arrived. Boo Boo carried Mad Dog, while Pope slung Rookie's body over his shoulder. That meant Bibby, Doolittle, Drac, Wolfgang, and Sapper were responsible for security on the way back. Sapper and Wolfgang took point. Boo Boo and Pope remained in the middle of the line. Drac, Bibby, and Doolittle brought up the rear, keeping Judas just ahead of them, squarely in their sights.

"I still can't believe you got in," Judas told Bibby. "Im-fucking-possible."

"So where'd you hear that question?"

"My grandpa told it to me. During the McCarthy era, when the witch hunts were on to find communists, he was a juror, and he heard a lawyer ask that to a defendant."

"Because the Aesopian language is all about covert communications. It's all about hidden meanings. Isn't that what you're about, too?"

"No shit. I didn't know that."

Bingo. Thank you, Judas, you ignorant fool.

Five minutes later, as Bibby and the rest of the team continued picking their way parallel to the riverbank, AK fire cracked behind them. Drac and Doolittle broke off from the line and began to return fire, the latter calling on the radio to say that it appeared the local guys from Tongaso had been overrun.

Meanwhile, Pope and Boo Boo were exhausted and had to stop, so Wolfgang and Sapper were directed by Mad Dog to fall back down the line and help out.

As they charged by, Bibby couldn't resist the temptation to open his laptop, establish another connection with the bank, and test out his theory.

An RPG struck the large boughs of a tree not three meters away, the explosion sending Judas into a fit of screaming: "I want a weapon! I want a goddamned weapon right now!"

"Shut up!" Bibby cried, just as the screen showed the prompt to answer Judas's question.

What did Judas know about the dialectics contained within the Aesopian language relative to the Marxist-Leninist theory?

Bibby typed in the word *nothing*.

ACCESS DENIED

Shit. He typed in *absolutely nothing*.

He typed in *jack shit, squat, fucking nothing, not a goddamned thing*, as Judas kept screaming, the gunfire rattled, brass thumped into puddles, and voices blared in his earpiece: "Get me some suppressing fire up here, goddamn it! Four, I need your ass up here now!"

"Give me your sidearm!" Judas demanded.

"Shut up!"

"Your sidearm!"

ACCESS DENIED

Bibby's face didn't just warm, it ignited as he burst to his feet, slammed shut the laptop, and reared back, ready to repeat his performance in *Murder by Computer*, only this time Judas would play victim.

But as he looked into the spook's eyes, the answer to the question came to him, accompanied by an amazing chill that began at his feet and spread across his shoulders, making him feel as though he had just grown magnificent wings.

He whirled back, reopened the computer while ducking behind a tree. "Come on, come on," he grunted waiting for the damned thing to wake up.

What do you know about the dialectics contained within the Aesopian language relative to the Marxist-Leninist theory?

Bibby typed in the answer to the sixteen-million-dollar question:

Ask grandpa.

ACCESS GRANTED

"What would I like to do today?" Bibby read aloud, then whispered, "Make a fucking transfer. A big one."

"Get off that goddamned computer!" cried Judas. "What are you doing?"

Bibby allowed himself a smile. If Mr. Spooky only knew. In fact, Bibby now felt so cocky, so giddy, that he pulled out his Browning high-power 9mm pistol and proffered it to Judas. "Here, asshole. Defend yourself."

Frowning, the spook accepted. "You play games with this weapon, too?"

Bibby wriggled his brows. "Put the barrel in your mouth, pull the trigger, find out."

"Blackhound One, this is Two," called Bibby, keeping his voice down.

Mad Dog was waiting for this call. "Go ahead, Two."

"We weren't good to go before. I was bluffing to get one more piece of data. I have it now. And the money, over."

"Roger that. I knew something was up. Just take the four million now, over."

"How 'bout six, just in case the diamonds turn out to be fake."

Pope had given Mad Dog the gems, which he now kept in his breast pocket. He patted them gently and nodded. "Okay, I like your style. Take six. If Kidman tries to fuck us over, we'll still have our reward, courtesy of Uncle Jimmy. By the way, you got eyes on him?"

"Roger that. Gave him my pistol. He's taking pot shots at those meatheads behind us, over."

Mad Dog swore under his breath. "Well, that was a fucking mistake! Why'd you arm him!"

"To shut him up, over."

"Well, get that weapon back. I don't care what you do. And find out how Dan's doing, out."

Perhaps that whack in the head had knocked all reason from the once-reasonable Brit.

Or perhaps the entire place had been sucking the life from all of them, and now they were weak and hallucinating in the desert—or drugged up and hallucinating in the jungle from painkillers given to them by sour-faced medics. The puddles were, after all, turning into amoebas, beating like hearts extracted from dying men.

Boo Boo set down Mad Dog, propped him against a tree, and shoved a pistol into his hand. Mad Dog raised the weapon, tried to aim at a fallen tree, his vision blurring.

Oh, this would be fun.

"What do you think?" Pope called to Wolfgang as the rebel fire began to die. "They're moving?"

Wolfgang, binoculars in hand, was spying two stands of trees about fifty yards off. "I see a couple of guys. One's on the phone. Maybe they found Kisantu. Maybe they're getting called back."

"That's enough for me. Let's move! Blackhound team, this is Four. Ready to move out!"

After the other replied, Wolfgang said, "Give me a minute."

"What? To be sure?"

"Uh, yeah, right."

Wearing a smirk, Pope jogged off, back up the line to fetch Rookie's body.

Wolfgang was still suffering from sniper's withdrawal caused by a vivid fantasy: his taking aim at Kisantu, the perfect headshot ringing out, and the envious looks from his colleagues at the assassination party. That's right, an assassination party—that's what snipers threw.

Hearing that Mad Dog had taken out the rebel leader was a major letdown for two reasons: the glory would not be Wolfgang's, and he'd have to carry out more large-caliber ammo than he had anticipated. That shit was heavy!

To compensate, Wolfgang knew he had to kill someone. Anyone. Well, maybe not anyone. Bad guys would be nice.

So he had two of them. Could he possibly get off a shot, taking out one guy, then nail the second one before he could react? Be fun to try. Wolfgang raised the rifle and thought of the rain, the wind speed, of becoming one with his bullet, imagining his hand reaching out toward the target.

Strangely, he began trembling, couldn't get a bead. What the hell?

The guy lowered his phone and turned. Wolfgang relaxed into his weapon, told himself to concentrate.

Pope called on the radio. Asshole.

Come on, what's wrong?

Wolfgang couldn't stop the trembling. He swore aloud, then suddenly lowered the rifle and realized he was losing his breath. He glanced up at the rain, then back toward the others, who were just moving off. He turned toward the rebels.

They were gone.

He sat there a moment, raised his jittery hand, stared at it as though it belonged to someone else.

Lack of sleep. He hadn't lost his edge. It was just lack of sleep. He rose quickly and tore off after the others.

Tongaso, Angola
Near Congo Border
1145 Hours Local Time

Mad Dog had ordered Pope and Sapper to go back for the Delta team. They had turned the bodies over to Morstarr reps, who would hold them for SoCom. Judas had wanted no part of that, saying that their presence in Angola was just another bad example of the right hand not knowing what the left hand was doing . . .

Mad Dog had risen from the small bed inside the hut and forced himself into a rickety wooden chair, facing Kidman, Morstarr's CEO. Mad Dog had pictured the guy as a rail-thin dweeb with an alabaster complexion, type of guy whose experience with the outdoors was limited to stepping from the terrace of a fancy restaurant to the valet's station to fetch his Lexus.

But Kidman seemed more like those Silicon Valley types, ruggedly handsome, a wannabe adventurer who looked the part but was just a poser. He wore an "outback"-style hat and described in great detail how he had designed it himself and had insisted it be constructed of real kangaroo leather.

Mad Dog hadn't asked, didn't care. Sure, Kidman's money afforded him some expensive toys, more elaborate experiences, but had he ever been on a real battlefield? Did he know what it was like to hold a dying friend in his arms?

All of which was to say that the hat, the long hair, and the attitude left Mad Dog underwhelmed.

Bibby, who sat to Mad Dog's right, wasn't impressed, either, his smirk growing as he stared at the computer in his lap.

Mad Dog let Kidman go on for another minute with the bullshit happy talk, then interrupted by slapping the leather pouch on the table. "Here you go. Now I know why they call them blood diamonds."

Kidman's expression soured as he opened the pouch, then examined a few of the rough gems with a jeweler's monocle jabbed in one eye. "Well, mate, let's see what we have here."

Mad Dog cocked a brow at Bibby, who did not falter. The Brit removed his glasses, rubbed the corners of his eyes as Kidman continued studying the diamonds. Bibby would make one hell of a poker player, but he refused to play, yet another of his oddities.

Kidman nodded. "I've been around gems all my life. Family business. I'm considered an expert. Make no mistake, this diamond rough is real."

Mad Dog leaned forward, eyes widening on the CEO. "It had better be real. That's all I can say."

The Aussie grinned.

Mad Dog didn't. "So you got your rocks back. Now let's hear the rest of the story."

Kidman nodded resignedly. "Croft, our finance director, is in bed with al Qaeda."

Mad Dog swore under his breath. "Can you prove that?"

"The phone records are a start." Kidman regarded Bibby. "Thank you."

Bibby frowned. "You need better security. And it sounds like Croft isn't your only problem. He had help in the field. We think Mbandi killed Jack Palansky, but there could be other moles in your organization."

Kidman sighed. "I know."

"Jack's dead," Mad Dog interrupted. "He was a good man."

"Yes, he was," said Kidman. "I always liked his attitude."

"Who are you kidding?" asked Mad Dog. "Guys like you don't give a fuck about people like Jack . . . people like me. We're just tools, a means to an end, so don't insult me."

Kidman rose. "I don't appreciate that, Mr. Hertzog. Not at all . . ."

"You just lost an employee. I lost a friend. And a member of my own team."

Bibby cleared his throat. "Mr. Kidman, of course we'll expect payment now."

"My assistant out in the truck is ready to wire-transfer directly to your account."

"Let's make it two-point-five mil," said Mad Dog. "I think we've earned it. I think we've earned it with blood."

Bibby gave him a look that said, *Don't push our luck.*

Kidman brought his lips together, furrowed his brow. "All right, I'll throw you an extra five hundred, but you should know that I was going to make you another offer, one much more lucrative." Kidman removed his hat and regarded Mad Dog, his expression hardening. "Bibby's right. My operation here is still vulnerable, my new security hires in dire need of training. I was going to hire IPG on a regular basis."

"Actually, we might be able to—"

Mad Dog grabbed Bibby's arm and squeezed. "We're not available." He leaned into the Brit's ear. "Go outside and get our money."

Bibby's cheeks grew flush. "Mr. Hertzog, I think we should—"

"No."

Kidman's lip twisted. "What's the matter, Hertzog?"

Mad Dog sighed loudly for effect. "We're taking our money, and we're going home. Angola? Fuck this place."

"Mr. Hertzog, you're making a big mistake."

"Nope." Mad Dog finally smiled. "I always go with my gut."

Agent James Moody was confused by what he saw on his computer screen. Six million was missing from his account, not the sixteen that Bibby had mentioned. He stomped out of his hut and marched toward the Brit as one of the mining company guys shut his computer and crossed to the back of their truck. "Bibby? I want to talk to you!"

"One moment, Mr. Moody." The man typed quickly on his keyboard. "I'm sure you have questions, but suffice it to say that if you check your account in a few moments, your original balance will be there. I've returned your two million, and taken back our four."

"You said you took sixteen."

"Mr. Hertzog had a change of heart."

Moody chuckled under his breath. "I'll tell you what, Mr. Bibby, as much as I hate you fuckers, I . . . well, I hate you fuckers."

"And we fuckers were never here."

"Neither was I." Moody returned the pistol that Bibby had loaned him.

"He didn't trust you with this."

"So why did you?"

"I'm not sure. I can't even say we're both Americans, but I figured we had your money. And my hands are as dirty as yours."

"You're a fool."

"We both are."

"So, did you get the diamonds? He'll never tell me."

"What do you think?"

Moody nodded. "Well, Mr. Bibby, I think our paths will cross again."

Bibby lowered his head and yawned. "If Dan dies, I'm sure they will . . ."

"Tell your boss I said it's been a real fucking treat."

"He'll be upset that he didn't say good-bye himself."

Moody snickered. "Oh, I'm sure he will."

Back on his computer, Moody wrote a report for his bosses in Langley: *Morstarr's own security team recovered the diamonds, but during an intense firefight between myself and the rebels, I pinpointed the location of and terminated the target.*

He smiled and sent off the report. Then he thought of Hertzog, wondered if the man really understood how they were two sides of the same coin.

"I'm just like you . . . fucked up. So fucked up that this is all we know."

Misery loves company, of course. And there was nothing worse than being alone to contemplate your sins.

Moody slammed shut his computer and began packing his things. Within two days he'd be in Bangkok. His usual girl would be waiting for him, and as they lay there in bed, he would tell her the story of Angola. She would not understand a word, but she would listen attentively, stroke him with her small, soft hands, and smile.

"The Dog Pound"
Talisay City
Cebu, the Philippines
Six Days Later
0920 Hours Local Time

"Hey, Dan? You know who called me this morning?" Mad Dog asked from his recovery bed, which had been set up beside the old man's. "Paul, from Chicago. You remember Paul?"

"Huh?"

"Paul, from Chicago."

"What was he doing there?"

Mad Dog rolled his eyes. "Forget it." The old man was on heavy painkillers. The gunshot wound wouldn't end his life. The diabetes would, but not yet. Not yet.

Mad Dog opened the laptop computer, figured he'd continue with his journal entry, ACCOUNT #A008, CODE-NAME: BLOOD DIAMONDS. While he couldn't keep official notes on all of IPG's activities because they could fall into the wrong hands, he'd been keeping a personal journal since the very start, remaining vague about the details of each job, but providing enough insights and reminders so that in the years to come he could reread the entries for lessons learned. He skimmed down to where he had left off:

Yesterday, while I was online and reviewing a shipment of supplies that I had just sent to Jumoke's village, Wolfgang came to me and said that something was wrong with him. He said that he just didn't feel right anymore, like he lost his mojo or something. I laughed in his face. I know what kind of a practical joker he is. But the son of a bitch didn't crack a smile. He just stood there like a cherry on his first day of basic training. I didn't know what to tell him. I asked if he wanted to quit. He said no but that he thought I should know about it. Fucking strange that he would even admit a problem to me, like deep inside he was crying out for help.

I asked Pope to get with him, work it out on the practice range, take Doolittle along. The rest of the guys were feeling pretty high, drinking and partying hard, especially Boo Boo and Sapper. I'd do the same if I weren't lying in bed with a gunshot wound in each leg. I divided that extra five hundred among them, plus gave each the hundred grand base pay. Do the math. Not bad for a couple days' work.

And, oh, yeah, Pope and Sapper each earned their shiny new nickels, which they received wearing broad smiles as they cursed through their teeth.

I've been thinking about visiting Rookie's parents because it's the right thing to do. I did have Rookie's share transferred into his father's account, and the guy called me back, confused, wanting to return the money. I forced it on him, and he caved in. Yesterday, we had a little ceremony in the backyard, but only Pope and I had something to say. I talked about how Rookie was talented and how we'd lost a potentially great friend before we'd really had a chance to know him. Pope said that he sensed a great future in the guy, but you could read the guilt in his eyes, hear it in his voice. I'll need time with him. I'm no expert, but I've been around a lot of guys with survivor guilt, including myself. I need to make sure he doesn't carry that around. But who am I kidding? This is a guy who has a Barbie doll in his ruck, and you just know there's guilt behind that. And it's not as though I've ever forgotten about Doc and Eddy.

I did talk to Jack's brother, who was a real asshole on the phone. I didn't remember Jack ever saying that he and his brother fought, but oh, yeah, they had. Politics, probably. Richard Palansky struck me as hardcore liberal with no use for anyone in the military, let alone mercs. He said that Jack got what he deserved. Nice . . .

Though I'm unsure if there are any lessons to be learned here (people die, family members can sometimes be assholes, life is meaningless), I do know that I've never been more proud of my team. What we do is not simple, and it's hardly admired. They call us scumbags without consciences who will do anything for a buck.

Damned thing is, I want the best of both worlds. I want to fight for money, get paid well, but never do anything that would compromise America's security or my own beliefs. I feel like I can affect a lot of change doing it this way—much more than I could in the Marines—but it's hard to soldier for profit without calling yourself a whore.

Yet that's the least of my problems right now. These gunshot wounds got me talking to a lot of docs. I casually mentioned to one that I'd been feeling a little weak for the past few weeks and had seen blood in my stool. I thought I had hemorrhoids.

But no, Murphy has caught up with me again. It's Stage IIB colon cancer, and it's spreading. I'm not telling anyone. Not even Dan. I'll go to the states and get it treated quietly, pray to God it doesn't get worse. My